Behind Enemy Bylines

"This sweet romance set in the early 2000s about a small-town Arkansas newspaper made me long for a time I didn't even know I was missing. By the time I finished *Behind Enemy Bylines* I wanted to pack my bags and travel down to Clementine so I could keep visiting all the new friends I'd made on these pages. (Hopefully at a hoedown with lots of funnel cake.) If you're in search of a charming second-chance romance full of lovable characters and satisfying emotional arcs, Kathleen Fuller has written you a great one right here."

—Becca Kinzer, award-winning author
of *First Love, Second Draft*

So Into You

"*So Into You* by Kathleen Fuller is an uplifting story about rising above your fears and letting go of your past. Secrets abound in this satisfying romance, and it's hard to look away when the house of cards comes crashing down. This satisfying tale will charm its way into your heart!"

—Denise Hunter, bestselling author
of *Before We Were Us*

Sold on Love

"The sweet third entry in Fuller's Maple Falls series (after *Much Ado About a Latte*) follows an unlikely romance between an ambitious realtor and an affable mechanic . . . their friends-to-lovers arc charms. Fans of wholesome romance will be eager to return to Maple Falls."

—*Publishers Weekly*

"Kathleen Fuller writes an 'opposites attract' romance that will leave you with a wonderful sigh and a silly smile. Harper Wilson overworks to cover up her insecurities, but when tenderhearted and gentle grease monkey Rusty Jenkins enters her life to save her Mercedes, an unexpected friendship grows into something both of them need. Love-authentic and sweet, this small-town romance with wonderful heart and a delicious male makeover will have you cheering for two people whose lives look very different on the outside, but whose hearts are very much the same."

—Pepper Basham, author of
The Mistletoe Countess and *Authentically, Izzy*

Much Ado About a Latte

"Fuller returns to small-town Maple Falls, Arkansas, (after *Hooked on You*) for a chaste but spirited romance between old friends with clashing entrepreneurial goals . . . The cozy atmosphere and spunky locals will leave readers eager to return to Maple Falls."

—*Publishers Weekly*

"You've heard of friends to lovers; now get ready for childhood friends, to coworkers, to fake-dating coworkers, to business rivals, to lovers. *Much Ado About a Latte* has it all—charming and sweet, with delectable dialogue and just enough biting tension to keep you on the edge of your seat. I fell in love with Anita's determined spirit, Tanner's kindness, and their slow-burning romance. A wide cast of side characters, including Anita's complicated but loving family, build the delightful feel of the town. Readers will love the beautiful setting of Maple Falls, the gratuitous food descriptions at Sunshine Diner, and Anita's adorable cat, Peanut."

—Carolyn Brown, *New York Times* bestselling author

Hooked on You

"Sign me up for a one-way ticket to Maple Falls. If you love small towns, charming characters, and sweet, swoony romance, *Hooked on You* is your next favorite read. Kathleen Fuller has knit one wonderful story yet again."

—Jenny B. Jones, award-winning author of
A Katie Parker Production and *The Holiday Husband*

"A charming story of new beginnings, family ties, love, friendship, laughter, and the beauty of small towns. Fuller invites you into Maple Falls and greets you with a cast of characters who will steal your heart, make you want to stay, and entice you to visit again."

—Katherine Reay, bestselling author of
The Printed Letter Bookshop and *Of Literature and Lattes*

"A sweet, refreshing tale of idyllic small-town life, family, and unexpected romance, *Hooked on You* is the perfect read to cozy up with on a rainy day."

—Melissa Ferguson, multi-award-winning
author of *How to Plot a Payback*

"The quaint Arkansas town of Maple Falls could use a little sprucing up, and as it turns out, Riley and Hayden are the perfect pair for the job. What neither of them is counting on, of course, is that their hearts may receive some long overdue TLC in the process. Kathleen Fuller has knit together a lovable cast of characters and placed them in a setting so rich and dear you may find yourself hankering for a walk down Main Street on a warm summer's evening. I loved every minute of my time in Maple Falls, and I can't wait to return to visit the friends I made there."

—Bethany Turner, award-winning author
of *Brynn and Sebastian Hate Each Other*

Behind Enemy Bylines

OTHER CONTEMPORARY ROMANCE NOVELS
BY KATHLEEN FULLER

Stand-Alone Novels

So Into You

The Maple Falls Romance Novels

Hooked on You

Much Ado About a Latte

Sold on Love

Two to Tango

Behind Enemy Bylines

A NOVEL

Kathleen Fuller

THOMAS NELSON
Since 1798

Published in Nashville, Tennessee, by Thomas Nelson. Thomas Nelson is a registered trademark of HarperCollins Christian Publishing, Inc.

Thomas Nelson titles may be purchased in bulk for educational, business, fundraising, or sales promotional use. For information, please email SpecialMarkets@ThomasNelson.com.

Publisher's Note: This novel is a work of fiction. Names, characters, places, and incidents are either products of the author's imagination or used fictitiously. All characters are fictional, and any similarity to people living or dead is purely coincidental.

Library of Congress Cataloging-in-Publication Data

Names: Fuller, Kathleen, author.
Title: Behind enemy bylines : a novel / Kathleen Fuller.
Description: Nashville, Tennessee : Thomas Nelson, 2025. | Summary: "Brimming with small-town charm, this latest clean rom-com from USA TODAY bestselling author Kathleen Fuller offers a second chance at romance for one local reporter and his big-city accountant ex"—Provided by publisher.
Identifiers: LCCN 2025010221 (print) | LCCN 2025010222 (ebook) | ISBN 9780840716156 (trade paperback) | ISBN 9780840716170 | ISBN 9780840716163 (epub)
Subjects: LCGFT: Romance fiction. | Christian fiction. | Novels.
Classification: LCC PS3606.U553 B44 2025 (print) | LCC PS3606.U553 (ebook) | DDC 813/.6—dc23/eng/20250325
LC record available at https://lccn.loc.gov/2025010221
LC ebook record available at https://lccn.loc.gov/2025010222

Printed in the United States of America

25 26 27 28 29 LBC 5 4 3 2 1

To James. I love you.

Prologue

"It's not my fault."

Jade sighed, closing her eyes as her foster brother complained on the other line. Although they hadn't lived in the same home for more than nine years after she aged out of the foster system and went to the University of Central Arkansas, she still felt responsible for him. She always had, from the moment he walked into Madeline and John Westin's house and was introduced to her as her new foster sibling. His wide, scared brown eyes, overgrown curly black out-of-control hair, and gaunt frame touched her fifteen-year-old heart. Logan Mitchell had held it ever since.

But that neglected, frightened child was now twelve years old, and once again he was in lots of trouble. And as always, it wasn't his fault. While he continued his tirade of blaming everyone else but himself for his predicament, Jade opened her eyes and glanced at the clock on the wall in her tiny office at *The Arkansas Democrat-Gazette*. In a little while she had to meet Sebastian for their lunch date. Despite her frustration with her brother, she smiled a little.

If anyone had told her when she joined the accounting department at the paper six months ago that she would be having weekly lunches with the most incredible man she'd ever met, much less date him for four months, she would have said they were crazy. Jade didn't date. She didn't do much socializing either. But that had changed since she met handsome Sebastian Hudson. He might be a newspaper columnist, but he had the body of an athlete—not surprising since he played football in high school. *"Tight end,"* he'd told her. *"Bench rider too, although I did play in a couple of games my senior year. My coach felt sorry for me."*

She had no idea what a tight end was, but she had no complaints about his backside or the rest of him. And she wasn't surprised he downplayed his role on the team. Sebastian wasn't just good-looking and charming. He was humble, which made him even sexier.

"When can you get me out of here?" Logan whined. "These people suck."

Her temple started to throb, and she was a little irritated that Logan had interrupted her Sebastian reverie. "Those people are trying to help you. And you wouldn't be in youth detention if you hadn't been caught smoking marijuana behind the school building. Henderson, right?"

"Pulaski Heights," he muttered. "You can't even remember where I go to school."

She tried to ignore the guilt his words triggered, and logically she couldn't be expected to remember all the schools he'd gone to over the past several years. Logan had been in one foster care and child home after another since she left the Westins. That made her feel guilty too. She could have stayed at their house as an adult, like they offered, and could have commuted to UALR instead of going to UCA and living on campus. She could have continued to be the surrogate mother she'd been to him since day one. If she'd given up her dream of finally living a normal life, maybe Logan wouldn't have gone off the rails.

"It was only one joint anyway." He sniffed. "I promise I'll follow the rules."

"You said that the last time—"

"I mean it now." His voice wavered. "Please, Jade. I just wanna go home."

Her heart broke. Logan didn't have a home—not a real, permanent one. Until she graduated college and got her own apartment, she didn't either. Not since she was nine. *It's not fair.* Logan didn't deserve to live a transient life like she did. Like so many other kids had to. "I'll see what I can do," she said, looking at her suddenly shaking hands. "I'll call Mr. Brink."

"Who's he?"

"My lawyer." She paused. Should she tell him? Get his hopes up when she wasn't sure she could deliver on the promise?

"Thanks, Jade," he said, sounding relieved. "You're the best. I miss you."

"Miss you too." Her fingers grew steadier now that he sounded appeased.

"I wish I could live with you."

"I know." He said that every time they talked on the phone or met in person, usually once a month and on holidays. Even though she wasn't around all the time, she made sure to be a presence in his life. Unfortunately she had limited influence on him. This time he sounded so dejected she had to give him some hope. "Mr. Brink is trying to figure out something."

"Like what?"

"Like me adopting you."

"Really? You're going to adopt me?"

She grinned, his excitement fueling hers. "I'm trying to." She heard someone yell his name in the background.

"I gotta go. Social worker time." His tone turned crabby again.

"Do what they say, Logan, and stay out of trouble."

"I will."

"I mean it. I love you, and I'll always be here for you—"

"Bye!" Logan hung up.

Jade put the phone in the cradle and sat back in her chair, worried she'd said too much. Now that she'd told him, she'd have to make sure Mr. Brink did everything possible to make the adoption happen. That would cost money—more than she had. But Logan was worth it.

She looked at the clock again and her stomach churned. Talking to Logan was easy compared to what she had to do next, and she had ten minutes to figure out what she was going to say to Sebastian.

A printed contract from Preston Ustace was on her desk, ready for her signature. She looked through the media company's offer one more time, then picked up her pen. The ballpoint hovered over the signature line. Once she signed this, her world would change, and she suddenly felt weary. She was tired of change. Her entire life had been one upheaval and disappointment after another, with a few victories along the way—making it through foster care almost unscathed, graduating from college in three years, finding an accounting job right away, then moving on to *The Democrat-Gazette* . . . and meeting Sebastian.

Her chest squeezed. But she knew what she had to do. With a surprisingly steady hand, she quickly signed the contract, sealed it in a brown envelope, and put it to the side of her tidy and organized desktop to mail on the way home. There. A done deal. She was doing the right thing—for her career and, most importantly, for Logan.

This wouldn't be the first time she'd had to put her happiness on the back burner. She doubted it would be the last.

———

SEB'S VIEW
BY SEBASTIAN HUDSON

In the immortal words of Snoopy, it was a dark and stormy night. But storms didn't deter fans of the Quisenberry Golden Rockers and the Sterling Spring Chickens as they watched the two senior teams vie for the coveted *We Ain't Too Old for This* bowling trophy at the Little Rock Professor Bowl. The sassy and steadfast septuagenarians battled through three close games, with the Spring Chickens emerging victorious.

"We'll get 'em next year," Horace Quisenberry, the Rockers' team captain, said, shaking off the loss as he spooned a stack of sauerkraut on his foot-long hot dog. "This is all in good fun, and we raised over two hundred dollars for the senior center."

Mr. Q.'s wife of fifty years, Pearl June, wasn't as magnanimous. "Those Chickens cheat," she muttered, her frosty pink lips pursed in a scowl while her good-natured husband strode off. "We should have won the second game

Briiiiiing!

Sebastian jumped at the jingling sound coming from the sleek black telephone perched on the edge of his desk. His fingers froze over his manual Smith Corona typewriter as he switched his thoughts from the Professor Bowl to his office. He shoved aside the ever-present stack of papers in front of him, found the phone, and picked up the receiver. "Hudson here."

"How are things in the big city?"

Seb smiled at Buford Wilson's gravelly voice. "Still hustling and bustling."

"That's why I like it here in Clementine. No hustle or bustle."

Leaning back in his creaky antique chair, Seb grinned. "It's good to hear from you, Buford. It's been a while."

"Far too long." A pause.

His grin faltered. "Everything okay? Glenda doing all right?"

"Yeah, she's fine. Everything's fine. I just needed to ask you something."

Seb glanced at the paper in the typewriter. His column was due by end of day, but he could spare time for his old mentor. Besides, it was his own fault he'd procrastinated so long on it. Not something he normally did, but the muse had struck during the weekend, and he'd spent both Saturday and Sunday working on his novel instead of the writing that paid his bills. "Sure," he said to Buford. "What's up?"

"My retirement."

Seb sat up. "Really?"

"Don't sound so surprised."

"I'm not surprised. I'm shocked. You said you'd retire when you were dead. Wait. You're not—"

"No, no. I'll be alive and kicking as long as the good Lord wants me to. It's just . . . I'm tired, Sebastian." His voice turned gruff. "And with my nephew, Bo, happy with his farm and having no interest in the newspaper business, I realized I need a succession plan. I want you to be a part of it."

That was the last thing he'd expected to hear.

"I want to sell *The Clementine Times* to you. Before you say anything, just listen to my offer. I talked it over with Glenda and Bo, and they agree with me—you should be the one to carry the paper into the future. But I know how important your work for *The Democrat-Gazette* is, and I don't want to pull you away from that."

Seb wouldn't call it important work—not really. After *The Arkansas Gazette* merged with *The Arkansas Democrat* and formed one paper with a rather uninspired yet self-explanatory moniker, Seb had moved from hard reporting to writing slice-of-life features for Seb's View. He didn't think his column would be missed all that much if it were to disappear tomorrow. His new editor sure wouldn't mind if it was gone. Frank had little respect for what he called "boring" little columns. *"Readers want excitement,"* he'd said more than once. *"They like stories with conflict, not fluff."*

He didn't share Frank's opinion, and he had enough reader mail to prove his column was popular. But how long would that last? He'd been in the newspaper business since he was twelve, working for Buford in Clementine, his hometown. The business had changed a lot since then, and the changes seemed to come at a faster clip the closer they approached the twenty-first century. "Why me?" he asked.

"You were the best carrier I had, and then you turned into the best reporter I'd seen in years, even at sixteen."

Seb grinned. He hadn't thought about those days in a long time. "I was just the local sports reporter. Not a big deal."

"There you go, selling yourself short again. Let me guess—all those awards you've won are in a box, right?"

He didn't have that many awards, but Buford was correct. "Just like yours are in the cleaning supply closet on the bottom shelf. They should have twenty feet of dust on them by now."

Buford chuckled. "Touché. I'll cut to the chase. You have the writing talent and reporter instincts. You've been around a newsroom for most of your life. You're the future of *The Times*, Sebastian. No doubt about it."

Seb was glad Buford couldn't see him blushing over the compliments. It meant the world that his mentor thought so highly of him. Yet there was one hang-up they both had to face. "I'm not a businessman."

"Exactly why I want you to continue my legacy. I don't need a bean counter who will put the bottom line before journalistic excellence and integrity. The people of Clementine deserve better."

Clementine, a tiny town nestled in the Arkansas Ozark Mountains, had exactly one general store, one gas station, one motel, a Southern-fried diner that was always packed with hungry patrons, and zero traffic lights. Not exactly the big time. But the paper's total circulation was larger than Clementine's population and included several smaller towns in the area. It was also Seb's hometown, and he hadn't been there since . . . huh. He couldn't remember the last time he'd made the two-and-a-half-hour drive to visit. Here his mentor was offering him the family business, and Seb had been too busy to see him, although they did keep in touch over the phone every once in a while.

"Sebastian, I'm prepared to offer you *The Clementine Times* for the princely sum of . . . one dollar."

For the second time since answering Buford's call, Seb's jaw hit the floor. "Now I know that's a joke."

"I'm serious, son."

And Seb didn't really doubt him. The man wasn't only his mentor, he'd been a second father to him after his own dad ran off with the Clementine High School secretary and never looked back, leaving Seb, his mother, and his younger sister, Evelyn Margot, to fend for themselves. They made it through some tough times, and Evelyn was still finding her way. Seb probably would be too, if it weren't for Buford.

Still blindsided by the offer, Seb said, "It's very generous, but I don't know. It's a big decision. Can I have some time to think about it?"

"Take all the time you need. I'm not in any hurry to retire, and there will be a training period before I turn the reins over to you."

"You sound pretty sure I'm going to accept."

"I'm cautiously optimistic. Just let me know when you're ready to talk."

"I will. Regardless of my decision, I appreciate the offer." A lump formed in his throat. "I'll be in touch."

They said their goodbyes and Seb hung up the phone. He leaned back in his chair, still dumbstruck. He'd never aspired to be anything more than a reporter, and now a columnist. There was the pipe dream of being a novelist too. But at the rate he was writing his first book, he'd be near retirement age, if he could even get it published.

But owning and running a newspaper? That wasn't on his radar, and he wasn't sure it should be. He also had more than a lack of business sense that made him hesitant. And there was something else—or rather someone else. *Jade.*

Simply thinking about her made him happy. For the first time in six years, since his last disastrous relationship in college, he was considering his personal future again. He and Jade had been casually dating for the past four months, emphasis on casual. But he wanted more. And if things worked out between them, he'd have to take her into consideration when thinking about Buford's offer.

He glanced at his watch. In a few minutes, he would meet her downstairs at her office in the accounting department, and they would go to the Sports Page for hamburgers and fries, their usual Wednesday lunch.

Seb got up from his chair and shoved Buford's offer out of his mind. Good thing Buford had given Seb plenty of time to think about it. He didn't like being rushed. Never had.

He was about to head out when he saw a female figure behind the frosty glass window of his door, which used to enter an empty closet that his former editor had agreed to let him change into a tiny but usable office. Seb grinned, his pulse quickening as she knocked. "Hey," he said as he opened the door with a smile, resisting the urge to take her hand even though they agreed no PDA at work. It wasn't a secret that they were dating, but they didn't draw attention to it either. "I was just heading downstairs to get you."

She nodded, her gaze focused on her black pumps. "Can we talk first?"

His smile tempered. "Sure. Come on in." He stepped back as she closed the door behind her and clutched her hands together. That wasn't a good sign. "Is something wrong?"

"No." She pressed her lips together. "Not exactly."

He didn't believe her. He was also more than a little distracted by how pretty she was in her brown pants and crisp white shirt. He'd always had a thing for redheads, and her pixie-cut auburn hair framed a flawless face with round malachite eyes and long russet eyelashes. Irresistible. When his eyes dipped to her rose-colored lips, he fought not to linger. They'd kissed a few times, and if he had his way, he'd kiss her a lot more. She'd made it clear in the beginning that she wanted to take their relationship slow, and he respected that. Hopefully he could speed things up soon, though. Very soon.

As she lifted her gaze to meet his, she said, "I, uh, have some news."

"Well, you're in the right place then. News is our bread and butter." He chuckled, but her expression remained unreadable. "What's going on?"

She moved toward his desk, her heels tapping on the wood floor. He half expected her to comment on how disorganized it was, and she'd have a right to. Twice she'd helped him get his office in order, and both times he vowed to keep it that way, only to immediately revert back to his habit of setting things down and dealing with them later. But when she faced him again, she remained silent.

"Whatever it is, you can tell me."

A quick nod. Then, "You know that new website? Thompson Recruiters?"

"Never heard of it." He didn't use a computer at the office, although Frank had given him one. Forced it on him actually. He'd never been on the internet and didn't plan to. He figured it was just a flash in the pan anyway. No one in their right mind would give up a tangible newspaper or printed book to read a screen all the time.

"It's a place to post your resumé and find jobs," she said. "I made a profile last week."

"You did? Why?"

"I've been looking for another job."

Whoa. She hadn't given any indication that she was wanting to work somewhere else.

Her hands were wringing now, and she shoved them behind her back. "I got an offer for an analyst position. I start next week."

"Oh." Well, that stunk. He wouldn't be able to see her every day. But if she was happy, he was happy for her. He put his arms around her, fully intending to give her a hug. "Congratulations," he murmured into her hair. She smelled so nice. Jade wasn't one to wear perfume or more than minimal makeup. He found her simplicity enticing, and before he could stop himself, he was kissing her. To his shock and pleasure, she melted against him, returning his kiss with more fervor than she ever had before, and he was happy to match her. Bliss, pure bliss.

Suddenly she jerked away, slipping out of his arms and turning. "I'm sorry," she mumbled, so low he almost didn't hear her.

He scrubbed his hand over his face. Even though his office was well out of the way of everyone else on the floor, he'd blown it. "I'm sorry. I shouldn't have done that. But I love you—"

"What?" She whirled around, stunned.

He froze, shocked he'd said the words when he hadn't even thought them before. No, that wasn't true. He had, but only once or twice . . . maybe a little more lately. But now that they were out there, he couldn't take them back. He didn't want to. After having his heart trampled in the past by someone he thought he loved, he realized what he felt for this beautiful woman was the real thing. She was smart, determined, caring. Sure, she could be a little uptight, a little overly focused on her work. But he liked the passion and fire he saw inside her. No, he *loved* it.

"I love you, Jade." He smiled, the phrase sounding more natural. More *right*.

She didn't move or respond. She stared at him, her mouth slightly parted and more than slightly red from their fierce kissing. As the seconds ticked by and she remained mute, his stomach turned into a sour mess.

Seb tried to brush it off. "You don't have to say it back." So awkward. "How about we just forget it and go to lunch? I'm starving." The last thing he wanted was food, but he had to leave his stifling office and get some air, because it was becoming clear that he had messed up. Big-time. He started to open the door.

"The job is in Atlanta."

The door latched shut and he turned around. "Georgia?"

"Yes."

Now it was his turn to remain silent as reality set in. She wasn't just leaving *The Democrat-Gazette*. She was leaving Arkansas. *Leaving me.*

"I'm sorry, Sebastian."

To her credit, she sounded genuine. That didn't make him feel any better. "I didn't realize you were so unhappy here."

"It's not that. I . . . need a fresh start. This is a good opportunity— one I couldn't pass up."

With every word, she deflated him. "What about us?"

Jade's hands stilled and she looked him straight in the eye. "We weren't that serious."

After his declaration of love, she didn't think they were serious? After kissing him like she couldn't get enough of him? Like she'd been telling him . . . goodbye.

"It's for the best," she continued, her earlier hesitation gone. "We're different people, we have different goals. It wouldn't have lasted."

"I just told you I love you." He shook his head, trying to make sense of what was happening. "Doesn't that mean something?"

A pause. Her bottom lip quivered. Then stilled. "No, Sebastian. It doesn't." She brushed past him and walked out the door.

He could hear her clicking heels down the hall, percussing in his spinning head. *It can't be over. Go after her. Tell her again that you love her. Don't let her go.*

But his feet wouldn't move. He'd done that before, chased after Karen, who in the end didn't want him either. They dated for three years in college, and he'd been so sure she was the one for him. Just like he'd been sure about Jade.

Seb plopped down on his chair and leaned his elbows on the desk, his head drooping. He was the guy who didn't like to be hurried or rushed, and then he prematurely and inexplicably voiced his love to Jade. While he blamed Karen for breaking his heart, in hindsight she wasn't the only one at fault. When he finally came around to wanting to marry her, she had moved on to someone else.

Now Jade was moving on too. He was a loser either way.

He could try talking to her again. Convince her to stay. But what would be the point? If she wanted to be with him, she wouldn't take a job hundreds of miles away. She didn't even ask him to go with her. He was truly confused by that, since he thought—felt—they'd been growing closer during their short relationship, even before that amazing kiss.

"Your girl picker's broken." Evelyn Margot's words entered his brain. She'd said that after Karen had dumped him, and considering his high school girlfriend had kicked him to the curb before graduation, his little sister might be right. He'd also been completely wrong about Jade. His own emotions too. Minutes ago, he'd been so sure he was in love with her. Now he never wanted to see her again.

His logical brain kicked into gear, instantly hardening his feelings. Fine. In fact, better than fine. She had done him a favor by ending things before they got too deep. He was the idiot who had read more into their *casual* relationship. He wasn't going to spend years moping over her like he had Karen. Jade Smith wasn't worth it.

Chapter 1

Clementine, Arkansas
2004

Seb glanced at his watch. Three o'clock and Haskell Panchak wasn't here yet. It figured. Clementine's earnest, friendly, and mostly capable mayor was terrible with time and deadlines. More than once he'd had to nudge the man to get his monthly column done and turned in before *The Clementine Times* went to press. But beggars couldn't be choosers, and Seb was having a hard enough time getting local content for the once daily newspaper that was now a biweekly publication that went out on Mondays and Thursdays. If circulation and advertising didn't change for the better, he would soon have to go to just Mondays.

But he didn't want to think about that now. Instead, he observed the cast of characters sitting at the long conference table in *The Times*'s conference room. They were all waiting on Panchak's arrival. Or Pancake, as Seb had christened him in one of his columns a couple of years ago. It was a joke at the time that ended up a part of Clementonian vernacular, much to the politician's consternation.

There were Cletus and Paul, cousins who were as good ol' boy as any two guys could get and had worked *The Times*'s press for thirty years. They typically didn't attend staff meetings, but Seb had invited them to this one. Across the table from them was his sister, Evelyn Margot—his advertising manager who also doubled doing layout and graphic design. Next to her was Flora Fisher, *The Times*'s bookkeeper, who had no idea what was in store for her as soon as Pancake arrived, and she was talking to Isaiah Boston, the sports beat reporter who also picked up breaking news.

Sitting next to Seb was Tyler Hernandez, an eighteen-year-old kid who was graduating from Clementine High next week but had been working for Seb for two years. Tyler reminded Seb of himself when he was younger—eager, willing to do the most menial of the jobs while also showing an aptitude for taking on more responsibility. Right now he was the unofficial circulation manager, and the only reason he was unofficial was because Seb couldn't afford to pay him an official salary. At best he'd been able to give him a bonus Christmas ham from the Piggly Wiggly, the nearest grocery store, last year. But Tyler didn't mind the pay or the measly ham, and he was quickly turning into Seb's right-hand man, much like Seb had been for Buford.

Seb shifted his gaze to the modest conference room that hadn't changed since the early seventies, complete with a picture of Buford and his wife, Glenda, on the opposite wall. It wasn't a large photo or a staged one. Just the two of them sitting on their patio at their cabin thirty minutes outside Clementine. It was the last picture of them together, taken a couple of years after Seb had bought *The Times*, two months after Buford first offered it to him, and for the one dollar the man had promised.

It wasn't often that Seb turned wistful, and maybe it was due to the real reason they'd all gathered in the conference room, but seeing Buford and Glenda during happier times tugged on his heartstrings. Little did anyone know that shortly after the picture was taken, and only two-and-a-half years into their retirement, the unthinkable would happen—a deadly car crash that took both their lives. The grieving process had been hard, but he'd been stoic and helped his staff get through it. But there were times, like now, that he wanted Buford to be here. He and Glenda *should* be here.

"Sorry I'm late." Pancake swooshed into the room, the three strands on top of his balding head hanging on for dear life as he took his seat on the other side of Evelyn. Grateful for the respite from his melancholy thoughts, even though he was irritated by the mayor's tardiness, Seb stood up. "Now that everyone's here," he said, giving Pancake a stern look, "we can start the meeting."

Pancake shifted in his seat.

"Ignore him, Haskell," Evelyn said in an exaggerated whisper. "He's just being his usual crabby self."

"No, he's right. I was late. I had a meeting with the Clementine Historical Society, and we ran behind. My apologies."

Considering the historical society was comprised of five women in their sixties and seventies who were all compulsive talkers and stealth gossipers, Panchak could be forgiven his tardiness. "No problem," Seb said, softening his stance. "Okay, a quick state of the union and we'll be on our way. The Memorial Day Hoedown is three weeks away." As far as Seb knew, Clementine was the only town that held a hoedown in the spring instead of fall, which elicited questions from non-Clementonians every year. He'd always liked the originality. "I want everything covered before the event. Evelyn, what's the advertising status?"

She flipped through her spiral notebook. "We've got a general ad going out this week, and next week three of the vendors who will be there have taken out small—emphasis on *small*—ads. I'm working on filling our empty spots in the next two issues."

While he wished those spots were already full, he knew she would do her best to complete the job. If not, she'd come up with some drawings and cartoon blocks to fill the empty space, but it would be nice to earn some needed funds from ads.

He asked Pancake for more info on the hoedown and the progress being made to get everything in place, and the mayor obliged. He then queried Isaiah and Tyler for their reports and assigned both of them to cover the hoedown. Isaiah, always cool and collected, just nodded. But Tyler's eyes lit up.

"Take plenty of pictures."

Tyler grinned and pushed up his large round metal glasses. "Yes, sir."

Ah, enthusiasm. Seb could use some of that.

Evelyn got up from her chair. "I'll be right back," she said, giving Seb a small nod.

Showtime. He faked a scowl. "We're in the middle of a meeting, Evelyn."

"Cool your jets. I'll be right back." She hurried out of the room.

As Seb pretended to be irritated, he noticed Pancake's gaze had followed her out the door. Well, well, well. Although Haskell's fading hairline made him look much older than thirty-four, he and Evelyn had gone to high school together, and she was actually three years older than him. But this was the first time he'd seen the man take a visual interest in his sister. Seb wasn't sure how he felt about that.

"Sebastian," Flora's resonant voice was butter-smooth as she spoke his name. "I've got an appointment at four—"

"Congratulations!" Evelyn burst into the room carrying a cake she'd picked up earlier that day from the Clementine Bakery. She set it in front of Flora as Flora's husband, Carl, and her mother, Florine, came into the room. Carl held two six-packs of Coke and Florine had a paper bag with the cups, napkins, and plates Evelyn had requested her to bring.

Flora looked at the top of the cake. It read: Retirement Suits You. Her gaze darted around the room. "I wasn't expecting this."

"There's no way we were going to let you go without a little celebration," Evelyn said, putting her arm around Flora's shoulders.

Seb stood to the side and watched as his staff celebrated Flora's retirement. The woman had been his bookkeeper for the past ten years, and she'd been Buford's for twenty before that. Thirty years of service to *The Clementine Times*. That deserved more than a cake, but he was waiting for the plaque commemorating her service to come back from the engraver. For now, a cake would have to do.

"Get over here, sugar." Florine waved her hand at him, her long, perfectly manicured coral nails a nice contrast to her dark skin. Ms. Florine was never without her nail polish or her pearls. "You'd better get your piece of cake before Carl eats it all."

"Hey," Carl said, scoffing at his mother-in-law. "I've only had two."

Chuckling, Seb uncrossed his arms and walked to the table where Florine had a slice at the ready. For the next thirty minutes, he was able to take off his publisher and editor-in-chief hats and just be Seb—a man hanging out with his friends.

At ten to four, the cake was put away and the mess cleaned up. Flora told Carl and Florine she'd see them at home. When everyone had left the conference room, Flora went to Seb, tears in her eyes. "You didn't have to make a fuss," she said.

"Sure we did." He smiled, keeping his emotions in check. "It was Evelyn's idea."

"I'm sure she didn't have to twist your arm." Flora dabbed at her eyes with a retirement-themed napkin and looked around the room. "I'm going to miss this place." She faced Seb. "I'll miss you the most."

He drew her in for a quick hug. "Same here. I don't know what I would have done without you all these years."

"You would have survived." She stepped back. "Just like you're going to survive now."

Doubt crept in. "I'm glad you're confident."

She touched his cheek. "Don't forget to come around on Thanksgiving. That's a standing invitation, no matter what."

"Of course. I wouldn't miss your collard greens and Florine's potato pie." While Evelyn usually spent Thanksgiving with their mother and their stepfather, Bill, in Tennessee, Seb didn't like to stray too far from Clementine and *The Times*. Flora and her family had taken him in on the holidays.

She nodded. "I best get to that appointment. You holler if you need anything . . . even though I know you won't."

She was right—he probably wouldn't. *The Times* was his responsibility, not hers. "I'll keep it in mind, though."

After she hurried out of the room, Seb stayed behind. He'd see Flora in town and at the Clementine Community Church, but not having her in the office was going to be hard. And then there was the fact that now he had added another job responsibility on top of being publisher, editor in chief, part-time columnist and reporter, and full-time owner. But that was the newspaper business in the twenty-first century, and despite the hard work and uncertain times, he still loved it.

He loved Clementine even more.

Seb turned off the lights and went to his office to check the messages on his answering machine. There was only one, which was unusual. Often his machine was full. He hit Play.

Hello, Mr. Hudson. Miles Harrington here, from Harrington Media. I'm following up on the three letters and five messages we've left with you recently. Our company is serious about discussing a possible deal with you—

Seb hit the Erase button. Geez, this guy was persistent. Seb had read his first letter and immediately balled it up and threw it into the trash, and did the same with the subsequent letters that he hadn't bothered to open. He also didn't listen much further to the other phone messages Harrington had left over the past two months. He'd figured if he ignored the man, he'd leave him alone. So far he hadn't, but Seb wasn't changing his strategy. Eventually he'd realize the answer was an emphatic and forever *no*.

The Times might be in dire financial straits, and he was taking on another job to keep it afloat, but he continued to hope that this was only temporary—that the newspaper business would make a comeback. He'd been very, very wrong about the appeal of the internet, and Evelyn had asked him more than once to start moving things to digital. Seb refused. If he changed the newspaper format, then that would irrevocably change *The Times*. He couldn't allow that.

Yes, he was a relic at age forty, but if someone didn't preserve the past, who would? When he bought the paper from Buford, he made a vow not to let it go under or stray from its original mission—to keep Clementine and the surrounding communities connected. And even though it was hard, even though at times it seemed impossible, he wasn't giving in.

Los Angeles, California

"And now here's the latest from No Doubt—'It's My Life'!"

"Ooh, I love this song." Kalista Clark pushed down her Chanel sunglasses and looked at the man cleaning the pool. "Turn it up."

The guy stopped pushing the long pole he was holding and looked at her. He was pretty old—at least in his forties. "The radio is right beside you, ma'am."

"I *know* that." She glanced at the small portable radio on the glass table near her lounge chair. "My nails are still wet."

The guy put down his pole—did he seriously just roll his eyes?—and walked over to the table. He turned the knob, and Gwen Stefani's voice carried through the speaker. "How's that?"

"Good. You can go back to"—she waved her hand at him—"whatever you were doing."

"Yes, *ma'am.*"

Ugh, Kalista didn't like his tone at all. She'd have to tell Daddy to get another pool man. She blew on her hot-pink nails, then lay back on the lounge chair and closed her eyes. The bright California sunshine warmed her skin, and the white string bikini she wore was very comfortable. She might wear it to the beach this afternoon when she met up with Abbie, Ryan, and their other friends. Having a huge pool was nice, but she loved being at the beach—or rather, being *seen* at the beach. *Let's be real.*

She was just about to turn over when the worst voice that ever existed hit her ears. "Kalista!"

Kalista cringed. Maybe if she didn't move, Bettany would think she was asleep. She kept super still, resisting a scowl when she heard her stepmother's kitten heels approach on the textured tile surrounding the pool.

"I know you're awake and you can hear me." Bettany kicked Kalista's lounger.

Rude. Kalista took off her sunglasses. The pool man was gone, but Bettany was looming over her. "What do you want?"

"Ray-baby wants to talk to you."

So dumb. "Why can't you call him Raymond like my four other stepmothers did?"

"Because he's my Ray-baby." Bettany's long blond extensions framed her face. Her very young face. Kalista had been shocked to find out her stepmother of three months was twenty-five—only seven years older than Kalista. So tragic. "He's in his office."

At least her father was home. Usually he was gone during the week, either at his office downtown or flying out somewhere to close some business deal. Kalista wasn't sure exactly what kind of business her father was in, but he was incredibly rich, and that's all Kalista cared about. She replaced her sunglasses. "Tell him I'm busy."

"He's not going to like that."

"Don't care."

"You're such a brat." Bettany stormed off.

Kalista frowned. Maybe she was being bratty, but not any more than her stupid stepmother. She wondered how long this marriage would last. The longest one was Megyn, and that had been eight years, when Kalista was in her early teens. She didn't like her either.

Another song started, this one by Maroon 5, and Kalista focused on the music and her tan and pushed Bettany and "Ray-baby" out of her mind. When Adam Levine crooned the last words, the radio shut off. "Hey," Kalista said, scrambling to sit up. "I was listening to that."

"Now you're going to listen to me."

Uh-oh. She whipped off her sunglasses at her father's stern tone. She hadn't expected him to come out here, and he didn't look happy. "Hi, Daddy," she said, giving him her sweetest smile.

His expression softened. "Hi, sweetheart. Are you enjoying the pool?"

"Yes, very much."

"Good." He looked at the crystal-clear water, tinted blue by the Moroccan tiles decorating the edge. "I need to spend more time out here," he mumbled. "Shame to have such a nice backyard and never enjoy it."

Kalista was surprised to hear him say that. Usually he was just in and out of the house, and every once in a while he'd call and check in with her. It could be annoying sometimes, like when she was at the mall or the movies or at a friend's house after school. But after next week, she wouldn't have to worry about school anymore.

He turned to her. "What are your plans after graduation, Kalista?"

Plans? "Hang out here. Oh, and hang out with my friends. Go shopping for sure, and of course go out with Ryan." They weren't official, but they were going out more frequently lately. She liked him, but she also liked to keep her options open.

"What about college?"

"Ew, no. I'm tired of school, Daddy." She laid back down. "I just wanna have fun, you know?"

He pushed his hand through his short gray hair. "That's what I'm worried about. It's time to grow up."

"I am grown, duh. I turned eighteen in March."

"I mean mature."

Where was this coming from? "I am mature. Just ask my friends."

"You overcharged four credit cards this month. Where did the money go?"

Oh. She didn't realize she'd done that. "Things."

"What things?"

"You know, stuff." She sulked. "You've never complained before."

"That's my fault. I should have taught fiscal responsibility to you earlier, but there's no time like the present."

"What do you mean by that?"

"After your ceremony next week, you're going to Arkansas."

She sat up again. "What's an Arkansas?"

Daddy's mouth dropped open. "You're kidding. Wait, you're serious. What did they teach you in school anyway?"

"Lots of boring stuff."

He shook his head, then said, "Arkansas is in the south . . . by Texas . . . Forget it. Vivian's there, and she's agreed to let you stay with her for the summer."

"Really?" Despite her confusion, she was excited to hear him mention her first stepmother, Vivian, or Viv as Kalista called her. She had married Daddy when Kalista was six, a year after her mother had died, and even though they divorced five years later, Viv was a formal model and had been in her life a few years after that. Although, since then they'd talked infrequently. Why was she in Arkansas? "Hold on, what do you mean 'for the summer'?"

"She's getting married in August, and she agreed to let you stay with her until after the wedding."

"But what about my summer here? I have plans with my friends." Very loose plans. Actually, nonexistent, but that was usually how her summers went—she just did what she felt like when she felt like doing it. "Does Arkansas have a beach?"

Daddy chuckled. "No."

"What about a mall?"

"Probably, but I'm not concerned about that. I'm worried about your lack of direction. I don't want you to get your trust fund and blow it on clothes and hair salons."

"I wouldn't do that." She'd known for a while she had a trust fund that she would get when she turned twenty-one. "I'm going to buy a Bentley. Oh, and a big house. I bet I could get Britney Spears to sing at my parties—"

"Good Lord," Daddy said, his scowl back again. "Are you listening to yourself? Having money involves lots of responsibilities. There's nothing wrong with a fancy car or a big house, but you need other goals. Like an actual job."

"Oh, I can get a job," she said, although the idea sounded dull. None of her other friends worked—why should she?

"You need to understand the value of hard work too. Vivian's fiancé is a farmer—"

"Yuck."

Daddy gave her an exasperated look. "You also need an attitude adjustment." He stood. "I bought the tickets and Vivian is expecting you. A week from today you'll be in Clementine, Arkansas."

She jumped to her feet. "But—"

"No buts, Kalista Louise. You have to prove that you're mature and responsible enough to handle your trust fund. The first step is getting a job and helping Vivian with whatever she needs. Understand?"

"And what if I don't?" She crossed her arms over her shoulders. He couldn't make her do this, could he? She was an adult, not a little kid.

"Then you won't get your trust fund until you're thirty. No, make that thirty-five. I must have been out of my mind to plan to give it to you at twenty-one."

No trust fund? "All I have to do is get a job?"

"And be responsible—don't forget that."

"Okay." She held out her hand. "Deal."

"Wow." He looked surprised. "That was easier than I thought." He shook her hand, then gave her a hug. "I'll miss you," he said.

She froze, unable to remember the last time he hugged her. Weird. She hugged him back. "Uh, me too."

"I'll let you get back to your"—he sighed—"tanning."

"Thanks, Daddy."

"I love you, Kalista."

"Love you too," she said and quickly turned on the radio. Instead of a cool song, a commercial played and she heard her father walk inside. Arkansas . . . hmm. She could do anything for three months, and it would be nice to see Viv again. This would be a breeze, as long as Clementine had a decent mall. Oh, and a Starbucks. And a spa. She couldn't survive without a spa . . .

Chapter 2

Atlanta, Georgia

Y ou don't know what he wants?"

Jade looked up from her computer at Charlotte Rae, her coworker in the next cubicle. The fiftyish woman was standing next to Jade's desk, her thin eyebrows raised above surprised eyes. She'd heard Jade talk to Miles's secretary when she called a few minutes ago, and as soon as Jade hung up, she came right over.

"I have no idea." Jade's nerves started an unpleasant tap dance under her skin. In the ten years she'd worked for Harrington Media—eight of those had been when it was Preston and Ustace Communications—this was the first time she'd been summoned by Miles Harrington, the owner's nephew and an up-and-coming junior executive. Thankfully, her hands weren't shaking. With a lot of practice and self-talk, she'd overcome that outward show of her inner anxiety.

"Maybe he's got the hots for you." Charlotte gave her a sly look. "He's about your age and quite handsome. In fact, if I were fifteen years younger—"

"You're not and you wouldn't."

She sighed. "I suppose it would put a tiny crimp in my marriage."

"Only a crimp?"

Charlotte laughed. "I'm joking. But you're single and ready to mingle, and from all accounts, so is he."

Jade put a stack of data sheets in the folder she'd been instructed to bring to her impromptu meeting. "I'm not mingling with anyone."

"Obviously."

What did she mean by that? Jade frowned and pushed back from her desk. She had to meet Miles upstairs in fifteen minutes, and she needed to get there early to collect her thoughts. The last thing she wanted was to think about her nonexistent social life, which was nonexistent by choice. "He's not interested in me."

"You don't know that." She quickly undid the top button of Jade's blouse.

Jade gasped and pulled back. "What are you doing?"

"You're too uptight. Showing a little skin—emphasis on *little*—wouldn't hurt."

She redid the button. "If you're finished being ridiculous, I've got a meeting to go to."

Charlotte sighed. "One day you're going to realize that all work and no play makes for a dull life."

"My life is fine." She softened her tone. "Really, I'm happy." At least as happy as she could be.

"It's a shame you can't see that you're such a catch." Charlotte's smile was sweet but bordered on pity too. "I don't want you to end up an old maid like my cousin Gert."

"There's nothing wrong with being single, and I have to go."

"Good luck!" she called out as Jade hurried down the hall. "And if he gives you bedroom eyes, flirt right back!"

Bedroom eyes? *She's lost her mind.* She meant well, though. Jade had worked with Charlotte since she joined Preston and Ustace—or PU, as it was informally called, much to the chagrin of the owners who hadn't quite thought through the ramifications of combining both their names. Her cubicle mate was a little eccentric, nosier than she should be, but it was nice that she cared.

As she made her way to the elevator, she shifted her thoughts to Miles. The only encounter she'd had with him was at last year's Christmas party, and that had been in passing. She stayed fifteen minutes, a suitable length of time for a drop-in. She couldn't stand small talk, and what little free time she had, she preferred to spend volunteering at one of the women's shelters in Atlanta or helping with charity events for the children's home and foster children's association.

But Charlotte didn't know that. No one at Harrington did, and neither did they know about her past. She intended to keep it that way.

When she stepped onto the elevator to go upstairs to the executive offices, she felt the phone in her jacket pocket buzz. She pulled it out and saw an unfamiliar number on the small screen. She let it go to voicemail and straightened the collar on her white shirt to make sure the button was securely fastened. "Bedroom eyes," she mumbled. She had no idea what bedroom eyes were. "And I'm not going to flirt with Miles—"

The elevator doors slid open, and an office worker she didn't recognize tilted his head at her, confused.

Jade's cheeks flamed. "I, uh . . . Never mind." She brushed past the man and hurried down the hall toward Miles's office. When she was halfway down the hall, she turned to the right. A plaque right outside the door read Miles Harrington, Vice President. She took in a big breath and opened the door.

A beautiful young woman with long blond hair, French tip

nails, and burgundy lipstick smiled at her from behind a modest-sized desk. "Ms. Smith?"

"Yes. Hi." She gripped the folder.

"I'll let Mr. Harrington know you're here." She gestured to a chair on the other side of the room. Jade nodded as the woman buzzed her boss, but before she could sit down, Miles came out of his office.

"Ms. Smith. Or can I call you Jade?"

"Jade," she said.

"Perfect." He smiled and waved her in. "I promise this won't take long."

Jade followed him into a simple office adorned with photos of Miles and various people, mostly on golf courses. She noticed a few golf trophies on a shelf behind his desk, and on the opposite side were several diplomas. Near the desk was a medium-sized round table with three neat stacks of folders on it.

"You can sit here." He held out one of the chairs at the table for her.

She sat down, and he sat opposite her. "Sorry about the mess," he said, moving one of the stacks to the side. "I'm in the middle of research."

As someone who liked tidiness, she didn't think it was even a little bit messy. She'd seen worse. Much worse.

"Thanks for meeting me on short notice, Jade." He folded his hands and rested them on the table. "I'll get to the point. I need your assistance."

That explained the data sheets he asked her to bring regarding several newspapers in Oklahoma and Missouri. She handed it to him. "I'm happy to help."

"I was hoping you'd say that." His smile widened, and she had to admit Charlotte was right—he was a nice-looking man. A little too nice-looking for her taste. His short black hair was slicked to the side, his dark eyebrows perfectly groomed, his chin appearing freshly shaven despite it being three in the afternoon. His navy blue suit and crimson tie looked perfectly pressed and expensive. All things she would expect from the nephew of a very rich CEO with an impressive financial portfolio.

"I want you to go to Arkansas," he said.

She froze. "W-what?"

He took one of the folders near him and opened it. "I'm putting together a huge acquisitions deal, but I've run into a snag." He pushed the folder toward her.

Jade looked at it. *The Clementine Times?*

"It's been a thorn in my side for months." He tapped the folder. "This small newspaper is the last piece I need to make this deal work, but I can't get to the owner."

She lifted her gaze. Clementine sounded familiar, but she couldn't place it. And she didn't want to. She'd left that state behind a decade ago, and after her failure with Logan, she never looked back.

"I need you to go to Clementine and open negotiations with him."

"But I'm just an accountant."

"Now, you're more than that, Jade." His smile widened, to the point she thought he might hurt himself. "You're a valuable member of the Harrington team."

So valuable he never bothered to talk to her before this, but she shoved that thought aside and looked at the folder's contents again. The top page was mostly specs about the newspaper's circulation, expenditures, history, other business things. Then she got to the list of employees.

Sebastian Hudson—Owner, Publisher, Editor in Chief.

Her gaze flew to Miles. "I can't do this," she blurted.

"Sure you can. In fact, I think you're the only one capable of getting through to him. I did some digging and found out he used to work for *The Arkansas Democrat-Gazette*. Imagine my surprise when I discovered you worked there too." He sat back, extremely satisfied. "What are the chances?"

"Yeah," she mumbled, glancing at Sebastian's name. She hadn't thought about him in years. Not too much anyway. When she packed up and left Arkansas shortly after their last conversation, she'd been filled with guilt over how she'd handled ending their relationship. His telling her he loved her had thrown her for a thousand loops . . . and it had also felt nice. Like when he surprised her with that intense, amazing kiss that nearly made her lose her mind. Those heavenly moments in his arms had nearly made her lose her resolve too, and she almost told him she wouldn't take the job. Somehow, she had regained her senses. Logan was her priority, not her feelings for Sebastian. Better to end it then instead of breaking it off later. That would have inevitably happened—no man would want to be saddled with an instant family and a troubled teenager.

In the end, she didn't even have a family anymore.

"Jade?"

She shifted her focus to Miles. "I'm sorry," she said, pushing the folder toward him. "I'm the last person Sebastian wants to see."

"Because you used to date?"

Her brow lifted, and she almost asked him how he knew that. Then again, she shouldn't be surprised. His uncle Mayfield Harrington and the executive team were very thorough, conscientious, and successful. Of course Miles wouldn't have left a stone unturned. "It didn't end well."

"That was ten years ago. Surely bygones are bygones?" He

leaned forward. "Even if they're not, you can both be professional. I want *The Times*, Jade. It will complete our acquisition of all the community newspapers in that region. The other owners were eager to sell. They understood our mission—to keep newspapers alive in an uncertain industry."

Miles was making sense. And while her time at *The Democrat-Gazette* had been brief, she knew how newspaper employees loved and believed in their work—Sebastian in particular. Besides, he was probably married with a family by now. She had been a quick blip in his life, an unimportant one at that, despite his declaration of love. There was no way he still harbored any feelings for her. Still, doubts persisted. "I've never negotiated anything."

"You don't have to negotiate. Just convince him to talk to me. Once that door is open, I'll take over from there." He stood. "Tifanni has your itinerary, your flight information, where you'll be staying in Clementine."

"But—"

"You'll also have plenty of information about *The Clementine Times*. I'm sure once you've read my proposal, you'll understand we're doing the right thing by purchasing the newspaper. Then you can convince Hudson he's making a mistake by not talking to us."

Jade opened her mouth, then closed it. Miles wasn't looming over her, not exactly. But he was leaning forward and staring intently at her with piercing black eyes that weren't as friendly or eager as his smile. She didn't like that he was making her feel obligated, or that he assumed she would say yes. Then again, she couldn't exactly afford to lose her job or be demoted because Sebastian was being obstinate. "I just have to get him to talk to you?"

"An open line of communication, that's it." He straightened a little. "Once you've accomplished that, you'll return to Harrington and receive a raise and a bonus."

Both? That was unexpected. She stared at Sebastian's name again. She could use the bonus money, and the raise would be nice too. It wasn't like she could say no. Technically she could and he wouldn't fire her, although she didn't think he had that kind of clout . . . yet. But she could kiss any career advancement goodbye if she refused to do what he asked.

"We have a deal then?"

When she glanced up, his smile was almost gone and his expression turned impatient. Clearly he was ready to mark this off his checklist and move on. "Okay," she said, her fingers slightly trembling. She gripped them tight, just as her phone rang in her pocket again.

"Excellent." He gestured for her to leave. "I'm sure you want to get that call."

What she wanted was not to have to go to Arkansas. Instead, she nodded.

"Don't forget to get your packet from Tifanni. I'll be in touch." He went to his desk and back to work.

As Jade left his office, her phone thankfully stopped ringing. She paused at Tifanni's desk.

"Here you go," the secretary said with a smile, handing her two glossy folders with the Harrington Media logo on them. "Have a good trip."

"Uh, thanks." She took the folders and left the office, still in a daze. When she got to the elevator, she almost changed her mind and turned around, then realized she was being silly. Or to be more accurate, cowardly.

She straightened her shoulders and pressed the elevator button. Her assignment was a simple one. She didn't need any special negotiating skills, and she expected her trip to Clementine would be short and sweet. She would be professional, and so would Sebastian. No emotions involved.

If only her nerves would get the message.

———

A week after Flora's retirement, Seb stared at the mess of papers spread across his desk. He needed to work on his column, Seb's View Part Deux, but he'd put off dealing with The Clementine Times's financials long enough. Before she left, Flora had explained her bookkeeping method, and Seb had taken notes. But it wasn't easy looking at a balance sheet that had been in the red more often than the black over the years, and now that he was solely responsible for keeping track of the books, he dreaded opening the ledger. The only thing he was thankful for was that Flora had resisted using a computer bookkeeping program. He definitely didn't want to have to use one of those things.

He shoved his bangs back from his forehead and reached for the ledger. What he really needed, besides a sudden influx of cash, was a haircut.

"Mr. H.?" Tyler poked his head inside the door.

Seb motioned for him to come in. He kept telling the kid to call him Seb, but Tyler refused. Even though Seb was editor in chief, he didn't cotton to formality much, but they finally settled on Mr. H. "Thanks," he said as the young man shut the door behind him.

Tyler's fuzzy, dark brown eyebrows furrowed. "For what?"

"Saving me from this." He swooped his hand over the dreaded book and set it on one of the several crooked piles on his cluttered desk.

"You're, uh, welcome?"

"What brings you by?"

The kid frowned. "Wish I had some good news for you, Mr. H."

Just what he needed—more problems. "Lay it on me."

"We lost Daniel."

Oh no. Seb sat back in his chair, stunned. For eighteen years Daniel had been the carrier for *The Times*'s most difficult route, a zigzag through a rural, mountainous region that was mostly one-way back roads. Seb would know—Buford's cabin was at the highest elevation on the route, and after he passed, he'd bequeathed the cabin to Seb, who tried to spend as much time as he could there. Arkansas didn't experience snowfall, but ice was a problem, and the route was brutal in winter. Daniel rarely missed a day, even during the worst storms. "Was it his heart?" he asked, bracing himself.

"No. Florida." Tyler parked on the chair, and his leg immediately started to bob up and down. The skinny eighteen-year-old go-getter could never keep still. "He and Becky finally decided to retire."

"Oh. *Oh.*" Seb smiled, relieved the septuagenarian hadn't kicked the bucket like he presumed. "Good for him."

"But bad for us."

Seb sobered. "Yeah. Any of our current carriers interested in taking the route?"

Tyler's leg stilled. "No, sir. One even said she'd rather, and I quote, 'Drink a castor oil cocktail.'"

"How specific. And descriptive." He frowned and leaned back in the chair, the creaky noise resounding in the office. This room was larger than the cracker box closet he had at *The Arkansas Democrat-Gazette*, not that he'd needed a big office to do his job. But other than his typewriter, chair, a few reference books, plus the mess of folders and papers on his desk, everything else was still Buford's. Seb didn't want to get rid of any of it, and Buford's nephew Bo was happy to keep his uncle's things here, where they were appreciated.

Bouncing up from the chair, Tyler said, "Don't worry, Mr. H. I'll figure something out. Until then, I'll take the route."

"I can split it with you, if that helps."

"It might, if I can't find anyone. I'll keep you posted."

"Sounds good. Hey, great job on your Witfordville City Hall exposé. I hear rumblings that the mayor might resign because of your reporting."

"He needs to." He turned somber. "Hard to believe there's so much corruption in such a small town."

Seb merely nodded. There was corruption everywhere, especially when politics were concerned. Witfordville, a town only slightly larger than Clementine and about an hour north, wasn't immune from problems, and right now they were mostly instigated by its crooked mayor. But there were plenty of good, solid local politicians interested in the job who hadn't traded in their integrity. Seb had a few friends in Witfordville, and after Tyler's article hit the stands, it looked like things were going to change for the better.

"Thank goodness Mayor Pancake seems to be an all right guy." Tyler broke out a toothy grin. "Catch you later, Mr. H." Tyler dashed out the door.

Seb smiled, but it quickly dimmed. The day was coming when Tyler would put Clementine in his rearview mirror and move on to bigger and better things, just like Seb had when he was the same age. But until then, Seb counted himself lucky to have him. Maybe at some point Tyler would be interested in running *The Times* and following in Seb's footsteps. *If* The Times *is still in business.*

He glanced at the bank statement folder and set it aside. Facing reality could wait another day and he turned to the small desk that was perpendicular to his larger one, where his black Smith Corona manual typewriter made its home. Due to his shoestring staff, he was having to depend on AP and UPI feeds to pad *The Times*— something he didn't care for because, up until the past several years, the newspaper had always been locally focused. At least he could keep his own column going.

He picked up a piece of crisp white paper and wound it into the typewriter. A Macintosh computer with the dust cover still on it was on one of the shelves behind him, untouched since his arrival at *The Clementine Times*. He flexed his fingers with unnecessary flair and started typing his column for tomorrow's paper.

SEB'S VIEW PART DEUX
HOEDOWN LOWDOWN

With the Clementine Annual Memorial Day Hoedown at Wilson Farms coming up this weekend, I've been asked to disseminate the following information:

1. There will be horses, cows, pigs, and chickens at the farm, so plan your footwear accordingly. I suggest old cowboy or rain boots for field and barn touring. Trust the voice of experience: You don't want to bring home anything fragrant on the bottom of your sandals or Air Jordans. If you're planning to congregate around the event tents, dance floor, and food areas within the white oak fence, you're in the clear.

2. Junior Rankins is roasting plenty of oxtail, pork butt, and spareribs, with sides provided by local

Clementine cooks. There will also be food stalls, including the perennial favorite funnel cakes. Bring a big appetite!

3. Bo Wilson is cordoning off a kiddie area with a bouncy castle, crafts, and face painting. A big thank-you to the student volunteers from Clementine High School for helping out with the lil' darlin's.

4. Straight outta Flippin, Arkansas, the Flippin Biscuit Boys will again be providing the music this year, complete with fiddle, banjo, washboard, and jaw harp. For the tenth year in a row, Ms. Eugenia Pickles will be giving square dance lessons, so take advantage of that if you desire. Be ready for a boot-scootin' good time!

5. Per tradition, the last musical number of the night is a Sadie Hawkins one, so, ladies, you still have time to figure out who you're going to ask. Don't be shy now!

6. Finally, have fun, be safe, put on your best smile, and leave your bad attitude at home, 'cause you know Sheriff Thistle and Mayor Pancake won't abide any trouble.

Remember, summer officially begins sundown after the hoedown. See ya Saturday!

"Seb?"

He jumped at the sound of Bo's voice.

"Sorry." Buford's nephew was standing in front of the desk. "I knocked a couple of times. Didn't mean to scare you."

"It's okay." Sometimes he got so caught up in his writing that he tuned out the world. He stood and shook Bo's hand, then gestured to the chair Tyler previously occupied. "Good to see you," he said, sitting back down. "It's been a while."

"Sure has." Bo sat and placed his folded hands over his portly stomach. "Between the hoedown and wedding plans, I'm plum busy, and you know how summertime is on the farm. Lots of work to do up until after the harvest."

"How are the crops this year?"

"Looking good so far, as long as the weather holds. We could use a drenching rain, though."

Bo's words were normal enough, but Seb could tell he looked a little off-center. He definitely wasn't here to shoot the breeze. "What can I do for you?" Seb asked.

Bo ran his palm over his bald pate. "I have a big favor to ask."

"If I can do it, I will."

"It involves Vivian's stepdaughter, Kalista Clark."

"I didn't know she had a stepdaughter."

"I knew about her, but we've never met. Viv and Kalista's father, Raymond, divorced a long time ago, but she and Kalista kept in touch for several years after and then lost touch again. It's a long story, but Kalista's coming to visit for the summer. Viv's missed her. I don't think she realized how much until Raymond called."

Seb nodded. While he'd known Bo almost all his life, the man was thirteen years older than him. Everyone in town was shocked when he announced he was getting married, not just because he was Clementine's oldest bachelor but also because Viv was a former model who lived in California. Not exactly the type of woman one would peg as farmwife material. But she'd proven her mettle when she moved to Clementine earlier this year after they'd gotten engaged. She lived in Bo's small, fifties-era house, and Bo stayed in the bunkhouse with his farmhand on the back forty of the property. The relationship worked for them, and they were getting married later this summer.

Bo adjusted his left suspender over a red short-sleeved shirt. "Kalista arrives tomorrow, and Viv's going to help her find a job so she'll have something to do while she's here. I thought I'd try you first, though."

"You want me to hire her?"

"I was hoping you could. See, Kalista's lived a pampered life. Spoiled rotten is what Viv says, even though she loves her. She says that deep down Kalista is really sweet. It's just hard to find that sweetness when it's swimming in vinegar."

"Does she have any journalism experience?"

"I reckon she doesn't. I know this is a big ask, but since we're family . . ."

They weren't, not technically. But in Seb's book, they were in every way that counted. He didn't believe you had to be blood related to be family. "I'd be glad to help out, but I don't have anything—" He thought about the abandoned route. "Does she know how to drive?"

"She's eighteen, so I assume so. I don't know for sure."

"We have a delivery route open. If she wants to apply for it, send her over. That's the only job I can give her right now. We're low staff as it is."

"Things aren't getting any better?"

Seb shook his head. He could admit that to Bo. "It's hard on newspapers all over, especially since everything's moving to digital. You know how your uncle felt about digital."

"Sure do." He glanced at the MacIntosh. "Bought him that computer over there, thinking he'd appreciate it. He wasn't interested. I can see you're not either."

"My manual typewriter and some good old-fashioned paper are all I need."

"And that's one of the reasons Buford liked you. You're an old soul, Seb. A throwback even. Kinda like myself." He stood and grinned. "I'd better get back to the house. Viv and me are cake testing this afternoon." He patted his large stomach. "I ain't been into all the wedding planning, but today's gonna be a good day."

"Sounds like a delicious one too."

"Sure hope so. Thanks again. I knew I could count on you."

Bo left, and Seb turned back to his column. He was glad he could help Bo and Viv, although he wasn't thrilled with the idea of hiring a spoiled kid. If she worked out, though, it would help him and Tyler, at least in the short term until they could find a permanent carrier.

He started typing, only for the door to open again. "Now what?"

"Good morning to you too, bro." Evelyn Margot paused in the doorway, holding five eight-by-ten pictures of him. She thumbed through them, then showed him the one with a scowl and slid it into the clear frame right outside the door, altering his staff photo to match his current mood. He frowned as she came back in and sat in front of him, placing the rest of the pictures on his desk. "Sorry I'm late."

"For what?"

"My yearly reminder that you're not allowed to duck the Sadie Hawkins dance at the hoedown."

"Not this again. Don't you have some vendors to call? Some ads to create? A lawn to mow?"

She gave him an annoying smirk, bothering him even more. Her smirk looked like his smirk, and if his smirk annoyed other people as much as her smirk annoyed him—

"Lawn's mowed, ads will be done by the end of the day, and I'll make some calls in a bit, so stop dodging the conversation."

"I don't duck the dance." He just made sure he wasn't available when the time came.

"Quack, quack." She crossed her legs, clad in flared jeans with a wide belt, her olive T-shirt tucked inside the waistband. "Or should I say, 'Cluck, cluck'?"

"You're one to talk. When are you going to tell Haskell how you feel about him?"

Evelyn rolled her eyes. "Not this again."

He faced the typewriter. "Payback's a pain, isn't it? And as much fun as this banal conversation is, I have a column to finish."

"I need to talk to you about something else."

He turned to her. "What's that?"

She pushed a lock of her long brown hair over her shoulder. "Piggly Wiggly doesn't want to renew their contract."

Seb groaned. "Why?"

"George wouldn't say, at least not right away," Evelyn said, referring to the grocery store's advertising representative. "But they don't think *The Times* has a big enough circulation anymore. They're going to look at more regional advertising instead of local."

"That's just great." The store was one of their biggest accounts.

"Sorry," she said, her teasing mood completely gone. "I tried to convince him otherwise."

"I'm sure you did." Evelyn was a good salesperson, and he had confidence she'd done everything she could to get them to stay. "Would it help if I called them?" He and George were on friendly terms.

Evelyn shook her head. "I mentioned that. George said the decision's been made."

Seb sighed and rubbed his forehead. So much for the paper being in the black anytime soon. He did some quick calculations in his head. If he didn't hire Kalista—Bo would understand—and he and Tyler split the mountain route until Evelyn found another large advertiser, the paper would bleed less money. But that would also give Tyler a third job and Seb would have . . . He lost track of how many jobs he had. No, they had to hire someone for that route.

There was another thing he could do, but it would take time. Lots of time—something he didn't have. And even if he had the time, he wasn't sure he could pull it off again. The sophomore slump was real.

Evelyn took the rest of the pictures off Seb's desk and stood. "Cheer up, bro. I'm sure we'll get another advertiser soon." She left his office.

He wanted to believe her. And he could carve out some time to make vendor phone calls and help Evelyn in her advertising search. He hated sales almost as much as bookkeeping, but it had to be done. He glanced at his half-finished column. He'd work on it tonight. With another sigh, he picked up the phone, moved his Rolodex closer to him, and started dialing.

Chapter 3

Water cascaded over Jade's car as she leaned back in the driver's seat and closed her eyes. She barely had time for the deluxe car wash, and after the seven-minute-and-thirty-second cycle was complete, she'd have to rush to the airport to catch her flight to Little Rock. That's what she got for procrastinating—something she normally didn't do. Usually she was ahead of schedule.

After reading Miles's information about *The Clementine Times* and his plans to keep the paper afloat after the acquisition, she was convinced he was correct. She just wished he hadn't tapped her for this assignment. The thought of going back to Arkansas filled her with dread. She had had trouble sleeping the past two nights, and her continued self-reassurances that she and Sebastian would both be professional and let the past stay where it belonged didn't help.

Colorful soap bubbled across her white sedan and the industrial scent filled the car interior. She closed her eyes, pushing her impending trip and Sebastian Hudson out of her mind and focusing on the sound of swishing brushes. For a few moments she felt a little peace . . . until her phone rang.

Her eyes flew open, and she grabbed her purse from the passenger's seat and took out her Razr. When she saw the number appear on the small gray screen, her chest tightened. *Logan.* He'd called her at the end of her meeting with Miles but didn't leave a voicemail. She didn't call back, and neither did he. She hadn't heard from him in nearly two years, and it figured he'd pick the worst time to call.

She slipped the phone back inside her purse and closed her eyes again. The water from the rinse cycle crashed against her car, causing it to rock slightly. There. She was getting her bearings back.

The phone rang again, but she refused to answer it. As the huge blow-dryers dried off her car, her cell rang a third time. She grabbed the Razr just in case it was someone else, but it was Logan again. Worry set in. He never called her three times in a row. What if something was seriously wrong? She'd never forgive herself if that were the case. Against her better judgment, she answered. "Logan?"

"Finally," he said, relief in his tone. "I was starting to think you wouldn't pick up."

His voice was raspy and old sounding, especially for a twenty-three-year-old. A side effect of years of drug and alcohol abuse. He also didn't sound upset or panicked. Which was good, but she couldn't stop feeling that he would try to manipulate her again. "What do you want?" She winced at her harsh tone, but she couldn't help it. She couldn't let down her guard.

"I know you're still mad at me," he said. "Just give me a few minutes. Please."

The dryers shut off and she put her car in Drive and inched forward. Something in his tone made her pull over by the manual car wash stalls, although she kept her foot on the brake. "I'm not mad." Well, not as mad as she had been the last time she bailed him out of jail and he promised not to get into trouble again, only to call her a week later for more bail money.

"You sure sound like it."

"Logan—"

"I've changed, Jade."

She tapped her fingers against the steering wheel, resisting another snide remark. How many times had he said those very words? Had promised to get his act together? She believed those promises, just like she believed her mother when she said the same things. And just like her mother, he continued to use, continued to break the law, continued to drain her financially and emotionally. Lydia had finally left her alone after five years of bleeding her bank account, and Jade had to cut off Logan just to keep from going bankrupt.

"I'm telling the truth this time. I'm sober and living in a halfway house."

She could almost picture him, his ebony eyes darting around as if trouble constantly followed him, because it usually did. "If you're okay, then why are you calling me?"

"We need to talk."

"We're talking now."

"Not over the phone." His tone turned urgent. "In person."

She tilted her wrist and glanced at her watch. "No. I told you the last time we talked I was done helping you out."

"But—"

"Bye, Logan." Before he could say anything else, she cut him off and tossed the phone onto the passenger seat. She hung her head and tried to settle down. This was the first time he'd mentioned a halfway house. Was he finally getting his life on track? *Or is he trying to play me again?*

Jade lifted her head, her teeth clenching as she left the car wash and drove to the airport. She wasn't responsible for Logan anymore, and she wasn't going to support or fund her little brother's self-destruction. She'd told him that right before she'd cut off contact, and he'd been upset, spewing vile things at her—words that cut her to the core, even though she knew they were coming from a drug-induced haze.

Her watch glinted in the sun, and when she saw the time, she panicked. If she didn't hurry, she'd miss her flight. She zoomed off to the Hartsfield-Jackson airport. Whatever Logan wanted, he'd have to figure it out himself.

Two hours later, she was settled in her seat on the airplane, waiting for takeoff. In about ninety minutes she would land at Little Rock airport, then pick up the rental car reserved for her, and drive nearly three hours to Clementine. Even though she'd grown up in Little Rock, she'd never been to the Ozarks. As an adult, she'd been too busy, and it wasn't like her mother would have ever taken her anywhere during the infrequent times she was able to keep custody of Jade.

She pushed off those thoughts and switched to Sebastian. Miles hadn't set up a meeting time with him, and she had sent him an email asking why. *"How busy can he be? I'm sure he'll fit you in,"* was his response. At first she was confused and almost asked him for clarification, only to realize that surprising Sebastian at his office would make it harder for him to say no. Theoretically anyway. She'd find out if that was the case soon enough.

The plane lifted off, and she pulled out her handheld personal digital assistant and worked on her plan, although there was nothing left for her to do but a few tweaks. It was straightforward—she'd explain Miles's position and how it would benefit Sebastian and *The Times*. Miles had revealed how much Harrington Media was willing to pay, and the offer was more than generous. From a business standpoint, Sebastian would be a fool not to accept, considering *The Times*'s desperate financial position.

But would he be willing to hear that information from her? She wasn't sure. All she could do was hope he would be reasonable.

———

"Rise and shine!"

Kalista shielded her eyes from the bright light that suddenly came on in Bo's spare bedroom. She grimaced and sat up as Viv approached her with a wide smile, showcasing straight white teeth that had graced many a fashion magazine cover in the seventies and early eighties, her chin-length bob smooth and sleek. Her former stepmother had almost reached supermodel status, only to walk away from the business when she was at the top of her game—something Kalista never understood.

"What time is it?" Her bleary eyes glanced at the old-fashioned alarm clock on the equally old-fashioned bedside table. "Six thirty? I slept all day?"

Viv sat next to her on the soft mattress. "It's six thirty in the morning."

Kalista fell back against the pillow and groaned. "You know I don't rise and shine until after ten."

"That's about to change, young lady." Viv's cultured voice held a slight Southern twang. "I let you sleep in today."

Six thirty was sleeping in?

Viv's salt-and-pepper bangs were pulled back with a red scarf. "There's lots to do on the farm. Bo always takes care of the heavy farmwork, but we have chickens, pigs, and goats to feed."

Kalista felt faint. "I have to feed pigs?"

Viv's smile widened. "You'll love them. Their snorts and grunts are adorable."

It was official. Vivian had lost her marbles.

"We also have to get ready for the hoedown on Saturday."

"The what?" It was like she was in a foreign country.

"The Clementine Memorial Day Hoedown." Viv went to the window on the opposite side of the room and pulled open the red-and-white gingham curtains. Light poured inside. "You'll have a great time. Everyone does."

Doubt it. The excitement of seeing her former stepmother after so many years was starting to wear off. Viv had changed, and she barely recognized her. The old Viv loved to shop, get mani-pedis, peruse fashion magazines, and attend lavish parties. She'd lived to be seen, and Kalista had loved being seen with her, even as a preteen, although the parties had always been off-limits.

The Viv sitting next to her was a different woman. Completely barefaced and wearing a blue gingham sleeveless shirt and knee-length blue jean shorts, she looked like she'd come in straight from the barn. She didn't even appear to be wearing lip balm. Unthinkable.

Kalista covered her face with one of the fluffy white bed pillows. "I'm going back to sleep."

"Nope." Viv grabbed the pillow, dropped it on the bed, and stood. "You're getting dressed and going to your first job interview."

"I have one already?"

"Bo arranged it for you. He had to call in a favor, so you don't want to be late."

Kalista scowled and shoved off the covers. She shouldn't have let Daddy make her come to Podunk, Arkansas. She should be back in Los Angeles with her friends having fun, hanging out at the beach. She was a California girl through and through. She was also starting to think Bettany put her dad up to this. She wouldn't put it past her current stepmother to use the time Kalista was away to dip her paws further into Daddy's bank account.

"But Daddy has to teach me a lesson," she muttered as she got up from the bed.

"What?" Viv was inside the closet, pushing hangers across the clothes bar. She poked her head outside the door. "Oh boy," she said, looking at Kalista from head to toe before ducking back into the closet again.

"What?" Kalista walked toward her.

Viv tossed a robe at her. "Put this on. You can't walk around the house wearing next to nothing."

Kalista looked down at her plum-colored negligee. "What's wrong with this?"

"It's inappropriate."

"It's a nightgown, Viv. You've worn less than this at the beach."

"And I regret being so immodest."

"A bikini isn't immodest. Neither is a little nightgown." Kalista rolled her eyes. "It's not like it's see-through."

"It's too short and leaves too little to the imagination." Viv crossed her arms. "I don't want you to embarrass Bo if he drops by. There are also men working outside and getting the property ready for Saturday."

Although Viv's tone was kind, Kalista scowled anyway and slipped on the frumpy housecoat. Her skin recoiled at the polyester fabric, the pattern straight out of the seventies—large yellow flowers on an avocado green background. "Where did you get this thing?"

"It belonged to Bo's mother." Viv shut the door. "It's vintage, by the way. Don't be so condescending."

Kalista put her hands on her hips. "You wouldn't have worn this a few years ago."

Viv faced her. "I've grown up since then. Do you want sausage gravy with your biscuits?"

"Ew, carbs."

Viv sighed. "Suit yourself," she said, and walked out of the room.

Kalista plopped down on the edge of the bed and folded her arms over her chest. Viv had picked her up from the airport in Little Rock yesterday, and they had caught up during the drive to Clementine. But it wasn't long into their conversation that Kalista realized Viv was different. When they got to Bo's house where Viv was living until they got married, he'd already gone to bed in something called a bunkhouse. Kalista was still trying to comprehend that Viv was engaged to an almost fifty-year-old farmer who'd never been married before.

Then there was the house—a fifties-era cottage with only two bedrooms, one bathroom, a tiny kitchen with linoleum flooring, and a small living room that featured a TV on a stand. How could anyone live in a place so small, even if they were single? When Viv and Daddy were married, she decorated their massive LA house in the latest style, and everything was expensive and chic, not country bumpkin. The woman had gone all *Little House on the Prairie*.

She reached for her phone and checked for any texts or voicemails. She'd let her friends know she was leaving "on vacation" but didn't tell them where—just gave hints that it was somewhere tropical and expensive and that she'd be gone awhile. Huh. Not a single call or message, not even from Ryan. She thought about calling him, then remembered it was way too early. Her friends rarely stirred until noon.

Scratching her arm, she felt the polyester fabric again and jumped up from the bed. Her skin didn't need this kind of abuse.

She opened one of her Louis Vuitton suitcases and searched for something to wear to her interview. Finally deciding on a crimson off-the-shoulder dress and sandals, she got dressed, then squeezed into the minuscule bathroom and peered at her reflection. Ugh, the humidity was already frizzing her blond hair, so she swept it up in a long ponytail to hide the state of it.

"Kalista, breakfast is ready!" Viv called from the kitchen.

"Be there in a minute." She needed to do her makeup and apply a generous amount of hairspray to the flyaways that were already escaping her ponytail.

"Kitchen's closing in ten minutes," Viv said. "You eat now, or you don't eat at all."

"What a crabby patty," Kalista muttered. She didn't remember Viv being so militant either. Oh well, she'd scarf down a piece of bacon, finish getting dressed, then find a decent coffee shop for a much-needed cappuccino. Surely there was one in downtown Clementine.

Viv was at the kitchen sink washing dishes in a white apron with a frilly red hem. She turned and tilted her head toward the round table. "Help yourself . . . Wait." Viv dried her hands and faced her. "You're not wearing that to your interview."

"What's wrong with this?" First, she'd criticized her nightwear, and now she was fussing about her cute outfit. It was certainly modest enough. There was nothing indecent about a bare shoulder.

"You look like you're going to a cocktail party." Her expression grew soft. "You've never been to a job interview before, have you?"

Kalista lifted her chin. Until now, she'd never needed to. What was the point of having an über-rich father if she had to work for her money?

Viv pulled out a chair. "Let's have breakfast first. Then we'll look at the clothes you brought. Surely you have something suitable."

"This *is* suitable," she muttered and sat down.

Viv placed a small plate with one boiled egg and two pieces of bacon in front of Kalista. Then she poured two cups of coffee and joined her at the table. Kalista had just picked up one of the bacon strips when Viv took her hand.

"We pray before our meals," she said softly.

Kalista set the bacon down. Viv closed her eyes and prayed silently while Kalista stared at her plate. She'd never prayed or gone to church in her life. Her daddy always played golf on Sundays, and her other stepmothers always slept in. *Like I should be doing.*

When Viv finished, she picked up her coffee cup and took a sip. "Bo's coming over for supper tonight. He's eager to meet you. We're having pork chops, baked potatoes, and salad. Would you mind going to the Piggly Wiggly after your interview and picking up a few things?"

"The wiggle what?"

"Piggly Wiggly. That's our closest grocery store, and there's been so much to do lately I haven't had time to stock up for your visit. I'll give you a list and some money. Feel free to get what you want to eat too."

"Do they have a sushi bar?" She bit into the bacon. Wow. It was delicious.

"Ah, no."

"Do they have an organic section at least?"

She shook her head. "Not at this grocery store. The pork and chicken we raise here on the farm is organic, but Bo doesn't have a garden, and I didn't have time to put one in this year. I will next spring. If you need other organics, we can go to Harrison or take a trip to Russellville. Maybe even go to Little Rock, although that's quite a drive."

"How do you live so isolated, Viv?"

"I love it." She sat back in her chair. "I got so tired of the fast-paced life. It was burning me out."

"Is that why you left modeling too?" She'd always wondered, but until now she never asked. As a kid, she hadn't wanted Viv to get mad at her and not see her anymore after the divorce, and when she got older, well, she wasn't really interested. Seeing Viv's shocking change piqued her curiosity again.

She shook her head. "The industry was soul crushing, Kalista. I used to lament that I'd never made it to the top, but now I'm glad I didn't."

"You could have, though. You could still model now." Despite the lack of glamour, Viv had kept her figure, and for an older woman, she still looked stunning.

"I'm happy here in Clementine, and I love the farm and small-town life. Bo is the best thing that ever happened to me." She took Kalista's hand again, her eyes misty. "Did I tell you how much it means to me that you're going to be at my wedding?"

Surprised, Kalista felt a lump form in her throat. "I'm glad I will be too." From what she could tell, Viv's wedding was the only thing she had to look forward to, other than going back to California. It was nice to hear someone wanted her to be around. Until the past week or so, her daddy didn't seem to care, and of course Bettany and her other stepmothers had seen her as a nuisance. But not Viv. Kalista smiled—her first real one since leaving LA.

Viv glanced at the rooster clock on the wall. "You need to hurry or you'll be late for your interview with Sebastian." She jumped up from the chair and dragged Kalista to the bedroom. "You'll barely have time to change clothes."

"But I still have to put on my makeup." That was a thirty-minute process, minimum.

"There's no time for that." At Kalista's shocked look, Viv added, "Don't worry. You're lovely without it."

Kalista grimaced, doubting her words. Her hair looked awful, she had no idea what kind of dowdy clothes Viv would insist she wear, and now she couldn't put on makeup. What a disaster. *It's going to be a long three months.*

Chapter 4

I hope you enjoyed breakfast, Ms. Smith."

"It was delicious." Jade dabbed at the corner of her mouth with her napkin as she looked at Mabel, owner of the Clementine Inn. The inn was expectedly small, with only eight rooms, and each one had a different country theme. Jade was in the cowboy room, and she had to admit that while it wasn't her style, it was tastefully done. Although she could do without the steer head hanging on the wall above her bed.

"Clyde is famous for his biscuits around these parts." Mabel beamed with pride as she referred to her husband, a slim man who was just as friendly as his wife. She straightened the black napkin holder on the table. "Are you here for the hoedown this weekend?"

Mabel was friendly, but Jade wasn't in the mood for a chat. She'd planned to get a cup of coffee, her normal breakfast of champions, but she'd skipped dinner last night and the scent of biscuits and gravy from the modest breakfast buffet had been irresistible. Sausage gravy was her weakness. "No, just a meeting." If only it were *just* a meeting. Her nerves started up again. Ugh, she shouldn't have eaten so much for breakfast. When she stood and started clearing her plate, Mabel intervened.

"Don't worry, hon, I'll clean this up. Just let me, Clyde, or the staff know if you need anything else."

"Thank you." Jade forced a smile at Mabel's kindness, even though she could barely contain her anxiety.

"Sure thing. You have a blessed day."

Jade's smile relaxed into something more natural. Even though she still lived in the South, she missed this kind of sweet Southern hospitality that was in short supply in a large city. She was certain she could find it in rural Georgia, but she never ventured past the Atlanta suburbs. She never had the time. *Or made the time.*

She had twenty minutes before she needed to leave for downtown Clementine where *The Clementine Times* office was located, so she hurried back to her room. She half expected Logan to call her back, but so far he hadn't. She felt some relief that he was respecting her boundaries, but there was a part of her that wondered if she was doing the right thing by not listening to what he had to say. He didn't ask her for anything, just to talk, and that was new. What if . . . ?

No. There were no what-ifs when it came to Logan. For her own sanity and financial health, she had to keep her distance, even if he was telling the truth. Even if she missed him. *Even though it hurts.*

Blocking off her feelings about Logan, she went into the bathroom to touch up her hair and makeup, pausing to stare in the mirror. Her hair had been short ten years ago, and now it was shoulder length. Despite watching her diet—that went out the window this morning—and exercising when she could, she wasn't as thin as she was a decade ago. Would Sebastian notice? Would he care?

And why was she wondering whether he would or wouldn't?

Shaking her head, she left the bathroom. All she needed was to look presentable and professional, which she always did. Even on business casual Fridays, she still wore her power suits and sensible pumps. She grabbed her briefcase filled with spreadsheets and other persuasive sales collateral, just in case Sebastian had questions. The latch opened on its own, her papers falling to the floor.

"What in the world?" She looked at the latch. It seemed fine, and it had never failed before. She grimaced, picking up the papers, organizing them in their original stacks, and putting them in the case, making sure it fastened tightly. Giving it a shake, it stayed shut. She must not have closed it properly the last time she opened it.

Mustering confidence she didn't feel, Jade marched out of the Clementine Inn to her rental car, a black two-door Nissan that had a little pep but not much room. She hadn't expected Miles to splurge on a Cadillac or some other luxury rental, but the Nissan seemed cheap. Fortunately she wouldn't be in Arkansas for long. Despite it being mid-May, it was already humid and warm, making her sweat. Or was it her nerves? Probably both.

The drive from the inn to downtown Clementine was quick. Too quick, and when she pulled the Nissan into one of the three parking spaces in front of *The Clementine Times* office, she didn't get out of the car. Instead, she put it in Park and flipped the air conditioner dial to its highest setting.

Only the quaint, historic building separated her from Sebastian, and she felt her tenuous resolve slip away. What if he refused to see her? What if he was still angry about the past? What if he agreed to see her but simply wouldn't listen to reason? She might not be able to get him to talk to Miles or anyone else from Harrington Media.

She pressed her fingertips to her temples. The spiral was getting her nowhere. Miles had faith in her—why didn't she have it in herself? And if she did fail, it wasn't like she was going to be fired . . . right? Oh no. What if she was? She couldn't afford to lose her job. She still had a loan and credit cards to pay off from trying to help Logan and Lydia—

Thump. Thump.

She jumped at the sound on the driver's side window. When she turned, she could see only the beltline on a pair of well-worn khakis. "Can I help you?" she asked through the glass. Years of living in a big city had taught her to be cautious.

"You can't park here."

Jade froze, recognizing the man's voice before he bent over and peered at her. And when she raised her gaze—*oh . . . my*—she was face-to-face with Sebastian Hudson.

———

Seb blinked as he stared at the auburn-haired woman in the car. When he saw she'd taken his reserved parking space—the only perk he allowed himself as publisher and editor in chief—he was irritated. Everyone in Clementine knew not to park here. Then he saw the Illinois plate on the back of her car, and he settled down. He couldn't blame an out-of-towner for stealing his spot. He parked in the next space, got out of his thirteen-year-old red Nissan Altima, and knocked on the window. When she turned and faced him, he froze.

She looked familiar—so familiar that he . . . no. It couldn't be her. And for a minute he was sure she wasn't. The Jade Smith he remembered had a short pixie cut, and this woman had long hair with luxurious waves that fell past her shoulders. Yowzah. Green eyes too, but green eyes and red hair weren't a rare combination.

Besides, there wasn't a single reason on earth for Jade to be in Clementine, much less Arkansas. She'd shaken off the dust of the state over a decade ago. This must be her doppelganger—

Honk!

He jumped and pressed his body against the woman's car as an old truck almost hit him. He spun around and saw the vehicle slow down, hitch and jerk, and finally park crookedly in one of the last empty spots in front of the news building. He peered at the truck. Hold up. That was one of Bo's junkers. But his friend wouldn't drive like that unless he'd been drinking, and that was impossible. Bo had been a teetotaler all his life.

Knock. Knock.

The woman seated in her car now at his back tapped on her window a third time. Oh, right, the Jade look-alike. He stepped aside as she opened the car door. "Lady, I know you're new here, but this is my—"

"Hey! Are you Mr. Hudson?"

Seb turned as a very young woman advanced toward him. So Bo wasn't driving the truck, thank goodness, and this must be Kalista, Viv's stepdaughter—

"Sebastian?"

Slowly he turned. This was no doppelganger. This was Jade. *His* Jade. He shook off the thought. She'd never been his.

"Mister?"

Kalista's high-pitched question pulled his attention away again. He glanced at her, seeing her tapping one sandaled foot. How did he manage to get sandwiched between these two?

"Excuse me, we were talking before you pulled up," Jade said, peering around Seb.

"Whatever."

Seb's gaze bobbed between them as they stared each other

down. Jade's cool-as-an-ice-bath expression had met its match in this high-and-mighty teenager. He'd seen Jade in this mode plenty of times at work. Business Jade was all business, and she could be a bit intimidating.

Kalista was undeterred. "I have an interview."

"I have a meeting," Jade responded.

Meeting? What meeting?

"And I was here first," Jade added.

"Beauty before age, right?"

"*Excuse* me?"

Unnoticed, Seb slowly backed away, hurried into the building, and went straight to his office, quickly shutting the door behind him. He sank on the chair behind his desk. Now that he'd met Kalista, he wasn't impressed. She was haughty, and he wasn't about to subject any of his employees to her entitlement. Besides, she probably wouldn't take a lowly delivery job anyway. Then there was the fact that she seemed to be a terrible driver, at least with Bo's truck. He'd go through the motions of the interview for Bo's and Viv's sakes, then move on to finding someone else.

But he had no idea what Jade was talking about. Surely, she wasn't here to meet him. But who else would she be meeting with? Evelyn Margot was working from home this morning—something she did fairly often. She could call advertising leads from her apartment just as easily as she could from her office here.

He searched his desk for his calendar and opened it to May. Nope, nothing written here about a meeting with anyone, although he didn't exactly use his calendar very often. He hadn't even made a note of Kalista's interview. Maybe Evelyn had scheduled Jade and not told him. If so, he'd have a word with her about keeping him apprised of stuff like this. He didn't like being unprepared. Especially not where Jade was concerned, although his sister had no idea who she was.

Then he thought of a more likely explanation—Jade had a meeting with someone else in the building. Including the press and circulation rooms in the basement, The Times's operation took up most of the 1920s brick structure. But there were two other offices on the third floor that housed businesses—Larry Wilson's insurance company and Benji Mason's fledgling chiropractor practice. Good, he had nothing to worry about.

Except his accelerated pulse. That could be explained by his hurrying to his office, although he'd never had a heightened heartbeat before from fast walking. Surely it wasn't because of Jade. He'd blocked his feelings from her many years ago. One glimpse of her wouldn't cause them to resurface. No way, no how—

"Mr. H.—"

"What!"

Tyler flinched, his head poking inside the door. "Uh, sorry to disturb you."

"No, I'm sorry, Tyler. I'm . . ." *Confused.* "Is Kalista ready?"

Tyler frowned. "Kalista?"

"Yeah, the girl, um, woman, that's interviewing for the delivery job. Blond hair, uh . . ." He couldn't remember what she was wearing. Although he did notice that Jade had on a plum-colored blouse, navy blue pants, and she still sported plain black pumps, the same kind she wore back in the day—

"The one wearing the pretty blue-and-white flowered dress?" Tyler asked.

"Uh, sure. That one."

"Yes, she's here too." His eyes turned moony. "Kalista. That's a nice name."

"What do you mean 'too'?"

"There's another lady who wants to see you."

His stomach sank. "Please tell me it's not the redhead."

"Okay, but I'd be lyin' if I did."

Seb shifted in his chair. Okay, so Jade was here to see him. But what could she possibly want after all these years?

"Mr. H.?"

"All right, send her in."

"Which one?"

He paused. He was extremely curious about Jade, but he already agreed to interview Kalista right now. "Kalista," he said. "Tell Jade, er, Ms. Smith to wait in the reception area."

"Will do. Then I'll head over to Cherry Hill to cover their library reopening."

"Right. Thanks, Tyler."

"Sure thing, Mr. H."

When Tyler left, Seb fell back in his chair, questions flooding his mind. After Jade had told him about the job in Atlanta, she quit immediately without notice and without talking to Seb again. He'd been hurt over that too, but more frustrated with himself for jumping to the wrong conclusion about their short relationship. After she was out of his life, he moved on. Not with a new girlfriend, but with his job, and then he'd bought *The Times* and moved back here. Buying the newspaper had been a godsend in more ways than one, since it kept and continued to keep him extremely busy, to the point that Jade Smith moved to the recesses of his memory. Eventually he stopped thinking about her.

But seeing her again, even for a few minutes, and knowing she would be in his office soon, sent him inexplicably reeling. Had she moved back to Arkansas, and was she just dropping by for a visit? Or was she passing through and wanted to say hello? He discarded both of those. She'd specifically said meeting, which denoted business. But what business could she possibly have with him and/or *The Times*?

Kalista sat in the reception area at *The Clementine Times* and crossed her legs. She tapped her nails against her elbow and glanced around the old, tired-looking space. Framed newspaper columns were all over the walls. Two seats down sat the redheaded woman she'd argued with earlier. She was a piece of work, all high and mighty and demanding in her boring navy blue business suit. It was sweltering out and she had a jacket on. She did have pretty hair, though. Kalista would give her that.

She brushed off the old dress Viv had given her to wear, certain that there was dirt on the country blue-and-white flowered fabric. Polyester again, although she had to admit that she liked the fit of the dress, which reached to her mid-calf. With its three-quarter sleeves, it certainly was modest. And hot. How did people back in olden days deal with this heat when their fabrics didn't breathe?

And then there was the truck—an old green jalopy that backfired when she turned the ignition key. She'd never driven such a big vehicle before, much less one with no power steering. The radio was broken and only played AM stations, so she couldn't even listen to her music. She did feel a little bad she'd scared the tall man who had been talking to the redheaded woman, but she was in a hurry and didn't want to miss the interview.

The Hispanic guy who told them to sit down as he went to get "Mr. H." reappeared. He looked like someone who worked at a newspaper—owlish glasses, skinny as a ski pole, emo-looking black hair pressed against his head. His cargo shorts and white

T-shirt were way too baggy, and one of his raggedy high-top tennis shoes was untied. *And Viv said I dressed unprofessionally.*

"Mr. H. says he'll see you now." When the redheaded woman started to stand, he shook his head. "Not you, ma'am." He turned to Kalista and grinned. "He's ready for your interview."

Hmm. He was kind of cute when he smiled. "Thank you . . ."

"Tyler." His cheeks turned rosy as he looked down at his shoes. Then he turned to the other woman. "He said you can wait here."

The woman didn't say anything, but her lips were pressed into a thin line. She yanked something that looked like a cell phone with a big screen out of the pocket of her jacket and started tapping on it.

"Mr. H.'s office is down the hall and around the corner. It says Editor in Chief on the door." He grabbed a steno pad and pencil from the empty desk in the reception area. "I've got to run to Cherry Hill," he said, tucking the pencil behind his ear before dashing out of the room.

Kalista's fingers and toes suddenly turned cold as she headed down a dark hall that could use another ceiling light. When she neared the corner, she had the urge to run off, call Daddy, and tell him she wanted to come home. She could get a job in LA, easy. Maybe she could even work for her father, although he'd never offered her a job before. Come to think of it, that was a little insulting. Didn't he think she would be responsible?

No, he didn't. He'd said as much that day by the pool, and she barely listened to him. Now she remembered his words clearly.

She couldn't go home anyway, not until after Viv's wedding. She didn't want to disappoint her. There was no choice but to go through with the interview. She stopped in front of the door, hesitated, then knocked.

"Come in," a super deep male voice said.

She opened the door and saw that the guy in the parking lot had indeed been Mr. Hudson. He was sitting behind a messy desk. A really messy desk, and the rest of his office didn't look all that neat either. Not dirty, just crazy cluttered. He had on a crumply short-sleeved green-and-white plaid shirt, and even though his shaggy, grayish, light brown hair and two-day scruff made him look a little disheveled, he had striking blue eyes. Decent looking for an old man.

"Kalista, right?"

"That's me," she said with a little wave.

"Have a seat." He gestured to an old leather chair in front of the desk, then got up and walked to a tall filing cabinet. As she sat down, she noticed an old-fashioned typewriter on a short desk next to a larger desk with stacks of papers precariously balanced on the corners.

Mr. Hudson opened one of the drawers and thumbed through file folders, stopping in the middle and pulling out a sheet of paper. He shut the drawer and handed it to her. "Fill this out. I'll be back."

She took it and looked at the header. *Clementine Times* Application for Employment.

"Want some coffee?"

Coffee would be heavenly. "Espresso."

His scruffy face broke out in a smirk. "Yeah. Right." Then he walked out.

Humph. The sooner she finished this interview the better. Although Viv didn't know the job Kalista was interviewing for—Bo hadn't mentioned it to her—she assumed it was for the receptionist job since there was a desk but no receptionist in the waiting room. That gave her a little confidence. She would be the perfect receptionist since she was a pro at talking on the phone and telling people hello.

But she wasn't sure she should take it if he offered it to her. She didn't want to work in an old newspaper office. There had to be something else in Clementine that would be more suitable and fun. A salon or a spa. A cute little boutique even. This was all a formality.

She fished through her designer bag, found a pink pen with a fuzzy pom-pom on the end, and uncapped it, then filled in her name, address, and other simple-to-answer blanks until she got to the job history section.

List your last three jobs/positions.

What was she supposed to put here? The section was a table with the headings What, Where, and When. She wracked her brain and was about to skip the section entirely when an idea hit.

What: Office Aide.

Where: Beverly Hills High School

When: 2003

She smiled. That would work. Next question.

List any previous experience or skills you have for this position.

Kalista relaxed. Since she wasn't accepting the job, she just wrote one sentence.

I have a gorgeous smile, extensive experience talking on the phone, and a lovely demeanor.

The last section asked for references, and she wrote down Viv's name and phone number. She didn't remember her exact address, although it was something Country Road and she had the directions in the truck. She thought about putting down Daddy's name but didn't bother. No one here would know who he was anyway.

The door opened and Mr. Hudson appeared with two mugs and placed them on the desk. One had *The Clementine Times* logo on it and the other one said I May Be Wrong, but It's Highly Unlikely. Kalista got the logo mug.

"I'm finished," she said, grinning proudly as she handed him the application. He started to read over it while Kalista took an eager sip of coffee. Instantly she started to choke.

"Too strong?" he said, still looking at the application. He took a sip, unaffected.

"No," she rasped. What in the world did he brew this with—nail polish remover?

"I made it weaker than normal." He took another drink and set down the mug, then started to frown. The frown deepened as he kept reading. Finally, he looked at Kalista. "This is . . ."

She folded her hands on her lap and smiled.

He kept watching her, and she kept smiling. His expression was blank, and she couldn't tell what he was thinking. Her smile dipped as he remained silent.

Finally he shrugged and tossed the application aside. "Doesn't matter. You don't have to have experience to do the job. Tyler will train you. Wait, one question. Have you ever thrown a baseball?"

"What does that have to do with being a receptionist?"

Mr. Hudson tilted his head, then chuckled. "Didn't Bo tell you what you were interviewing for?"

"I haven't met him yet, and Viv didn't know."

He leaned forward. "This is a delivery job."

Kalista frowned. "Delivering what?"

"The paper."

Her jaw dropped. "I applied to be a delivery boy?"

"Girl. Woman." He waved his hand. "I saw you driving Bo's truck. It's got four-wheel drive, so you should be fine in the mountains, if you can get your parking under control."

"Mountains?"

"You'll start at 3:00 a.m. A little earlier than our other two delivery guys."

That was insane. So was driving in the mountains. She'd only ever skied on them. And throwing newspapers? No way. "I think there's been a mistake."

"Is that right?" He slowly sat back in the chair, his gaze landing on hers. "Obviously you can't do the job."

She went very still. How dare he tell her that? How hard could it be to toss a paper on the porch? Did he think she couldn't do such a simple task? "Oh, I think I can."

"And I'm sure you can't."

The nerve of this man. He didn't know her, or what she was capable of. "You're wrong, and I'll prove it to you."

A slight smile. "So you want the job?"

"Yes." Wait, what was she saying? She didn't want to deliver newspapers. She was above that.

"Then you're hired. I'll let Tyler know you'll meet him in the press room tomorrow at three for training until noon. After that, your hours will be three until you finish the route, usually by five or six o'clock."

Kalista's stomach slowly sank inward. "Uh . . ."

"Great. Welcome to *The Times*." He motioned to the door and turned to his typewriter, then began tapping on the keys like she wasn't even there.

Humph again. She snatched her purse and shot up from the chair. Spinning on her heel, she headed for the door. Then she stopped and almost turned around to tell him to forget it when she realized what had just happened.

She had a job. *I have a job!*

An unexpected giddy feeling went through her as she opened the door and left Mr. Hudson's office.

But as she made her way down the hall, her giddiness disappeared. She was glad she could call her father and tell him she'd found a job so quickly. That would show him she was responsible. However, under no circumstances could she let her friends find out that she was going to be a newspaper boy ... girl ... whatever. She would never live it down.

Chapter 5

After Kalista left his office, Seb sat back in his chair wondering if he'd made the right decision hiring her. He surprised himself when he changed his mind. Her application answers were a joke, and he initially thought she was treating the interview in kind when he saw the fluffy pink pom-pom pen she'd used to write on the form.

But there was something in her eyes—a defiant steeliness that he'd almost missed at first. Maybe she would work out after all. Viv certainly thought she was worth helping. And if Kalista couldn't handle the job, he could let her go, although he hated firing people. He'd only done it twice since owning *The Times*, but both had been necessary. He'd give her a week or three to learn and do the route, then reevaluate. He'd have to remind Tyler to keep his mind on the job and not on his trainee's looks, though. He already seemed a bit sweet on her.

That settled, he gulped another swig of coffee and shifted his focus to Jade. He set the cup down and absently ran his hand through his hair, patting down the stray ends, then stopped when he realized he was primping. Ridiculous. "Let's get this over with," he muttered, shoving Kalista's paperwork under one of the stacks on his desk, then walking out of his office to the reception area.

When he saw Jade, he stilled.

She was sitting with one leg crossed over the other, her gaze focused on the screen of her PDA, a small stylus in hand. He'd never owned one of those either and didn't intend to. He'd lived forty years without all these electronic gadgets everyone was entranced with, and he was doing just fine without them, although he did have a simple cell phone. That came in handy when he was working as a reporter.

Seb's eyes traveled to her profile. Her hair hung in waves, partially obscuring her face. Back in the day, he thought her pixie cut was cute. But the style she wore now was sophisticated. Elegant. Sexy.

As if she heard his thoughts, she looked up, their eyes locking like they were in a schlocky romance novel. His mind whirred with memories of their short, and for him intense, relationship.

"Mr. Hudson?" she said, coming to her feet.

Her formality came as a jab, and any idea that she might still harbor feelings for him sailed out the door. No problem. He could be professional. He could forget about the past and pretend they weren't an item. Because apparently they hadn't been. Only in his mind. "Ms. Smith."

"I apologize for not contacting you sooner to arrange a meeting. I should have been more considerate of your schedule." Her gaze flicked away for a split second, the only glimpse that she wasn't completely in control. "If you have some time, I'd like to discuss something with you."

"And what would that be?"

His question seemed to catch her off guard. "I, uh, would prefer if we talk in private."

Now his curiosity was fully piqued. He glanced at her hands. She had them loosely clasped and, more importantly, they weren't shaking. Cool as the proverbial cucumber—that was Jade Smith. Although he knew she ran much hotter underneath the surface. He also saw that her fingers were bare. No wedding ring, or any other rings. Interesting.

"C'mon back," he said, motioning for her to follow him. He'd give her a chance to explain why she was here. At this point he was dying to know.

———

Jade followed Sebastian down a dim corridor to his office. The words Editor in Chief were etched on the glass door, and there was an empty space for a photo next to it. She tried to pay more attention to her surroundings than to the man in front of her, but it was difficult. Keeping her cool in the reception area had been hard enough, because being around Sebastian Hudson was bringing emotions to the surface that she thought she'd buried long ago.

While waiting on him, she realized she'd made a huge mistake by not contacting him prior to coming to *The Times* office, something she would be sure to tell Miles. Then when Sebastian entered the room and she heard his deep, rich voice, took in his casual yet somehow appealing appearance, she had to double down on her business voice as she apologized. She could tell by his irritated expression he didn't like the formality. He never did, and it seemed weird to call a man she had kissed more than once—and so passionately the last time they were together—by his surname. If she didn't cling to professionalism, her toes would continue curling in her pumps at the sight and sound of him, and that wouldn't do.

He opened the door and gestured for her to walk inside. She nodded her thanks and entered the office, pausing a few feet from the door. The room seemed to be frozen in time, and *Clementine Times* mementos took up almost every inch of wall and shelf space in a room filled with furnishings from the fifties. Her gaze landed on the large, scuffed desk piled high with paperwork. She almost laughed. His penchant for clutter hadn't changed.

"Have a seat," he said, pointing to another old chair in front of the desk.

She set her briefcase on the floor and sat down while he moved to his own seat. Against her will, her heart skipped a beat as she took in his thick sandy-brown hair threaded with gray and touching the collar of his plaid shirt, his shaggy bangs hovering over his eyes. He'd never been one to embrace the corporate look, and he'd probably thrown away his one and only tie when he moved to Clementine. She pressed her toes into her pumps.

Then she noticed he wasn't wearing a wedding ring. That didn't necessarily mean anything—he could still be married and prefer not to wear one for some reason.

"All right, Ms. Smith. I'm listening."

The emphasis on *Ms.* was a pail of cold water, and she quit admiring his looks and got down to business. As he stared her down, her doubts about her capabilities set in once again. "Uh, thank you for seeing me."

"You already said that."

"Oh. Right." She grabbed her briefcase and clicked the latch, only for it to stick. Seriously? She pushed on it again, but it wouldn't budge. "Stupid thing," she mumbled. Then it instantly opened, making her almost drop it. With fumbling fingers, she pulled out the folder with the sales information Miles had given her and handed it to him.

He didn't take it. "What's that?"

"I'm a representative from Harrington Media," she said, repeating the speech she'd written down and practiced for the past two days.

Sebastian's eyes narrowed slightly. "In Atlanta?"

"Yes."

"You've been there all this time? Since you left Arkansas?"

She shook her head. "I worked for another company prior to PU—I mean Harrington." Wow, Harrington hadn't been PU for years. Where did that come from?

His brow raised and his mouth formed a slight smile. "PU?"

"Preston Ustace . . . Never mind." She held the folder out to him. "I'm here to discuss the possibility of you discussing a possible deal . . ." Uh-oh, that wasn't part of the script. She grimaced, her words disappearing. What was she supposed to say again? "I, um— just take this, will you?"

He put it on his desk without a second glance. "Is this about selling my paper?"

Jade nodded.

Sebastian leaned forward. "The answer is no."

"But you didn't even look at the folder. Or listen to my pitch." If only she could remember the pitch.

He scowled and sat back. "Your company has been hounding me to talk to them."

"Hounding is a little harsh," she said. "They're just eager to save *The Times*."

His expression turned stony. "*The Times* is just fine."

"Not according to your financials."

"What do you know about them? Have you been spying on me?"

"Of course not. All the information Miles has gathered about the paper is public knowledge."

"Is he your boss? Or your . . . Never mind, it doesn't matter. The answer is no. It will always be no."

She tried to regroup, although it was difficult, considering Sebastian's irritated expression was beyond unnerving. "If you'll look at the information I provided—"

Suddenly the faint ring of a cell phone came from inside the briefcase that held her small pocketbook. She ignored it. "If you'll look at the folder, you'll see our offer is generous."

"I don't have to." He crossed his arms, exposing his very nice, well-defined forearms. "Better yet, I don't want to."

"You're being unreasonable, Sebastian—"

"So now I'm Sebastian. What happened to Mr. Hudson?"

The phone kept ringing.

"Do you need to get that?" he asked.

"No." She set the case on the floor again. How could he just shut her down like this, without giving her a chance? At least the phone had stopped. Sometimes she hated cell phones. They were convenient, except when they weren't. Maybe she should start at the beginning again. "Mr. Hudson," she said, clasping her near-trembling hands. "I'm a representative of—"

Brrrrring!

Her teeth clenched. Why, oh why didn't she think about turning off her cell before the meeting?

"Just get the phone, Jade."

Not bothering to hide her scowl, she dug into her briefcase and pulled out the cell. Logan again. If she didn't answer now, he'd just keep calling until she did. Flipping open the phone, she turned away from Sebastian. "I'm in the middle of a meeting—"

"I'm sorry, Jade, but it's an emergency. I'm serious this time."

He did sound serious. And different than during his call back in Atlanta. "I have to take this," she said to Sebastian.

He nodded, and she didn't miss the flash of concern in his eyes.

Quickly she went into the hallway. When she was safely out of earshot, she asked, "What's wrong?"

"I need to get out of Little Rock ASAP."

"Why?"

"I can't say. Please, Jade, help me out. I promise this will be the last time. I can get a flight to Atlanta right now."

"I'm not in Atlanta." She paused, conflicted. If she told him where she was, that would open a door she'd already closed. But the urgency in his voice had her worried. "I'm in Arkansas," she said, wincing.

"Really? How long have you been here?"

"Not long. Logan, what's all this about?"

"I'll tell you when I see you. Are you in Little Rock?"

"Clementine."

"Never heard of it, but I'll be there in the morning. Where are you staying?"

If she saw him, she could assess his condition. He didn't sound under the influence, but that didn't mean anything. "The Clementine Inn. But I'm not paying for your room," she added. At least she could keep that boundary up.

"I don't expect you to." His voice lowered again. "Thanks, sis. I promise you won't regret this." He hung up.

Sis. Despite her worry and frustration with herself that she was so easily cajoled, the word stirred warmth inside her. That didn't mean he wasn't trying to get something out of her, however. She stared at her Razr. "I already do."

Seb drummed his fingers on top of the Harrington Media folder. Jade's skin was fair, almost porcelain, but when she saw her phone screen, she went pale. And as she talked on the phone outside his office, he saw her pacing back and forth behind the frosted glass on his door. He doubted she even knew what she was doing. The conversation was clearly tense.

His fingers had stilled, and when he glanced down, he was surprised to see his hand clenched. He relaxed, then rubbed both palms down his thighs. Jade wasn't his concern, so whatever was going on wasn't his business. However, her company wanting to buy *The Times* was.

He shook his head, his back teeth grinding. After all these years, Jade Smith had come back into his life, and she was intent on taking his business from him. Un. Believable. What made it worse was that after the last time Harrington left a message on his voicemail, Seb made a rare venture onto the internet, found the company, and discovered they were buying small newspapers left and right. They were destroying the community newspaper trade one acquisition at a time.

He found it hard to believe that Jade was okay with this. Then again, maybe she was just fine reducing Seb's hard work and Buford's legacy to a number on a spreadsheet and an afterthought in a bloated conglomerate. She was an accountant, or she used to be. Apparently she was in acquisitions and mergers now.

Even more concerning, annoying, and irritating was that, despite her wanting *The Times*, despite knowing that she never felt as deeply for him as he did her, and despite the possibility that she belonged to someone else, he couldn't stop looking at her. He really, *really* liked what he saw, especially when she turned around and left his office to take her phone call.

Jade came back in, her expression shuttered as if she'd just ordered takeout instead of having an intense conversation, and sat back down. "Sorry about that." She kept her phone in her lap. "Did you look at the offer?"

There was no point in talking about the offer since he wasn't going to sell. But he could get a few questions answered. "Why are you here?" he asked.

She frowned. "I told you, I'm a representative from—"

"But why you in particular? Are you still an accountant?"

"Yes." She shifted in her chair. "I don't see what that has to do with anything."

"Companies don't usually send accountants to discuss buyouts, do they?"

"No," she said quietly, glancing at her lap.

"Then why . . . Oh, I get it." He shook his head. "You thought you could use our past to convince me to sell."

Her head popped up. "No! I would never do that."

He sat back, the wheels of his antique chair squeaking.

"Is that your old chair? You never got it oiled?"

Her question stopped his interrogation. "It is. And, no. Kept meaning to. But"—he shrugged—"life—"

"—gets in the way."

"Yeah." He met her gaze, mesmerized by her pretty green eyes. That was why her mother named her Jade, she'd told him. When she was born, her eyes had a slight green tint to them. That was the one and only time she mentioned her family. He figured he would meet them eventually . . . but that never happened.

She didn't look away. Neither did he.

"Jade," he said, surprised at his gentle tone when a minute ago he was angry at her. But he couldn't ignore the sudden stirring inside him, a feeling that knocked him back to the past. To the good times, not the bad. When they—

The door flew open, and Evelyn Margot barged in. "Guess what! I—" She stopped. Looked at Seb, then at Jade, who had swiveled around in her seat, then at Seb again. Her eyebrows slowly lifted. "I didn't realize you had a meeting."

His sister's entrance diffused whatever was going on inside him, bringing him back to reality. "It's over," he said, picking up the folder and handing it back to Jade.

Her expression turned to shock, then exasperation. "Keep it," she said, grabbing her briefcase and rising to her feet. "We can discuss this later."

"No we—"

She breezed past Evelyn and left the office.

"Won't."

Evelyn slid over to his desk. "Who was *that*?"

"No one." He set the folder back on his desk. Just what he needed—more clutter.

"Come on, big bro. She's certainly someone, the way you two were looking at each other."

How exactly were they looking at each other? The last few moments seemed like a dream as he'd gotten lost in her eyes. Or had he just imagined she was also reminiscing about their better times. He blinked. Shook his head. Looked at his annoying little sister and snapped, "What do you want?"

"You need a new picture," she groused, putting her hands on her hips. "A snarling beast."

"Sorry."

She grinned. "You just confirmed that there's something between *you* and *her*." Evelyn sat down and crossed her legs. "Spill."

Seb pressed his fingers to the bridge of his nose. "I assume you barged into my office for a reason?"

She put her elbow on one knee and peered at him. "You're being cagey. All right, I'll let this go. For now." She sat back, then said, "I found another advertiser. They're nowhere close to Piggly Wiggly, but they're willing to do a small advertisement."

His expression relaxed. "I'll take everything I can get." Especially since Jade confirmed that *The Times*'s financial problems weren't a secret. He wasn't sure how Harrington Media had figured that out, not that it changed anything. "Tell me about them."

After Evelyn had explained that a new car wash had been built in Cherry Hill and they wanted to drum up business, he struggled to focus on the rest of what she was saying. Jade loved car washes. He remembered when she had revealed her secret to him shortly after they started dating. She worried he would think she was weird. Of course he didn't, and he'd gone to a couple of car washes with her on their dates. One time they'd even made out in one—

"Sebastian? Are you even listening to me?"

"Sure, sure. Cherry Hill Car Wash. Glad to have 'em. Is that all you needed?"

"That's all." She got up from her chair. "I'll leave you to your thoughts about . . . *her*."

"Shut up," he said only half-heartedly. She just delivered good news, and he wasn't going to get bent out of shape over her teasing. Evelyn Margot was practically a professional at it.

After Evelyn left, he looked at the folder again. The Harrington Media logo was emblazoned on the front in blue-and-white letters. Seb had always had a curious streak, something that was both a blessing and a curse, and this time he was poised to give in to temptation. What kind of deal was Harrington offering—not that it mattered. His fingers touched the edge of the folder.

He recoiled and threw the folder in the trash. No matter what Jade tried to do, she wouldn't convince him to sell. She might as well go back to Atlanta. *To Miles.*

He whirled in his seat and faced the typewriter. He was making an assumption about her and Miles when he shouldn't be thinking about anything but his job. *The Times* and his writing were his focus and solace, not Jade Smith. *Definitely not her.* His fingers hit the keys with gusto. After today's meeting, he doubted he would ever see her again.

Chapter 6

Disappointed didn't begin to describe Jade's feelings when she left Sebastian's office, and not only because she hadn't sealed the deal. She walked out of the building into the hot, sultry air and went straight to her rental car. Now what was she supposed to do? He was an immovable object, and she had no idea how to push him forward. Ugh, her neck and back were sweating, whether from the heat, nervousness, stress from Logan, or Sebastian's rejection, she didn't know. Probably all of it. For sure she had to get rid of this jacket. She whipped it off, thankful she wore a short-sleeved blouse underneath, then opened the car door and tossed it on the passenger seat, along with her briefcase. There, that was better—

Brrrrring!

She sank against the car. Couldn't she get just one break? She got inside, closed the door, and started the engine. Cool air flowed from the vents. *Much better.* She opened her briefcase without a problem and grabbed her phone, expecting Logan's name to pop up on the screen. Instead, it was an unknown number with an Atlanta area code. She quickly answered before it went to voicemail. "Hello?"

"Good morning, Jade!" Miles's bright voice sounded in her ear. "Were you able to talk to Mr. Hudson yet?"

Oh no. Should she lie and tell him no? That would put him off for a bit. She didn't like lying to her boss, though, and invariably lies were always exposed in the end. Better to rip off the Band-Aid now. "Uh, yes. I just finished speaking with him."

"Wonderful. What did he say?"

She gulped. "He, um, isn't interested in selling."

Silence.

Jade squirmed in her seat, waiting for him to respond. When he didn't, she wondered if he heard her. She was about to tell him again when he finally spoke, his tone no longer upbeat.

"Try again."

"I don't think I can convince him—"

"Do whatever it takes, Jade. I'm not going to let some country bumpkin get in the way of my deal."

She flinched. Sebastian was smart, driven, and extremely capable. The newspaper business was going through tumultuous times, and he was committed to keeping his paper alive. She found that admirable. Besides, there were plenty of so-called bumpkins who were also smart, driven, and capable. It wasn't the slur Miles thought it was.

"You're an attractive woman, Jade." His aggravated tenor switched to a near murmur. "Use that to your advantage."

Blech. His oily compliment gave her the creeps. She wanted to tell him to go stuff his shirt, but ticking off her already ticked off boss was the last thing she should do.

His suggestion wouldn't work anyway.

Sebastian had already accused her of trying to use their past to get to him, and she truthfully denied it. If she tried, he'd see right through her. He made it clear that he wasn't interested in her, not even enough to listen.

There was also another problem. She couldn't deny there was still something inside her that was drawn to him after all these years. Attraction for sure, although any woman in her right mind would be attracted to him. How had he managed to get even sexier at forty? If he wasn't taken, she was sure he had plenty of female interest.

Still, there was an undeniable flash, a spark inside her, especially when their eyes met. A little tickle appeared in her tummy just thinking about it. If she had to act on that, either by pretending, or worse, by unleashing her real feelings, she would be making a huge mistake.

There were so many reasons she and Sebastian would never work out, but the number one was crystal clear—he was over her. His tone, body language, and the overall sense she got from him was that he had moved on. Good, because she was over him, despite the tickle and the nerves and the weird spark thing. Stress, her brother, and the fact that she absolutely stunk at negotiations explained all that.

"You can do this," Miles said, a sudden smile in his voice. The man could alternate moods with whiplash speed. "I believe in you. Give it another shot, okay?"

She squeezed her eyes shut. It wasn't like she could go back to Atlanta anyway—she had made a commitment to see Logan tomorrow, although she half expected him not to show up. Maybe there was a sliver of hope that Sebastian would be open to talking to her again. She just had to figure out another angle that didn't require flirting, or as Charlotte Rae would say, *bedroom eyes.* "Okay," she agreed, without a shred of confidence.

"Great! I'll be in touch."

Jade threw her phone inside the open briefcase and leaned back on the headrest, trying to decide on her next move. She could go back to the inn and regroup. Or . . .

She glanced to her left. The Clementine Diner was a block down from *The Times* office, and despite the large breakfast she had this morning, she was craving something to eat—preferably fried. She could have a snack while she figured out a new way to approach Sebastian, and then return to his office and meet with him this afternoon. This time the element of surprise was crucial, because if she tried to call and set up an appointment, he would absolutely refuse to see her. Zero doubts there.

With renewed focus, she closed the briefcase and took it with her as she exited the car and locked it. While she walked to the diner, she thought about the woman who barged into his office. Sebastian hadn't bothered to introduce her, not that she expected him to. She was cute—petite, slim, with long brown hair and dark amber eyes. Quite striking. Was she his girlfriend? Or something more? She bounded into the office like she owned it, or owned Sebastian at least.

Jade shook off the thoughts. She needed to give all her attention to her goal of getting Sebastian to talk to her again. This time she wouldn't let him interrupt or distract her. She would read the folder contents to him if she had to. And she would for sure turn off her phone.

As she neared the restaurant, the scent of delicious food made her stomach growl. A few minutes later she walked inside, once again thankful for the air-conditioning. The diner had a Southern feel to it with plenty of down-home kitsch.

The sign near the door said Seat Yourself, so she found a booth near a window and sat down. As soon as she did, a young waiter wearing a stained apron appeared.

"Welcome in," he said, putting a menu in front of her. "What can I get you to drink?"

"Coffee. The strongest you have."

"Sure thing. Cream or sugar?"

"Black, please. Oh, and a glass of water."

He nodded and walked away. Jade fell back against the seat, tension draining from her body. The diner wasn't that crowded, and eighties music piped in through the speaker. Her gaze landed on a bird clock on the wall, and she was shocked that it was only ten thirty. Seemed like more time than that had passed since she arrived in downtown Clementine. *Like an eternity.*

Jade eyed the menu. Everything looked fried, loaded, and mouthwatering, but there were also the requisite chef, taco, and side salads. She should get one of those, but the crispy chicken tenders were calling her name. She'd eat more strictly when she returned to Atlanta. Right now she needed comfort food.

"Here's your coffee." The waiter set a white ceramic cup in front of her. "Ready to order?"

Jade looked at his name tag. She got the tender platter, which included a side of fries. "Thanks, Tad."

"Welcome."

After he left to put in her order, she took a sip of coffee and watched as an older couple walked in, followed by a pretty young woman, and she realized it was the one she'd argued with this morning. She didn't look nearly as angry or arrogant as she had earlier. Mostly just confused.

Jade watched as she sat down in a nearby booth and pulled a phone out of her expensive, soft pink leather purse with a gold Chanel logo on the front. Jade didn't collect purses or wear designer clothes, but plenty of her coworkers did, and she knew Chanel cost a pretty penny. The woman flipped open the latest cell phone model and punched in numbers. When she put the phone to her ear, she jerked it away, stared at it in disbelief, and punched the keys again. She repeated the action two more times before scowling and tossing the phone back in her purse.

The young woman wasn't just scowling. She looked scared and was trying to hide it. Jade understood that expression all too well.

Jade set down her coffee and frowned as she thought about her behavior this morning in front of *The Times* office. Not one of her better moments. Normally she wasn't snotty to strangers, but with her emotions already at the surface after coming face-to-face with Sebastian so unexpectedly, she lost her cool. She owed the woman an apology, although she wasn't sure if it would be accepted or not. She rose and walked over to her booth. "Excuse me," she said.

The woman looked up at her, her expression suddenly guarded. "What?"

Now that her nerves were more under control, she wasn't offended by the snippy response. "I wanted to apologize for my earlier behavior. I shouldn't have snapped at you the way I did."

Manicured eyebrows shot up in surprise. "Uh, thanks," she finally mumbled, looking down at the pale blue Formica table. "I'm sorry too."

"I noticed you were having trouble with your phone." At her questioning look, Jade pointed to her booth where Tad was setting down her salad. "I'm sitting over there. You can borrow my cell if you need to make a call."

Once again the young woman seemed shocked. Then she shook her head. "It's okay. I was just trying to reach my stepmom. I'll call her later."

"All right. Well . . ." She was about to say goodbye when an idea hit her. "Would you like to join me? I'm by myself waiting—" She couldn't tell her that she was killing time until she went to Sebastian's office again.

Three teenagers walked through the front door, one of them reminding her of Logan when he was young—tall, with tawny brown-toned skin, black curly hair, and a face dotted with freckles, all an appealing blend of his biracial heritage. He laughed with his friends as they sat at a table, and he stretched out his long, jean-clad legs. Seeing him happy reminded her of the good times she and Logan had amid the horrible ones.

But those good times had been nonexistent for a long while, and she had to keep her guard up when she saw him tomorrow. If he sensed any kind of opening to get to her, he would plow on through. He always had.

"Are you okay?"

She blinked and looked at the woman, not realizing she'd been staring at the wall in front of her, covered with old shoe advertisements. "Yes. Just a little distracted. It's been a tough morning."

"Tell me about it." She paused. "Sure. I'll join you." She picked up her menu and they walked over to Jade's booth.

When they sat down, Jade held out her hand. "Jade Smith."

"Kalista Clark."

"Nice to meet you."

Tad came back and Kalista ordered a salad. Considering her trim figure, no surprise there. "What brings you to Clementine?" Jade asked.

"How did you know I'm not from here?"

Jade smiled. "Your accent," she said, deciding on the most benign and recognizable feature. "Or lack of one, I should say."

"People do talk funny around here." Kalista took a sip of the water Tad had brought. "And slow. Really slow."

"It's the Southern drawl."

"You don't have one. Where are you from?"

"Atlanta." There were so many transplants in her company from other parts of the country, she was rarely around a true drawl anymore. And there was no reason to tell Kalista that Arkansas was her home state. She didn't belong here anymore, and as soon as she finished her business with Sebastian and found out what was going on with Logan, she would rush back to Georgia. She had no intention of staying here any longer than necessary. "I'll be returning home soon."

"I'm from LA. After my stepmother gets married in August, I'll go back to California. Until then . . ." She sighed. "I'm stuck here."

If she was only going to be here for the summer, why did she apply for a job? Unless it was an internship. That made sense. "How did your interview go?"

Their food showed up and they both started eating. "I got the job," Kalista said, "such as it is."

"That's great. What will you be doing?"

"Delivering newspapers."

"You're working in distribution?"

"No, I'm delivering newspapers." She made a small throwing motion with her left hand. "You know, chucking them out the window and onto porches."

Which was distribution, but Jade didn't want to embarrass her by telling her that. She'd figure it out soon enough. She was surprised, though. Kalista seemed more suited for a cub reporter or sales rep.

"It's not exactly what I thought my first job would be." Kalista sighed. "But it's only for the summer. It's going to be a drag having to get up so early, though."

Jade dipped a chicken finger into the honey mustard cup and took a bite. Yum. "What grade are you in?"

Her eyes narrowed. "I'm literally eighteen. I graduated a couple weeks ago."

Oops. "Sorry. You sound, er, look so young."

Kalista stabbed at a crouton, a little pacified. "Viv wouldn't let me put on makeup. She didn't want me to be late for the interview." She chewed on the crunchy bread square and swallowed. "She was right. I barely made it on time."

As they ate, an awkward silence fell between them. Kalista didn't seem interested in finding out more about Jade, and Jade was too distracted to carry the conversation. When her phone rang again, she was relieved. "I need to get that."

Kalista pushed her half-eaten salad away. "I'm done anyway." She opened her purse, but Jade waved her off.

"My treat."

Kalista scowled. "I'm not poor, you know. I can afford my own lunch."

Jade took out her phone, forcing an even tone. "I apologize."

Kalista opened her wallet and dropped a few bills on the table, then got up.

Jade frowned, her sympathy diminishing. "Have a nice day," she said.

Kalista gave a curt nod and left.

Oh well. Jade looked at the screen and saw Charlotte's name. She quickly answered. "Hey," she said, wiping up the remnant of ketchup on her plate with the last french fry. "Everything okay at work?"

"Work's fine. Dull as always. So, how's it going with your ex?"

Jade frowned. She was regretting her decision to tell Charlotte about her meeting with Miles, including her past relationship with Sebastian. She didn't get into details, only told her that they used to casually date. She should have known Charlotte would be nosy. "He's being stubborn. He won't even look at the pitch."

"Who cares about the pitch? I want to know how he was looking at *you*."

Definitely not with bedroom eyes. Her cheeks heated and she took a gulp of water. She had to stop thinking about Sebastian that way, or any other way other than a businessman. "He's taken," she said. Jade didn't know if that was true, but maybe it would stop Charlotte in her matchmaking tracks.

"Really?" Charlotte sighed. "Well, *fahrvergnügen*. I'd hoped you two had rekindled your old flame."

"Farfen-what?"

"You know, from that car commercial years ago?"

"Huh?"

"You need to watch more TV. There's this new show called *The Bachelorette* that's really good."

What Jade needed was to get back to work. "Nothing's going on with me and Sebastian, and nothing ever will. There. Case closed."

"Never say *never*."

"Charlotte—"

"I know, I know. You're doing fine and everything's fine and you don't need a social life because everything's fine. Got it. But just in case everything isn't *fine*, you should be open-minded. Just sayin'."

"Noted."

"Gotta go, meeting in five minutes. If you need any more advice, I'm here for you."

Jade smiled. "Thanks, Charlotte. I'll see you soon." She dropped the phone into her briefcase and rubbed both temples this time before glancing at her watch. Almost an hour and a half had passed since she talked to Sebastian. Was that long enough? Or should she wait another thirty minutes or so? Yes, that would be prudent. She didn't want to pop up there right away, and during that time she could go over her pitch, refine it, and memorize it again since she forgot it during their meeting.

She looked up and saw the list of desserts on the specials board. Coconut cream pie. Her favorite. But she couldn't. She shouldn't . . .

"Tad?" She lifted her hand and motioned him over.

———

Shortly after Evelyn Margot left his office, Seb finished up his column and delivered it to Paul and Cletus in the basement, trying to put the morning out of his mind. The cousins not only ran the press, but they also did the layout, although Evelyn was urging Seb to computerize the design process. "I can do it a lot faster on a Mac," she said. "I've looked into it. The learning curve isn't that steep."

No doubt she would do an excellent job, but he wasn't ready to give up tradition. Besides, with the paper moving to twice a week, he'd already cut back Paul's and Cletus's hours. He didn't want to take more work away from them or they might move on to somewhere else. He wouldn't blame them if they did.

He opened the door to the press room. The printing press was running, spitting out the Thursday edition of *The Times* while a large fan was blowing nearby, cooling off the room but not rustling the stacks of newspapers on the other side of the expansive area. Fortunately they had enough space to print and set up distribution so they didn't have to rent an additional space. "Here's my column," he said, handing Paul a manila folder.

The man took it with his dye-stained hands. "Thanks. Can't wait to read it." His jowls sagged as he frowned.

What now? Seb braced himself. "Something wrong?"

He nodded, adjusting the brim of his weather-beaten and ink-stained red Razorbacks baseball cap. Seb had never seen the man without it. He gestured to the printing press. "Ol' Bessie's having trouble again."

"What kind of trouble?"

"A lot of this, that, and the other."

Seb didn't pretend to fully understand how the ancient press worked, but he listened as Paul described in detail what parts of the machine were problematic as Cletus manned the controls. Seb had never been mechanically inclined, and the cousins knew the press inside and out. He trusted their judgment, expertise, and affinity toward the machine. They were the ones who christened her "Bessie."

"We can nurse her along for a little while," Paul concluded.

Dread filled him. "How long?"

"Not sure. I'd find a new press in the meantime."

That was a punch to the gut. New presses would cost tens of thousands, possibly more. Money he didn't have. He blanked his expression. No need to worry the guys. "I'll look into it," he said.

Paul nodded, looking at the press wistfully. "Bessie's a workhorse, that's for sure."

Seb said a quick prayer that their workhorse wouldn't need to be put out to pasture anytime soon. "Thanks for the info, Paul."

He nodded, taking Seb's file folder with his column inside and putting it on his tiny desk several feet away from the press.

Letting the men get back to work, Seb went upstairs and plopped down in his chair, mulling over this latest problem. He'd add searching for a printing press to his never-ending to-do list.

Even though it was only ten thirty, he took out a brown paper bag from the bottom drawer of his desk and pulled out a plastic bag that held the bologna and cheese sandwich he quickly made before dashing out the door this morning. A favorite of his since he was a kid, with a slice of American cheese, beef bologna from the deli, and of course, lots of butter on both slices of white Wonder Bread.

He took a bite as a memory struck him. Jade had looked at him in confusion when they had lunch together in *The Arkansas Democrat-Gazette* breakroom shortly after they started seeing each other.

"*Butter on a sandwich?*" she'd said, opening a Tupperware container filled with salad greens.

"*This is an American elementary school classic.*"

"*I'm more of a peanut butter and jelly girl.*" She'd smiled.

And it reached into his soul.

Was that the moment he was smitten with her? Or maybe it was the next day, when she returned with a matching bologna and butter sandwich and ended up loving it just like he did. Come to think of it, he never saw her eat peanut butter and jelly the entire time they were together.

There he was, reminiscing about her again. He had to stop doing that. He'd been clear about not selling *The Times*, and even though she said they would discuss the deal later, he didn't expect her to return. Which was what he wanted. She was on the other side now. She was, dare he say, the *enemy*.

He bit into the sandwich and searched for the ledger again. Flora had written pertinent account numbers inside the cover, plus a password or two. Apparently those were a thing now. "*Don't lose this, Sebastian,*" she'd said when she handed it to him on her last day of work. "*It's irreplaceable.*"

Seb had nodded, a tad miffed that she assumed he was so careless. Turned out she was right, and he had misplaced it a couple of times in his mess of an office, only to have it turn up again. In the last place he looked, naturally. He needed to have a designated spot for it and the folder that held the bank statements, but he was too busy to do that right now.

He took a bite of the sandwich and opened the ledger. Staring at the numbers didn't make the balance at the bottom any bigger, and he didn't want to think about how he would replace the press if it went down. "Tomorrow," he said, shutting the book and setting it to the side.

Eager for something far more pleasant, he picked up a half-filled spiral notepad, turned to a fresh page, and started jotting down random things that entered his mind while he finished his lunch. The notebook was full of ideas for future columns, articles, and features.

He paused, glancing around the office. Typically, he didn't notice his surroundings when he was deep in thought, but this time he saw Buford's picture on the wall, a broad grin on his face as he cut the ribbon in front of the building on the day he moved *The Clementine Times* to its current location.

Buford had won awards for both his writing and for the paper as a whole. The paper had won several AP awards over the years but nothing during Seb's tenure.

Seb sat back, letting out a sigh. He'd spent the past ten years learning how to manage a paper on his own and hadn't been able to nurture Tyler, Isaiah, or any of the other reporters and photogs he'd employed over the years who had moved on to grander journalistic opportunities. Tyler and Isaiah were doing well on their own, but when Seb had worked for Buford, he'd gotten a lot of advice and attention from his mentor, and he should have done the same for his staff.

Then there was his own personal work—the writing he did

when he was at his cabin in the mountains. He hadn't touched that story in months, and his inability to focus on his follow-up project had affected not only him but other people as well. Seb was determined that once he and *The Times* made it through this valley, he could go back to his cabin and fulfill that obligation. He just had to get the paper back to its glory days, or at least somewhere close.

Seb shut the notebook and was balling up the empty lunch bag to throw away when he glimpsed the Harrington Media folder in the trash can. He rarely second-guessed himself when it came to his job, and he was committed to keeping *The Times* a community-based publication. But was he making the right decision, maintaining a subpar paper that kept losing money and subscribers, was run on the tightest of budgets, and now might lose its printing press?

Yes, he was. *The Times* was worth hanging on to.

The alarm clock on his desk beeped, startling him. He shut it off, glad he'd set it before he left the office yesterday, or he would have completely forgotten about his interview with Mabel Winstead at the Clementine Inn. Her family had founded Clementine ninety-two years ago, and he was doing a series on the history of the town for publication at the end of June. Not only was she a fount of Clementine info, she was also president of the hospitality/literary/historical society. He was going to enjoy talking to her.

He retrieved a smaller notebook, slid a pen into his shirt pocket, and stood. Shoving the notepad inside the back pocket of his pants, he grabbed his keys and left the office, running into Tyler in the hallway.

"Did you hire Kalista, Mr. H.?" Tyler asked, hope in his eyes.

This kid had it bad, but hopefully he wouldn't get in too deep. Love in the workplace rarely worked out. Seb had learned that the hard way. "She's meeting you in the circulation department at 3:00 a.m."

Tyler grinned. Then, as if catching himself, he turned serious and nodded.

"Make sure you train her well." Seb went to the stairwell. "She's very inexperienced." To say the least.

"Don't worry, Mr. H."

Seb wasn't worried. Not too much anyway. He zoomed down the stairs and opened the door. The first thing he saw was Jade's car still in his parking space. He grimaced, wondering where she was. He expected her to be halfway to the Little Rock airport by now since he refused her. Shrugging, he got in his car. Whatever Jade Smith was doing right now, he wasn't interested.

Chapter 7

Kalista sped down the dirt road toward Viv's house, squeezing the old leather wheel in her hands. She didn't know the speed limit and she didn't care, although the plastic bags full of groceries sitting on the floor next to her were tossing back and forth. Whatever—she'd fix them when she got to Viv's. Then she'd use her stepmother's phone to give her father a very large piece of her mind.

After her interview with Mr. Hudson, she'd gone to the diner to try to call her friend Abbie, but her phone didn't work. It was like it was dead, but it still had more than half the battery life left. Before she went to the Piggles Wiggles or whatever that store was called, she saw her phone carrier's office in a strip mall and stopped to have them look at the phone.

"Your service has been shut off," a guy wearing a red shirt, square, dark-framed glasses, and a handwritten name tag that said John, told her.

"What does that mean?"

"You don't have service." He tapped on a computer keyboard. "Do you have your passcode so I can see your account?"

"Passcode?"

"For the account. I can't access it unless you have a code. It's like a pin code."

"Oh, for the ATM. Sure." She leaned forward and whispered it to him. There were a few people in the store, and she didn't want them hearing it. Ryan had had his pin stolen a couple of times.

"It should be five numbers, not four." The guy tilted his head at her.

Kalista mentally went over the pin in her head. She was sure it was four numbers. "Then it's not the one for the ATM?"

John's jaw fell open, then shut again. "It's a five-digit code specific to your phone account. Did you get your phone here?"

"No. In California."

"Then you would have given the tech the code when they were setting up the phone."

She waved her hand. "Daddy did all that."

He smirked and continued to type. "What's his name?"

"Raymond Clark." She gave him Daddy's address and phone number.

"Here he is. I see he's also on your account."

"Because he set it up. I already said that." She crossed her arms, her purse dangling from her left wrist. She didn't have the time or patience for this.

John scanned the computer screen. "Looks like he's turned off your phone."

"What?"

"There're some notes here . . . yeah. About an hour ago he asked us to put a lock on it too. The only person who can turn it back on is him."

"That can't be right!" she wailed, not caring that the customers were now looking at her. "I have to have my phone."

John's gaze darted from the customers and back to her. "Miss

Clark, you'll have to take that up with your father. I can't turn your phone back on. Only he can."

"Ooooooh." She snatched her cell off the counter. "Thanks for nothing!"

The trip through the Pig Wig wasn't much better. They had almost nothing she wanted, although she did find everything on Viv's list. At least she was able to get a few bottles of sparkling water. Harrison was definitely a bigger city than Clementine, but she was still in culture shock. And now that she didn't have a working phone, how was she supposed to talk to her friends? Or Ryan?

Kalista whipped into Viv's driveway and brought the truck to a stop near the tiny house. When she stepped out into the heat, her throat constricted from the dust and debris coming from the three riding lawn mowers that were mowing the huge yard on Bo's farm. She hated Arkansas. It was hot, everyone talked funny, it smelled like manure, and now she couldn't even speak to her friends or Ryan. Oh, and she also had a *job*. What a joke.

Workers were setting up tents, mowing the yard, working in the barn, and doing other stuff she didn't care about as Viv came out of the house, looking fresh, happy, and like she belonged here. "How did everything go?" she asked as Kalista stormed past her, leaving the groceries in the truck.

Then she stopped. Viv didn't deserve to be ignored. It wasn't her fault she didn't have phone service. She turned and faced her stepmother. "I got the job and everything on the list. I need to call Daddy right now."

Viv frowned. "Are you okay?"

She was very much not okay, but she didn't want to bother Viv with it. What could her former stepmother do anyway? She couldn't unlock her phone or send her back to California. Unfortunately.

"I'll get the groceries," Viv said, opening the heavy passenger door. "Go call Raymond."

Kalista hurried into the house where a light green phone hung on the wall. She lifted the receiver and saw the round dialing mechanism. She couldn't even remember the last time she *dialed* a phone. But dial she did, using her father's phone number.

"Hello?

Kalista groaned, her shoulders slumping at the sound of the breathy, high-pitched voice on the other line. Bettany. Ew, she did not want to deal with her. "I need to talk to Daddy."

"He's not available."

"Bettany, who's on the phone?" Daddy's question sounded in the distance.

Anger rose inside Kalista. "I thought you said he was busy?"

"I said he was unavailable. Which he is. He's *very* busy, Kalista."

A stab of pain burst through the anger. How many times had she heard those words—from secretaries, nannies, maids, his former wives . . . He was always busy. *Too busy for me.*

"I'll take it, babe," Daddy said.

"But Ray—"

"Hello, Kalista. I'm glad to hear from you—"

"Why did you turn off my phone?"

"Because I didn't want you spending all your free time on it. You're there to work and learn, not chitchat with your friends."

"But that's not fair!" She stamped her foot.

"And that right there is why I'm doing this. Sweetheart, you're not a child anymore."

Kalista rolled her eyes. "Daddy, I don't want a lecture. I want my phone turned back on. And if you won't do that, I'll buy another one."

"With what? You have no credit cards, no checkbook, and your bank account is suspended."

"Can't you give them all back to me?" she whined. "I don't understand why you're being so mean."

Silence. Then, "I'm sorry, Kalista. I don't like being mean to you, but this is for your own good. You have to learn responsibility—"

"I am. I have a job. I start tomorrow."

"Really?" he sounded shocked, then happy. "That's great! Where are you working?"

"I'm . . . in the newspaper business. At *The Clementine Times*." He didn't need to know she was throwing newspapers.

"That's wonderful, Kalista."

"Can I have my stuff back?"

"No. I'm proud of you for getting a job, honey. But let's see what you do with it first."

He's proud of me? The words sounded foreign coming from him. A small smile formed on her face. Then she realized she had an opening. "I could do my job better if I had my phone."

"If you've got a job, you can buy your own phone."

"Ray," Bettany whined in the background. "I'm *waiting*."

Ick. Kalista didn't want to know what she was waiting on. Or for. Double ick.

"Kalista, I have to go," Daddy said. "I'm glad you got a job."

"But—"

"Talk to you later."

She stared at the receiver. She had heard those words from him many a time. Later almost never came. He was paying attention to her now, somewhat, but it was all wrong. He should be giving her things, not taking them away.

Viv walked in with the bags looped around her wrists and arms. "Did you get ahold of him?" she asked, setting everything on the table.

Kalista put the receiver back in its cradle. "Yeah," she whispered.

"Good. Thanks for getting the groceries. You can tell me all about your interview while you help me put these away."

She almost rolled her eyes again. If Bo had such a big farm, couldn't he afford a maid? But she complied, answering Viv's questions with short ones of her own. If she noticed Kalista's distant mood, she didn't say anything. When they were done, she said, "I'm going to help with the hoedown setup in the barn."

Kalista held her breath, waiting for Viv to ask her to help. She'd never been in a barn before, and she didn't want to go in one now.

"Why don't you stay here and relax a little? You've had a busy couple of days."

Oh, thank goodness. She nodded as Viv left the kitchen, and a few seconds later, the back door banged shut. Kalista was tempted to go to her bedroom and take a nap. A long plane ride, having to get a job, and discovering she couldn't use her cell phone anymore was exhausting. Oh, and she'd gotten up at a tragically early hour. She huffed. Tomorrow would be worse.

Now that she had a minute to breathe and bemoan her circumstances, Jade suddenly came to mind. Kalista hadn't exactly been polite to her when she left the diner after parting with the last six dollars in her wallet to pay for her salad. But Kalista was always the one who treated others to lunch, like her friends and Ryan. And other boyfriends. She was the big spender.

And now she was one hundred percent broke and stuck in a tacky old house where the air-conditioning barely worked. Fanning herself with her hand, she glanced at the telephone on the chicken-and-egg wallpapered wall. Hmm. She might not have *her* phone, but she had access to one.

Kalista picked up the phone and dialed Ryan's number. When

he didn't answer—again—she left him a message. "Hey, it's me. I'm missing you so much. Give me a call when you get a chance. I'm in the worst place ever—"

Beep.

She scowled. Ryan needed to fix his voicemail. It always ended too soon. She dialed Abbie's number.

"Hello?"

"Hey, Abs." Kalista leaned against the wall. Finally, a sympathetic voice, other than Viv's, of course.

"Oh, hey—"

"You can't believe how messed up everything is." Kalista wound the cord around her thumb.

"I thought you were on your dad's yacht."

"Huh?" Then she remembered that she'd told her friends she was on vacation. "Ah, right. Yeah, his yacht is, um, messed up. We're docked, waiting for it to be fixed."

"That's nice. Listen, I have to go."

Disappointment coiled inside her. "Okay. Hey, have you heard from Ryan by any chance?"

Silence. "Um . . . sorta."

Kalista frowned. "What does that mean?"

"I . . . I'm sorry, Kalista. We were going to tell you."

She gripped the receiver. "Tell me what?"

"Like, he said you two weren't seriously serious, so when he asked me out—"

"He asked you *out*? I've barely been gone a whole day!"

"Yeah, but he said you weren't seriously serious. You know. Like on a break. Remember Rachel and Ross? He said it's like that."

"Abbie, you know how much he means to me."

"I never got the impression you were all that into him. Like, you two were only convenient when you needed something to do or were bored."

Her words hit home, but Kalista ignored them. "How could my boyfriend and my best friend go out behind my back?" she wailed.

"I said I was sorry. Geez, you're always such a drama queen. If you were so into him, then why did you leave him behind for a whole summer?"

"It's not my fault I had to . . . go on vacation! And I've tried calling him, more than once. Now I know why he's so busy. Fine, you two deserve each other."

"Kalista—"

She hung up, not wanting to hear any excuses—or accusations. She ran to the bedroom and flopped on her bed, tears streaming down her cheeks. Her life was upside down and now her boyfriend and best friend had betrayed her. Could things get any worse?

Suddenly the electricity shut off, and the only light was the sun coming through the small bedroom window. Dust motes danced in the air. She sat straight up as Viv knocked on the door. "Kalista?"

"Yeah?" Without thinking, she wiped her runny nose with the back of her hand, then realized what she'd done. Ew.

The door opened a crack, and Viv poked her head in. "A worker accidentally backed his pickup into one of the electric poles by the street. The power's going to be out for a while."

I hate this place.

———

Close to noon, Jade walked into *The Clementine Times* office building again. Now that she was fortified with the best coconut pie she'd ever eaten, she felt optimistic. A little. Okay, maybe not at all, but at least she was trying.

She thought about her phone call with Miles after her unproductive meeting this morning. Maybe he had a point, although she would never use her past relationship with Sebastian to get him to talk to her company. But perhaps she should have been friendlier and not just strictly business. They could have caught up on each other's lives, made some small talk, and then she could have asked him to talk to Miles. That might have worked a lot better.

Convinced she should do a soft sell rather than drop the info into his lap, she headed upstairs more positive than before. She didn't bother to put the small crossbody purse back in her briefcase after she paid for lunch, and it lightly bounced on her hip as she went up the stairs.

Tyler was sitting at the front desk in the reception area, using it as his workstation. His laptop was open, and he pushed his glasses closer to his eyes as he scanned the screen.

"Hi," she said, approaching him with a smile. "Tyler, right?"

He looked up, grinning. "Yes, ma'am."

"I'd like to see Mr. Hudson again, if he's not too busy."

Tyler frowned a little. "He wasn't in his office when I got back, but I've only been here a few minutes. He might be out on assignment."

"He's still a reporter?"

"When he can be. He likes being out in the field and talking to people."

Jade nodded. He enjoyed doing that when he worked for *The Democrat-Gazette* even when he wasn't officially on the job. "Is there any way I can find out where he is?"

"Well, he used to have a secretary, but that was before I started working here. Ms. Flora sometimes kept his appointments, but she retired last week." He held up his hands. "Sorry I can't help you."

"That's okay. Thanks for answering my questions."

"Anytime." He grinned. "When I have the time, that is."

What a nice young man. She headed for the front door, then had an idea. "Tyler?"

He kept typing. "Yes, ma'am?"

"Do you have a lady's room on this floor?"

"Just down the hall, past Mr. H.'s office."

Perfect. "Thanks."

A few moments later she was standing in front of Sebastian's door. On the off chance he actually wrote down his appointments, he might have them on a list or in a calendar on his desk. She looked to the left. To the right. Then touched the doorknob and gave it a twist. Unlocked. All she had to do was go inside . . .

She stared at her hand clutching the old-fashioned knob, then looked up and saw Sebastian's scowling photo in the picture frame beside the door. That made her reconsider, only to change her mind again. She had to try to find him. The sooner they talked again, the sooner she could finish her assignment and go back to Atlanta. She wouldn't stay long, just enough to scan his desk and then leave.

Before she talked herself out of it, Jade opened the door slowly, thankful that the doorknob wasn't as squeaky as his old chair, and tamped down the guilt as she walked inside. "Two minutes," she whispered. "That's it."

There was enough light coming through the dusty window that she didn't have to flip on the switch, so she slipped off her noisy shoes and crept to his messy desk. Her toe hit the metal trash can, and she saw her sleek Harrington Media folder inside. He must have trashed it after she left. *Jerk.* Now she wasn't feeling quite as guilty.

The piles of papers in front of her were daunting, and she carefully set her briefcase on top of two of them and started looking for something resembling a schedule. Nothing. She was about to grab her case and go when she saw a ledger book beside a pile.

She shouldn't.

She couldn't.

But a peek couldn't hurt, right? And it was in front of her—she didn't have to dig for it. While she had some of *The Times*'s financial info thanks to Miles, there might be something else here that could help her case. *He'll never know . . .*

Carefully she picked up the book and started opening it, then heard a female voice coming from down the hall.

"Don't worry, Tyler, he won't care."

Jade froze.

"I think he'll notice if the computer's gone," he responded.

Panicked, Jade clutched the ledger, grabbed her briefcase, and ducked under the desk, shoving her legs to her chest just as the door opened and the light flipped on.

"He never uses that thing." The woman and Tyler neared. "Besides, my PC is dying, and he's got a perfectly good Mac here, even if it's old."

Jade closed her eyes as she heard movement in the room just inches away.

"Oof, the monitor is heavier than I thought."

"I'll carry it," Tyler said. "You can get the keyboard."

"Hey, while I'm thinking about it—Seb had a meeting with a woman this morning. Do you know anything about that?"

Jade tensed.

"What did she look like?"

"Red hair—"

"Oh, that's Ms. Smith. I've never seen her before today."

"Interesting," the woman said. They were moving away from the desk. "I'll get the door for you."

"Thanks."

"No, thank you. This baby is getting a brand-new home, thanks to my brother being such a Luddite."

Brother?

The light turned off and the door clicked shut. Jade waited a few seconds before scrambling out from under the desk. She rushed to the door, eager to get out of Sebastian's office undetected, when she looked at her stockinged feet. Her shoes were right there by the door. Thank God neither Tyler nor Sebastian's sister saw them.

She slipped them on and, still clutching her briefcase, walked down the hallway. Peering around the corner to the reception area, she was relieved to see it was empty as she hurried out of the building. When she got to the car, she grabbed the handle of her briefcase.

The ledger fell to the ground.

Oh no! She'd forgotten all about it. She seized it off the ground and stood, just in time to see Tyler enter the building again. She gasped.

Jade jumped into her car, shut the door, and turned on the air. All she could do was stare at the building in front of her, wracking her brain to find a way to return Sebastian's ledger. But there was no way she could do it without looking suspicious.

I could just tell the truth. She discarded that idea too. Sebastian would never speak to her again if he found out what she did, and that would kill any chance of him talking to Miles. She would lose not only her raise and bonus, but probably her job. She broke the law, after all.

She wanted to throw up. How could she be so stupid? She'd never been underhanded in her life. It wasn't lost on her that she deserved this too. Could he prosecute her? Oh, the irony that Logan might have to bail her out—

Stop!

She couldn't think when her brain was on fire. After a few deep breaths, she decided to return to Clementine Inn to formulate a plan. She put the ledger in her briefcase, closed the clasp, and backed out of the parking spot.

On her way, she sorted out her whirling thoughts. Taking the ledger had been a mistake, one she could explain. Her biggest crime—shudder—had been to go into his office without him being there, despite her benign intentions. She was only snooping to figure out where he was, not to take anything.

By the time she reached the inn, she was a lot calmer and a little less nauseous. She could fix this. She still didn't know how, but being alone in her room and away from the scene of the crime would help her concentrate.

Jade pulled into a parking spot and turned off the car. Before she opened the door, she remembered what the woman had said. Sebastian was her brother. She was the one who interrupted her meeting with him. Jade had no idea he had a sister, although anytime he tried to talk about family, she changed the subject. Not because she wasn't interested in his, but she didn't want him asking questions about hers. Considering their quick breakup, it had been a good idea.

A slight wave of unexpected relief washed over her that she wasn't his girlfriend. Or wife.

She pressed the heel of her hand against her forehead at the rogue thought. Sebastian's relationship status shouldn't affect anything. *Or bother me.* She jumped out of the car, hustled into the inn, rushed past the front desk, and—

"Ms. Smith! Come join us!"

She screeched to a halt at Mabel shouting her name. Yikes. If she ignored the hospitable woman hollering across the lobby, that would look suspicious. And rude. For a split moment she considered doing just that. There was no time for chitchat—she had a hole to dig out of.

But that hole could wait for a few more minutes. Pasting on a smile, she turned to see Mabel waving at her from the eating area, sitting at a table with two glasses of iced tea and a man who wasn't Clyde. He actually looked a little like—

Oh no. *Oh no, no, no, no.*

Sebastian Hudson was motioning for her to join them.

Chapter 8

Seb had known Mabel all his life, but two things about her stood out—she was wise enough to marry Clyde, who made the best biscuits west of the Mississippi, and she was exceptionally observant. That second characteristic came into play when he spotted Jade scurrying into the inn, clutching her briefcase like she'd just escaped a heist at Fort Knox. Mabel immediately noticed him noticing Jade, and before he knew it, she was waving one bat-winged arm and inviting her to his exclusive interview.

He was ready to protest because he needed to get this interview done, and Jade had already distracted him enough today. As usual, though, his curiosity got the best of him. Seb had never been a patron of the Clementine Inn, but he'd covered plenty of events here over the years, including a massive lightning strike six years ago that took out half the structure. He also reported on the rebuilding process. He knew the place inside out, and before Mabel's friendly gesture, Jade was hightailing it to the hallway to where rooms 101–104 were located.

Then he saw her turn statue still, an unnatural smile on her pretty face. Yep, something was up. Not one to turn down an investigative opportunity, he motioned for her to come over.

She slowly walked to their table, her eyes shifting from his and locking on Mabel's before sitting down opposite him. She set her briefcase on her lap, protectively placing her hands on top. The strap of a small brown purse was slung across her body.

"Jade," Mabel said, a wide smile on her face. "Let me introduce you to one of Clementine's national treasures—"

He cringed at her overblown praise.

"—Sebastian Hudson. He's the owner, editor in chief, reporter extraordinaire—"

"We've met before," he interjected before Mabel shoved a crown on his head. The woman did have a flair for hyperbole.

Jade nodded, her expression still a little strained.

"Oh?" Mabel's gaze bounced between the two of them. "When?"

She was also a little nosy. Then again, who in Clementine wasn't?

"We both used to work at *The Arkansas Democrat-Gazette*," Jade said.

"In Little Rock," he added.

"Now isn't that a coincidence," Mabel said with a slight smile.

Seb turned to Jade. "Yeah. Coincidence."

Mabel pushed her chair back and started to get up. "Let me get another glass of tea."

Jade shook her head. "That's not necessary—"

"Sweet or unsweet?"

"Unsweet, please," she quietly replied.

Mabel disappeared.

Seb looked at the briefcase again. "Hmm."

Jade frowned. "Hmm what?"

"Nice briefcase."

She gave it a quick look as if she hadn't noticed she was holding it, then put it underneath her chair. "It's nothing special," she muttered, staring down at the tabletop.

"Looks like real leather."

"It's not. Real leather is expensive."

"Hmm."

She turned to him, exasperated. "What?"

"I just figured with you working at a fancy-schmancy company, you'd have a fancy-schmancy attaché."

"I've never liked schmanciness."

His lips twitched. "True. You were always unostentatious. That was one of the things I liked—" He shook his head, irritated at the almost slipup, even though it was accurate.

She looked at him, less guarded now.

Once again he was caught up in her eyes. When he and Jade first met, they were filled with determination and pluck. As they grew closer, he saw the kind softness that she kept carefully hidden. Then there was the desire, as they fell in love—

Seb's thoughts screeched to a halt.

Jade leaned toward him. Not too close, but the distance between them wasn't exactly businesslike. "Would you like to grab dinner tonight?"

His brows shot up to his hairline. "Huh?"

"We can have a bite to eat, catch up on the past ten years." She smiled, but there was something off about it.

Even though he had no idea if her offer was serious or if she was trying to manipulate him, he was tempted—more than he wanted to admit. What had she been doing for the past decade? Did she like living in Atlanta? Did she ever miss Arkansas? *Or me?* He was torn between wanting the answer and letting it alone. His curiosity was winning, though, and he knew a cozy restaurant fifteen minutes outside Clementine that served the tenderest sirloin steaks—

"Jade!"

They both turned to see a tall, biracial man with black curly hair and freckles stride toward them, a bright yellow backpack slung over one shoulder.

"Logan," she grumbled. "He wasn't supposed to be here until tomorrow morning."

While Seb was grateful the kid's unexpected appearance interrupted his insane thought that agreeing to dinner with Jade was even possible, much less a good idea, he wondered who this guy was.

Jade stood as Logan reached their table. "You're early," she said without preamble.

Logan's bright grin faded. "I was eager to see you." He glanced at Seb. "Am I interrupting something?"

"No," Jade said.

"Kinda," Seb added. He'd gotten sidetracked in his quest to find out what was so special about her briefcase, but maybe he'd read too much into it. She'd set it on the ground and now didn't seem concerned about it. Her attention was fully focused on the kid in front of her. Seb's gaze dropped to her wringing hands.

Mabel showed up with Jade's tea and set it on the table. She looked at Logan. "Now who do we have here?" she said.

"Logan Mitchell." He held out his hand. "I'm Jade's brother."

Seb hid his shock and saw Mabel's pleasant expression slip into the tiniest bit of confusion. He didn't blame her—he was just as confused. He didn't know Jade had a brother, and from appearances they weren't fully blood related, although genes were always unpredictable. Not that it was a big deal, just unexpected. Then again, neither of them had said much about their families when they were together. Other than one mention of her mom, she had avoided any discussion of the topic.

"Nice to meet you," Mabel said, back to her usual hospitable geniality. "Welcome to the Clementine Inn. I'm Mabel, the proprietor."

"Thanks. I'm glad to be here." He glanced over his shoulder at the front desk. "Is that where I can reserve a room?"

"For tonight?"

He nodded. "If you have one near Jade's, that would be great." He turned to his sister. "We have a lot of catching up to do."

Jade flinched.

"Oh dear." Mabel frowned. "We don't have any free rooms until after Saturday's hoedown. We booked our last one this morning."

Logan nodded, looking disappointed. "Is there another hotel I can stay at?"

She shook her head. "Not nearby. The Juniper Arms is about an hour away."

He turned to Jade. "Guess I'll have to bunk with you."

Her eyes widened. "I only have one bed. It's a double."

"No big deal, I'll sleep on the floor."

"You don't have to do that." Seb stepped forward and extended his hand. "Seb Hudson. I'm . . ." He glanced at Jade. "An old acquaintance of your sister's. I've got a cabin not too far from Clementine. You can stay there."

That suggestion brought Jade to her feet finally. "But—"

"Really? You have a cabin?" Logan adjusted his backpack. "Cool."

Jade was shooting quizzical arrows at Seb, but he ignored her. It didn't seem right for Logan to sleep on a motel room floor, no matter how clean Mabel and Clyde kept their premises. "It's about half an hour outside Clementine, in the mountains. It's remote, though. The nearest neighbor is more than two miles away."

"Sounds good to me. What do you think, Jade?"

Seb looked at her, and he could tell she thought this was a terrible idea. From Logan's crestfallen expression, it was obvious he could read her thoughts too. "Can I talk to you privately for a minute?" she said.

Logan nodded. "Sure."

"Not you." She turned to Seb, her eyes narrowing. "You."

––––––––

Jade tried to control her frustration as she dragged Sebastian by the arm to the patio outside, off the eating area of the inn. She shut the door and faced him, thrusting her trembling hands behind her back. "What do you think you're doing?"

He lifted his hands. "Giving your brother a place to stay."

"You had no right to do that!" She almost added that he didn't know what he was getting into. She wasn't even sure she knew Logan was sincere, although she was glad to see he was looking healthier and more clear-eyed than he had since their last meeting, when she cut off her financial and emotional support. She pushed the sudden stab of guilt away, remembering that he'd told her he had to get out of Little Rock. If he was in such a hurry to leave, then he had to be in some sort of trouble, even though he wasn't acting like it.

"You want him to sleep on your floor?"

"I want you to mind your own business!" She pushed her hair to the side and off her sweaty neck. Taking a small breath, she modulated her tone and crossed her arms so her unsteady hands were still hidden. "You don't even know him, Sebastian. Why would you take in a complete stranger?"

"He's your family." He held out his hands. "Why wouldn't I?"

His words caused warmth to spread in her chest. Of course he would do this. Opening his home to someone in need was quintessential Sebastian. Her hands stilled and she dropped her arms. "I . . ." She didn't know what to say without revealing Logan's past. If her brother truly had turned his life around, she didn't want to poison Sebastian's view of him.

"I'll rescind the offer if it means that much to you." He turned toward the door.

"Wait." She touched his arm. His bicep, in particular. Nice. Hard, firm, as if he still went to the gym like he used to back in Little Rock—

"Jade?"

Her eyes refocused and she saw him look at her, then at her hand. She snatched it away. "He can stay at your cabin."

"How kind of you to allow him."

She knew she was being unreasonable, and she wanted Logan to stay in a nice place. But his early arrival, along with her earlier, unexpected dinner invitation to Sebastian, had her all spun up. After Mabel left and they were alone for a few minutes, she simply wanted to open the door with him again and decided to be more personable. That had instantly turned into her practically asking him out on a date. Even worse, she thought it might actually be a decent idea, and after his initial shocked reaction, he almost seemed to be mulling it over. Then again, maybe she just wanted to believe he was. *So confusing.* For once, Logan's timing was spot-on.

"Thank you for giving him a place to stay," she said, measuring the speed of her words so they didn't come out in a mangled rush. "It will only be for one night."

"You sound sure of that."

"We'll go to another hotel tomorrow morning."

"An hour away?"

"There really isn't one closer?"

"Nope."

That did put a damper on things. She'd lose precious hours commuting back and forth, and Logan was going to take up some of that time too. "All right, we won't change accommodations. That way I can meet with you tomorrow to continue our discussion."

His hands went to his hips. "I made it clear to you this morning that our discussion was over."

She moved toward him, tilting her chin so she could look him directly in the eye. "It's only just begun."

And that ended up being a grave miscalculation. Her intent had been to show him how serious she was. Instead, she couldn't breathe. She'd forgotten what it was like to be this close to him, inhaling his scent, appealing and familiar. She could also see shades of brown mixed with a little gray in his scruffy beard. His blue eyes held hers, and a jolt of heat traveled through her.

The patio door opened. They jumped apart as Logan stepped outside. "Everything okay out here?"

Jade turned to him, stunned. When was the last time Logan had asked her if she was okay? She literally couldn't remember.

"We're cool." Sebastian went to him. "Everything's set."

"Thanks, dude," he said to Sebastian. "I owe you one."

For the first time since his arrival, she took a good look at him. He didn't reek of cigarette and marijuana smoke. His hair was clean, and he was dressed in casual clothes any twentysomething guy would wear in hot weather—a T-shirt and shorts—not ripped, torn, and stained clothing. It had been a long time since Logan had looked so . . . normal.

"No problem," Sebastian said. "I just need to finish my interview with Mabel, and I'll take you there." He turned to Jade. "You're welcome to come along."

She wasn't sure how to respond. His friendly offer and demeanor seemed surreal, considering they were in contentious business discussions and Logan was unknown to him. Since Sebastian had to talk to Mabel, Jade and Logan could go back to her room and she could find out what was going on with him—because something odd was going on. After their discussion she would decide whether to go to the cabin. It might give her another opportunity to talk about negotiations with Sebastian. All she needed to do was get her briefcase—

My briefcase!

How could she have forgotten? She was supposed to be figuring out how to return Sebastian's ledger. Hold on, she needed to keep her cool. She would just get her briefcase, go to her room with Logan, and take things from there. No need to act weird. "I'll be right back," she said, not waiting for a response, slowing her steps to an almost awkward gait to avoid rushing back inside.

When she entered the eating area, she halted. The entire room and lobby were packed full of guests. Some were at the front desk where Clyde was manning the reservations, and others were seated at the tables near the empty buffet. Where did they all come from?

She weaved through the small crowd to where she had been sitting with Sebastian and Mabel, looked under her chair, and freaked out.

Her briefcase was gone.

Her crossbody purse slapped against her hip as she rushed to the desk, pushing her way to the front.

"Hey," a woman said as Jade shoved her aside. "What are you doing?"

"Sorry, it's an emergency. Where's Mabel?" she asked Clyde.

"Wish I knew." His expression was pleasant, but there was a slightly stressed edge to his tone. "Hopefully she went to get Caroline to help us out. We weren't expecting everyone to show up at once. This has never happened before." He tapped on the computer and nodded to the gentleman in front of him. "Yes, sir, your reservation is here. Give me just a second—"

"Have you seen a briefcase? Brown with a big gold latch?"

"No," he said. "Sorry, Mr. Tate. I was saying that to her." Clyde looked at Jade. "I have no idea what you're talking about."

Panic anchored deep inside her. She couldn't lose her briefcase. She had other work-related papers in there. And if the ledger was gone, how was she going to explain that to Sebastian?

A swarm of people pressed against her, and she managed to slip away and get back to the dining area. When she couldn't see underneath the chairs, she dropped to the floor and started to crawl.

Logan was suddenly beside her as they avoided getting stepped on. "What are you doing?"

"I can't find my briefcase." How could she have been so stupid to leave it unattended? She'd had it close beside her the whole time since she left Atlanta, and that was before she'd taken Sebastian's file. She started to hyperventilate.

"It's okay, Jade. I'll help you find it."

Her brother's words calmed her, and they crawled around the dining area for a few minutes.

"This is impossible." Logan took her arm and brought her to her feet. "There's too many people here."

"You don't understand," she said. "I have to find it."

"Find what?" Sebastian asked.

She turned to see him standing behind her. "Nothing—"

"She's misplaced her briefcase," Logan said.

"Oh, right. It was by that table over there, wasn't it?" He looked at Jade. "I'll help you—"

"No!"

Logan and Sebastian drew back.

"I mean," she said, an ungainly chuckle escaping, "it's probably in lost and found by now. When things settle down, I'll ask Mabel or Clyde to get it for me."

"Are you sure?" Sebastian said.

"Positive." She clasped her hands behind her back. "One hundred percent."

He glanced at the crowd in the lobby. "Looks like I won't get to talk to Mabel for a while."

"Then why don't you and Logan go to your cabin?" She mustered a smile. "You can get him settled."

"Are you coming with us?" Logan sounded hopeful.

She shook her head. She would continue to look for her briefcase without having to worry about Sebastian finding it first. Just the thought of him picking up the case and the latch opening on its own terrified her. "I've got some things to do back in my room."

The men exchanged looks. "Sounds good to me," Sebastian said. He nodded to Jade. "See you later."

Logan put his arm around her shoulders. "We'll talk soon, sis."

Another surprise. Logan rarely hugged her once he became a teenager. When he was little, she used to cuddle him in her lap and read stories, mostly before bedtime. Her heart squeezed. She missed those days.

She watched her brother and ex-boyfriend make their way through the congested lobby to the exit. Unreal. When they disappeared, she blew out a breath and rubbed her temples. Once everything settled down, she could ask Mabel to check the lost and found. Surely it had to be there. No one would steal a briefcase. Would they?

———

As Seb made the twenty-five-minute drive to his cabin with Logan following in his small gray sedan, he took the chance to process the last hour with Jade. He hadn't expected her to get so upset, not only about his offer to house Logan, but also about the briefcase. He was still puzzled that she'd been against her brother staying at his cabin. The kid seemed nice, and like Seb told Jade, he was her family. It was almost as if she didn't want to trust Logan with Seb. Or was it the other way around?

Then there was the briefcase debacle. Her strong reaction to losing it brought his curiosity back. He'd seen fear in her eyes when he offered to find it, and she quickly covered that up with a bizarre laugh and enthusiastic suggestion that he take Logan to the cabin, when a short while earlier she'd been against it.

Strange, strange, strange.

The rest of the way to the cabin he made a mental note to get with Mabel again after the hoedown. He could push back his Clementine series. He was the boss after all.

Reaching the top of the curvy mountain road, he pulled into his driveway and Logan parked right next to him. He got out of the car and breathed in the Ozark air. It was fresh. Invigorating. He loved it up here. He saw Logan exit the car, a cell to his ear.

"Gotcha," Logan said into the phone. "I'll call you tomorrow morning. Hopefully I'll have some news." He hung up and slid his cell into his short's pocket, then reached inside and pulled out his backpack. When he turned toward Seb, he looked a little green around the gills.

"You all right?"

"I will be now that we're stopped." Logan leaned against the car.

"Sorry. Should have warned you about all the curves."

"That's okay. I'll be fine." He paused, his eyes filling with concern. "You think Jade's all right?"

Not really. But he had no way to explain that answer, so he said, "As far as I know."

"How long have y'all known each other?"

Ah, the inquisition. He would do the same if he'd met an "old friend" of Evelyn Margot's he'd never heard about. "About ten years. We met at the paper."

"That's where she was working before she moved to Atlanta, right?"

"Right." He shoved his hands into his pockets. "She went on to greener pastures."

"I don't even know what she does there," Logan said. "Not exactly. Something with business."

"Yeah," Seb said. "Business."

"I'm proud of her. She's always done well for herself."

"Seems to have. It's been a while since we last talked." No need for him to know how long.

"Same here." Logan was staring straight ahead, looking past Seb, his jaw set.

For once, Seb didn't pry.

Logan blinked and looked at Seb again, this time with a grin. "Nice place."

"Thanks." He walked down the incline to the cabin's front steps and unlocked the door. It had been a few weeks since he was last here, and as soon as he walked inside, he pulled down the window on the screen door and left the wood-paneled front door ajar. "I'll open a couple more windows in here to air it out," he said as Logan entered.

Logan glanced around the cabin. "Wow," he said.

Wow was an exaggeration, but the place was a gem. Seb had been shocked when Buford had bequeathed it to him, and worried that Bo would be upset. *"Nah,"* Bo had said. *"You went up there more than I did to visit him and Aunt Glenda. I'm glad it's yours."*

Seb was glad too, and while the cabin was his retreat, he wished he had more time to spend up here. Maybe someday he would again, once his problems with *The Times* were settled.

Buford and Glenda had designed and built the one-bedroom, one-bath home with chocolate-brown wood flooring, maple walls, and a high ceiling. The living area and kitchen were one continuous space, and a red cast-iron stove stood in the corner, cords of firewood stacked nearby. The weather was too warm to use the stove now, but in the late fall and winter, there was nothing better than a warm fire, some stout coffee, and a good book to read. *Or possibly write.*

"The bedroom is down the hall in the back." Seb opened up another window. "You'll see the bath right across from it."

"Thanks. I'll put up my stuff."

After Logan disappeared, Seb checked the near-empty fridge, save for mustard, ketchup, a jar of pickles, and two cans of Coke. The pantry had more supplies, but if he had been thinking, they probably should have stopped at the store on their way here.

"This is really cool, Seb." Logan walked into the room. "Thanks for giving me such a great place to stay."

"It's not the Clementine Inn, but it'll do." He turned to Logan.

"Supplies are pretty low. I can run to the grocery store and get you a few things."

"It'll be okay for one night. I brought some stuff with me in my pack. I wasn't exactly sure about Jade's reception." He shrugged. "I don't want to keep you if you have to get back to work." Logan stood by the brown suede recliner next to a matching overstuffed couch. "I can take care of myself."

Independence. A quality the young man shared with his sister. "You sure?"

"Positive."

Seb was tempted to stay but needed to get back to town. Even without the Clementine history series to work on, he had plenty to do. "Make yourself at home. There are some wicker chairs on the back porch and a hiking trail in the woods behind the house. It's about a mile and a half around and will bring you back to the cabin."

"Thanks, but I'll stick around and wait for Jade. We were supposed to talk tomorrow, and I can tell I threw her off schedule. But maybe she'll change her mind."

Seb didn't miss the hope in Logan's voice. "Oh, before I forget, cell reception can be spotty up here, so I can't guarantee your phone will work. I have a landline just in case." He opened up the junk drawer and pulled out a small pad of paper and a pencil that was worn to the nub. He scribbled down his phone number, address, and his nearest neighbor's same information. "Just in case," he said, handing the paper to Logan.

After saying goodbye, Seb headed back to Clementine. Before he reached his office, a crazy thought came to mind. Should he go to the inn and check on Jade? Make sure she found her briefcase?

No. She wasn't his concern or responsibility. He did hope she would go see Logan and work out whatever was going on between them. Whatever that was, he had to remind himself once again that it wasn't his business. And she was after his actual business. That was enough to maintain his distance.

Chapter 9

Earlier than she had ever been awake—if you could call it that—Kalista dragged herself down the stairs to the basement where she was supposed to meet Tyler for delivery girl training. Yesterday afternoon she managed to fall asleep, even though the electricity didn't come back on until eight o'clock. Viv woke her up for dinner, and when she left the bedroom, Bo was outside grilling steaks while the electric company truck was parked at the end of the driveway working on the damaged pole.

The three of them had a delicious supper, minus the baked potato since the oven wasn't working. Bo was incredibly nice, and he clearly loved Viv and vice versa. Their dinner was the highlight of her time in Arkansas so far and she'd easily fallen back to sleep.

But getting up at two in the morning was an absolute pain. She didn't even bother to brush her hair—just put it up in a scrunchie and slipped on shorts and a long-sleeved sweatshirt with UCLA on the front. It wasn't like she had anyone to impress.

When she reached the last step on the basement stairwell, Tyler appeared in front of her. "Hi," he said, way too cheery for this hour in the morning.

She nodded and yawned again.

"I know it's early," he said, pushing up his glasses. "But you're late."

Kalista looked at her watch. "Only by fifteen minutes."

"When you're delivering papers, fifteen minutes is a lot. Our customers expect their papers to be delivered on time. I'm sorry, but I have to give you a warning. Company policy."

"Fine." She waved him off as he stepped aside.

"Unless you have an acceptable reason, if you're late again, you're fired," he said, with all the force of a golden retriever.

Don't tempt me. She could already tell she wasn't going to like this job, and getting fired would be a relief. But she was just as sure that her father would probably apply more restrictions if she lost her first job on purpose. "I'll be on time from now on."

Tyler grinned. "Great. Let's get started." He headed for the other side of the basement where the huge stacks of newspapers were on long tables against the wall, plenty of pep in his step.

Ugh, he was annoyingly energetic. She shuffled behind him and half listened as he explained which newspapers were for her route.

"Sometimes you'll have to put flyers inside before you roll them."

"Roll them?"

He picked up a flat paper and, in a flash, the pages turned into a tube. Sliding a rubber band over it, he said, "You'll have to roll these before you can deliver them."

"Doesn't someone else do that?"

"When we had a bigger circulation, yes." He grabbed another paper and moved closer to her. "But we're small now, so we do it ourselves. It's easy, just watch."

He stood close enough she could tell his hair was damp, and he smelled clean, like he'd just taken a shower. No cologne, like Ryan always wore—sometimes too much—and her other male friends and guys she dated. Great hair, though. Thick and shiny.

"Now you try." He handed her a flat paper.

Oops. She should have been paying more attention to what he was doing and less attention to his hair. Still, how hard could this be? She took the paper and started to roll it. The sheets slipped out of her hands and separated, floating to the floor. "Sorry," she said, cringing that she'd messed up such a simple task.

He bent down and picked up the papers. "That's okay," he said good-naturedly. "It takes practice." He placed the separated sheets on the table and grabbed another flat newspaper from the stack, then stood in front of her. "Okay, watch carefully this time."

She did and realized the mistake she'd made. She grabbed a paper from the stack. "I think I've got it." When she finished, she'd rolled it perfectly.

"Awesome," he said. "Try another one."

Kalista continued to roll up papers as Tyler watched, getting into a rhythm. This wasn't too bad, and she was getting used to the smell of ink and newsprint. When she finished rolling the last paper, she grinned at the neat line of papers ready to be delivered. "I did it," she said, feeling accomplished. Then she looked down at her hands and almost freaked out. "My fingers are black!"

"It's from the ink." He handed her an old blue rag with stains all over it. "You can wipe your hands on this."

She eyed the rag dubiously. "Isn't there a sink around here?"

"Upstairs in the restroom." Tyler pushed a cart to the table. "But we don't have time for that. We've got to get these loaded into your car."

"Truck," she corrected. Bo had told her she could use it for the rest of the summer. *"I don't need it,"* he'd said, picking up a toothpick after they'd finished supper. *"I've got two more I use for work."* He also gave her tips on how to drive it, and she did better on the drive over here this morning than she had yesterday.

Her father had a fleet of cars, and right after he and Bettany had gotten engaged, he'd given Bettany a new Bentley, making Kalista seethe with jealousy. She was stuck driving a Mercedes.

"Great," Tyler said. "A truck will handle the back roads better."

Mr. Hudson had said the same thing yesterday. Exactly how treacherous were these roads? This was probably the wrong time to admit she'd only gotten her license a couple of months ago—something else her father had made her do instead of his driver taking her places. At the time she'd thought that was the only thing he was going to force her to do. *Little did I know.* She had learned to drive in LA traffic, though, and from what she could tell, Clementine barely had any traffic at all, so that was in her favor.

They loaded up the cart with the papers and went outside the door to the back parking lot, which was empty save for one beat-up looking car. "Where's your truck?" Tyler asked.

"Up front."

"Didn't Mr. H. tell you to park in the back?"

"He might have," she admitted. Once he hired her, she hadn't exactly been listening to him.

"No problem, you can do it next time. Just go and bring it around here." He flashed her another easygoing grin.

Did this guy get ruffled about anything?

After she parked the truck in the correct lot, they loaded up the papers and she got in the driver's side. Tyler squeezed in on the passenger side. Fortunately he was so skinny he didn't take up room, but he still had to push some of the papers over.

He withdrew a map from the back pocket of his baggy jeans and handed it to her. "This is your route," he said turning on the overhead light in the truck.

She glanced at a winding, circling trail that didn't look too bad.

"You'll need to memorize this as soon as you can, but while I'm here, I can help you with the directions."

Kalista nodded, and they were on their way. For the next couple of hours, she drove as he gave directions and showed her how to deliver the papers. Some of them she could put into a box underneath the mailbox, while other customers were fine with the paper being at the end of the driveway.

"We do have five customers that are very picky about where they want their newspapers," Tyler said. "They all happen to live near the top of the mountain. You'll have to get out of the truck to place them where they want them. We're coming up on Mr. Jackson right now. I'll go with you and show you where he wants his paper."

They parked in front of his gravel driveway, and faint streaks of daylight appeared in the sky. When they reached a wraparound porch, Tyler took the paper from Kalista and placed it near the front door. "He wants it to the left of the welcome mat. Not the right."

"The right," Kalista said. "Not the left." Or was it the left and not the right? There was so much she had to remember, she wasn't sure, even though he'd just given her the instructions. "What if I forget?"

He frowned. "I don't know. I've never forgotten, and neither did Daniel. He's the guy that had the route before you. Just try to remember."

"But what's the big deal?" she asked as they made their way down the driveway. "He could just as easily pick it up from the other side of the mat."

"That's not the point. He's our customer and we do our best to make our customers happy, even if it might seem . . ."

"Ridiculous?"

"I wouldn't say that." He opened the passenger door. "It's just their preference."

Fair enough. Kalista was known to be finicky herself. When she went shopping, she expected the salesperson to give her un-divided and personal attention because she was spending money. Her father's money, but the point still stood. She deserved to be catered to. Apparently Mr. Jackson felt the same way.

They finished the route, and Kalista marked on the map where the other four persnickety people wanted their paper. Then they headed down the mountain and back to Clementine. By the time they got to Main Street, the sun was already above the horizon.

"You did pretty good," Tyler said when she put the truck in Park. It lurched forward.

Pretty good? Humph. "What did I do wrong?"

"Not wrong, exactly," he said. "You're not used to driving a truck, are you?"

She fell back against the seat. "How can you tell?"

"You're taking your turns too wide. You have to be careful on some of the narrow parts of the route. You don't want to have an accident."

No, she certainly did not. She also didn't want to wreck Bo's truck. No doubt if she did, her father would make her take a second job to pay for it. Besides, now that she met him and saw how good he was to Viv, she didn't want to damage his vehicle in any way.

"Now that part of the job is done, it's time to finish up."

"I thought we were finished." She was ready for coffee and then back to bed.

"You have to tidy up the loose papers and get everything ready for Monday."

"Isn't Monday a holiday? It's Memorial Day."

"Not for us." Tyler smiled again. He was almost always smiling, even when she'd gotten turned around shortly after they left Clementine. "If you have everything ready for Monday now, then all you'll have to do is roll the papers, load them, and deliver them. Except if you have to put a flyer in, and that won't take long."

They went back inside, and she did everything Tyler told her to do to get ready for Monday's delivery. When he said she was free to go, she was relieved. And also surprised. This wasn't going to be too bad. Granted, driving up the mountain had been a little perilous, and she thought she was the only one who had noticed she was having trouble with some of the terrain.

"Well," Tyler said, shuffling his feet a little. "Guess I'll see you Monday."

"Uh-huh." She was already halfway across the room.

"Kalista?"

She turned around. Now he had his hands behind his back. "Do you know about the hoedown on Saturday?"

Not this again. She rolled her eyes. "Yeah. I'm staying at Bo's with my stepmother."

"Vivian is your stepmother? Cool. She's a great lady."

Kalista had to smile. "She definitely is."

"Are you going then?"

She sighed. "It's not like I have anywhere else to be."

He smiled again. "Then I'll probably see you there."

"Sure." She opened the back door and walked out, not wanting to think about the hoedown. Between Viv, Bo, the farmhands, and all the people working to get things ready and not having electricity for several hours yesterday, it was all so annoying.

She did ask Viv last night if there was a coffee shop anywhere close, and she said only the bakery in Clementine. But it didn't open until nine. She was stuck drinking Viv's coffee, and although it was pretty good, Kalista was really missing her daily cappuccinos.

"Bye, Kalista!" Tyler said, standing in the open doorway.

She gave him a less than enthusiastic wave and went to the truck, yawning as she got inside. Now that she was finished working, she suddenly felt tired again. Maybe she'd skip the coffee and go straight to bed. But she also felt satisfied. She'd made it through her first day, and she was determined to make it through the summer. Once she proved to her father that she could be responsible, he'd give her access to her phone, bank account, and charge cards again.

And once she had her trust fund money, she'd buy that Bentley—one twice as expensive as Bettany's. *Time to make her seethe with jealousy.*

———

At four the next morning, Jade yanked the hood of her purple hoodie over her head and crept toward the dumpster behind the Clementine Inn. After searching the premises as much as possible yesterday afternoon, Jade still hadn't found her briefcase by the time Mabel and Clyde had processed the rush of guests and checked everyone in. Right after that, Mabel had disappeared and hadn't returned until after six o'clock.

"I'm sorry I wasn't here to help you look," Mabel said when Jade met her at the front desk. "Our daughter called and asked if I'd pick up my granddaughter Millie from daycare. She was running a fever, and Kim couldn't get off work. I didn't have a chance to let Clyde know before I left. I felt bad about leaving him to deal with the rush of reservations. I had no idea everyone would show up at once."

"Is she okay?" Jade asked.

"Yes. I gave her some Tylenol and she was sleeping when Kim arrived. She had a low fever and some sniffles, so I think it's a cold."

Jade was glad it was nothing serious—and said as much—but she still had to find her briefcase. "Clyde and Caroline said it wasn't in the lost and found or the office."

"It's possible Phoebe picked it up before she got off her shift." Mabel tapped her fingers on the reservation desk counter. "She's one of our housekeepers."

"Where would she have put it?"

"In the lost and found." Mabel frowned.

"Could she have taken it with her?" Jade knew she was grasping at straws, but she was growing frantic.

"I don't know why she would do that."

"Can you call her and check?"

Mabel shook her head. "I wish I could. She finally got hitched to that navy boy she's been dating forever, and they left for Miami right after she got off work."

"Did she leave a phone number?"

"Not with us. Besides, she and Gary are going on a two-week cruise to Turks and Caicos. She's gonna be out of pocket for a while."

That put Jade into almost full-blown freak-out mode. She crossed her arms to hide her trembling hands.

"I'm sure Phoebe didn't take it," Mabel said. "That would be stealing, and we frown on that here in Clementine."

Jade bit the inside of her cheek and nodded.

"Don't worry, we will keep looking. I'll also ask our guests if they've seen it."

That was all Jade could ask for, but hope was slipping away. She thanked Mabel and spent the rest of the night in her room, kicking herself for being so irresponsible and dishonest.

Somehow she'd managed to fall asleep only to bolt awake an hour ago. Could the briefcase be in the dumpster? It was a long shot, and it didn't make any sense why someone would throw away a perfectly good briefcase and not just take it to the front desk. Although she tried to dismiss the idea, she ended up pursuing it anyway. She found the hoodie she'd packed in her suitcase at the last minute, slipped it on, and left the inn. It was warm outside, but the hooded sweatshirt gave her a semblance of disguise.

Unlike other hotels she'd stayed at in the past, the Clementine Inn had only one streetlamp, and it was situated between the front parking lot and the back of the building. Fortunately it gave her enough light to see by because she didn't have a flashlight. It was also fortunate that no one was around, and all of the rooms were dark on this side of the inn. She walked around the medium-sized dumpster and didn't see anything, not even a single piece of trash. The outside of the container looked as clean as a freshly washed car.

The inside probably was not.

Jade stared at the dumpster lid on top of the container. It was split in two, with one side open and the other closed. She had to be certifiable to even consider climbing it and looking inside. But what if by some miracle her briefcase was there?

Placing her hand on the top edge of the container, she planted her tennis shoe–covered foot on the side—

"Hey!"

She slipped at the sound of a deep male voice and nearly landed on her backside. Dread filled every cell of her body, and she searched her mind for a cover story as footsteps neared, then slowed down.

"Jade?"

Sebastian? Of all the people to catch her climbing a dumpster . . . Slapping a smile on her face, she slowly turned around. "Hi," she said, giving him an awkward little wave, as if they'd just run into each other in the frozen food aisle and not outside a huge trash receptacle. "What brings you by?"

While the streetlamp did provide some light, it wasn't enough to see his face clearly. He shined his flashlight on her. "Newspaper delivery. We're down a carrier, so I picked up this route. When I pulled into the parking lot and saw someone walking around the dumpster, I had to check it out."

"Isn't that dangerous?"

"No offense, Jade, but you're not the size of a linebacker. I can handle myself. Besides, this isn't the big city, and we don't have much crime here. The last time Sheriff Thistle had to arrest someone was over a year ago, and that was for drunk and disorderly, which I thought might be what was going on. Most folks around here are good, honest people."

She gulped.

"So . . . what's a lady like you doing at a dumpster like this at 4:00 a.m.?"

She tried to chuckle, hoping it sounded light and airy instead of deranged. "I . . . I'm looking for something." The truth, such as it was.

"Your briefcase?"

"No, we found that." She was disturbed by how easily the lie slipped out.

"Where was it?"

"Phoebe picked it up. She's one of the housekeepers. Did you know she finally got married to that navy guy she's been dating? They went on a two-week cruise to Turks and Caicos."

"Yeah, everyone knows about Phoebe and Gary. I'm more surprised that *you* know that."

"Mabel is quite informative."

"That she is. If you're not looking for your briefcase, then what are you looking for?"

Of course he would ply her with twenty questions, or more. "A bracelet." It was the first thing that popped in her mind. "I set it on the bathroom counter yesterday morning and forgot to put it back on. With, um, everything going on, I didn't remember about it until early this morning, and when I couldn't find it, I thought it might have fallen into the bathroom trash, but that had already been taken out. I didn't want to wake up Mabel and Clyde, so I came out here to see if it was in the dumpster." Oh no. Too many words. No way he would believe such an absurd story.

"Must be an important bracelet."

Her irritation rose. Why couldn't he just return to delivering the papers and let her be? "If it wasn't, I wouldn't be out here looking for it in the dumpster. I'm not an idiot."

"I didn't say you were. You're one of the smartest, most capable people I've ever met."

During the last two days, she'd been anything but smart or capable. The compliment was the last thing she anticipated from him, and it triggered that warm feeling she did not want to feel around Sebastian Hudson.

"Need some help?"

"I can do it." She resumed her climbing position on the dumpster. Immediately, her foot slid down the side. Nuts.

He moved closer to her, handed her his flashlight, and dropped down, threading his fingers together to give her a foothold.

Now that he'd gone to the trouble, she couldn't refuse. She put her foot on his hands, and he lifted her up. She peeked over the side of the dumpster, expecting to see full bags of trash, but it was empty. Whew, she wouldn't have to jump inside.

"Is it there?" Sebastian asked.

"No." Her disappointment was real as he helped her down. "It's gone." She handed back the flashlight.

"Sorry," he said, taking it from her.

"I'd better go inside and wash my hands. That was pretty gross."

"Glad it was you and not me. But if you need help again—"

"I don't."

"Got it." He turned around and stalked off.

Jade would have face-palmed if she hadn't just touched the dumpster. How was she supposed to get on his good side if she kept making so many mistakes? "Sebastian, wait." She rushed over to him. "I'm sorry. I'm just worried about the . . . bracelet."

Thankfully he turned around. "Someone special must have given it to you."

"I bought it for myself a while back," she said quickly. She had splurged on a pair of 24-karat gold hoop earrings shortly after she was hired at PU, so it wasn't a total lie, even though that was years ago.

They were closer to the lamplight, and she could see his face, relieved his expression wasn't as hardened as she thought. "Thanks for helping me."

"You're welcome."

Despite her frustration over the briefcase, she felt calmer. Sebastian wasn't doing anything special, just standing near her and accepting her apology. "I'm not used to asking for assistance."

Whoa, where did that admission come from? But in a conversation sprinkled with lies, that statement was the truth. She learned early on that the only person she could fully depend on was herself. Her foster mother, Madeline, was the closest she'd had to a reliable parent, but that had been during her teen years. Before and after her time with the Westins, she'd been on her own.

Except for the four months she'd dated the strong, solidly dependable man in front of her. He was never late for any of their dates, he never made her feel like a burden, and she could fully relax when she was around him—something she'd only been able to do in a car wash. *And I threw that all away.*

A lump formed in her throat, but she quickly swallowed it. Her reason for leaving Sebastian had been sound—she had to put Logan first. *Logan.* She was so focused on her missing briefcase, she'd pushed him to the back of her mind. They had to talk soon. She also had to meet with Sebastian again, but not here. In his office, preferably. Outside the business setting she couldn't seem to keep a handle on her emotions. "What's your schedule like today?"

"Busy. Always busy."

"Could you pencil me in this afternoon?" She took a step forward, but it was instinctual, not calculated.

"To talk about Harrington?"

"Yes. I'm not giving up, Sebastian. We haven't had a genuine discussion about the deal. Will you at least hear me out?"

He paused, and she fully expected him to say no. He didn't owe her anything. In fact, she owed him for giving her brother a place to stay. "How's Logan?" she asked, surprising herself by her sudden conversation shift.

"You haven't talked to him?"

"I will. This morning."

"Good. He's eager to see you."

Jade glanced at her tennis shoes. "I know. Things between us are complicated."

"So I gathered."

Her head tipped up. "Did he tell you what he wants from me?"

Sebastian frowned. "Only conversation, Jade. That's all he said."

There had to be more. While Logan had obviously made surface changes, she couldn't allow herself to trust him. "I'll call him. We can meet in town—"

"Or you can go to the cabin. It's more private there."

His offer softened her more. "Why are you helping us?"

Sebastian smiled. "Why wouldn't I?"

"There's at least one reason I can think of."

His grin flatlined. "Then you know more than me."

Huh? What did he mean by that?

"Logan can give you the address to the cabin." He turned on his heel and walked away.

She almost chased after him again, wanting an explanation for his cryptic comment. But as he went back to the parking lot, she realized she didn't need one. She unceremoniously dumped him and never gave him a good reason why. At the time a clean, uncomplicated break seemed necessary, and when she went to Atlanta, she poured her time and attention into her job and trying to adopt Logan. Other than the occasional feeling of guilt, she had closed that chapter of her life.

Now she was back in Arkansas, and the past surrounded her. Not just with Sebastian, but with Logan too.

She walked to the back entrance of the inn and inserted her key into the door, walked to her room, and washed her hands five times, then once more for good measure. Afterward she sank down on the edge of her bed, exhausted, her head falling into her hands.

It was too early to call Logan, but she would do that as soon as she could. She had asked Sebastian to hear her out—she had to give her brother the same courtesy. Even though Sebastian hadn't agreed to meet with her again, she would stop by his office this afternoon anyway. If she was lucky, he would be there. If she was luckier, her briefcase would show up before then.

She opened the top drawer of the bedside table and took out the phone book. She opened it to the Yellow Pages. There had to be a car wash somewhere around here.

Chapter 10

Midmorning, Seb entered his office and sat down on his chair. After he finished his route and returned to *The Times* building, he checked in with Tyler to see how things went with their new hire.

"She's great, Mr. H." Tyler grinned, his eyes bright and even more excited than usual, and that said a lot. "As long as she can get here on time, she's going to work out."

He hoped Tyler's assessment was unbiased and he wasn't letting his little crush on the California girl influence his judgment, but Seb would take his opinion at face value until further notice.

He then spoke with Isaiah, who was working in the office today. He, Tyler, and Seb were covering the hoedown at Bo's tomorrow. Seb then spent some time chatting with Cletus and Paul, who had come in to make some repairs on Ol' Bessie, then headed up to his office. Evelyn Margot was off-site today. She left a voicemail around seven this morning that she was going to be working from home again—

"Good morning, *older* brother!" Evelyn sailed into his office, holding the pictures once again.

Someday he was going to find her stash of his photos and throw them away. He wasn't thrilled with the picture idea in the first place when she had instigated it three years ago, but she'd insisted that his staff needed advanced warning of his grumpy days. Unfortunately those had been more frequent lately.

She held up a photo and glanced at him. "Let's see, who is Sebastian Percival Hudson going to be today?"

He rolled his eyes at her use of his full name.

She slid the photo back in the stack and chose another one. "There, this one will work. You actually look a little cheery this morning. Emphasis on *little*."

"I thought you were working from home."

She walked back to the door. "I was, but I decided I wanted to come in. A female reserves the right to change her mind."

Jade sure did . . .

Seb grimaced. After his encounter with Jade by the dumpster, he managed to put her out of his mind as he finished his route. Considering how much work he had on his plate, it was fairly easy. But one statement from Evelyn had him thinking about her again.

He didn't believe the story about the bracelet, mostly because she wasn't wearing one yesterday. A piece of jewelry worth crawling around in a dumpster for had to be important, so why not wear it every day?

He played along, though, hoping she'd reveal the real reason she was there. Too bad she didn't. He was glad to hear that the briefcase had been found, so that wasn't what she was actually looking for. Hmm . . .

Evelyn plopped herself on the chair in front of him. "So who's Ms. Smith?"

Seb paused, then busied himself moving papers on his disaster of a desk. "I know lots of Smiths," he said, not looking at her.

"I'm talking about the Ms. Smith that was in your office yesterday."

"Oh. Her." He tried to wrangle a pile of papers into a neat stack. Like Jade used to keep her paperwork. The documents slipped from his hands.

"Yes." She leaned forward. "Her."

"Former coworker. Just here for a visit." He grabbed a plain sheet of paper and rolled it into his typewriter.

"A friendly visit?"

He turned to his sister, who unfortunately possessed the same inquisitive gene he had. "Business."

"What kind of business?"

Seb scratched his left eyebrow. "I can order you out of my office, Evelyn Margot. I am your boss."

"You won't." Evelyn sat back and grinned. "You're too nice."

"More like desperate," he muttered, referring to his lacking the payroll to hire extra employees. He needed every single body currently employed at *The Times* and that included his talented, irritating sister.

But she wasn't wrong. He was too nice. Now that he had some time to think about it, he probably shouldn't have interfered with Jade and Logan. Not that he regretted giving Logan a place to stay, but when she brought him up this morning, he should have kept to a one-word answer and not mentioned she go to his cabin. In fact, he should have steered clear of her the moment he saw her at the dumpster instead of helping her. It didn't matter what she was looking for, fake bracelet or not. Because as soon as she mentioned the jewelry, he wanted to know if someone special had bought it for her. A male someone special. Bah, he didn't need this mental drama.

"She's pretty," Evelyn said. "How long did you work together?"

"Not long." He faced the typewriter again.

"Long enough to date?"

He paused, and that was all the opening Evelyn Margot Hudson needed.

"Ooh, why didn't you mention her before?" She clasped her hands together. "What other secret girlfriends have you been keeping from me?"

"We barely dated. And I don't have any secret girlfriends. You know better than anyone else that I don't have the time."

"You could make time."

He glared at her. "You're the one who said my girl picker was broken, remember?"

Evelyn balked. "I did? When was that?"

"After Karen and I broke up."

"Karen, yuck. You two were *not* compatible."

Apparently he and Jade weren't either.

He stared at the empty paper in the roller. A writer's worst nightmare—the blank page. He usually didn't have a problem starting on columns and articles. Those were a breeze most of the time after all his years writing them. It was only when he tried another kind of writing, a more personal kind, that he froze up. He wondered if he'd ever thaw that fear enough to do it again.

When he noticed Evelyn had grown quiet, he glanced at her. She was staring at the mess on his desk but clearly not seeing it. "Ev?"

She blinked, then looked at him. Gone was the teasing and nosiness. Evelyn Margot was uncharacteristically serious. "Do you think there's something wrong with us?"

He turned his chair toward her. "What do you mean?"

"You're forty. I'm thirty-four. Neither of us has ever been married." She sighed.

Where was this coming from? He and Evelyn had never talked

much about their social lives over the years. "Does this have something to do with Pancake?"

"Haskell? Pshaw." But her cheeks turned red as she averted her gaze. "He's like you. Consumed with his job."

"He's an excellent mayor."

"Yeah." She shrugged and got to her feet. "Never mind," she said, sounding morose now.

"Hang on." He gestured for her to sit down. "There's nothing wrong with us. At least not too much." He cracked a small smile. "I don't believe there's a set age to get married. Considering Mom and Dad, I think it's better not to marry until you're absolutely sure and committed to the other person."

"Agreed. She's happy now, though. Do you ever wonder about Dad—"

"No. I don't. He made his choice. If he wanted a relationship with us, he could have made it happen."

She nodded. "I used to be angry about that. Now I'm just sad."

"Me too. But we've got Bill. He's been a great stepdad." Seb paused. "You've been talking to Mom recently, haven't you?"

"This morning. She said to tell you hi and remind you that you still had a mother."

That was a bit of a gut punch. "I'll call her today. I'm guessing she's been inquiring about your dating life?"

"Always. I'm sure she'll do the same to you."

Seb chuckled. "She wants us to be happy."

"And that's one of the many reasons why I love her." Evelyn brightened and stood again. "Thanks, bro."

"For what?"

"The talk. You don't cotton much to discussing personal stuff." She grinned. "I think I'll call Haskell. See if he's free for lunch."

Seb smiled. "You should do that."

"Oh, and about Ms. Smith—"

He raised his hand. "Off-limit topic. Get to work."

"Yes, sir." She saluted him and left, only to stick her head back inside his office and say, "I'm sorry I said your picker's broken." She popped back out again.

He sat back in his chair. Sorry or not, Evelyn had been right. He was 0 for 2.

Seb looked at the landline phone on his desk. He picked up the receiver. Bracing himself for another conversation about his social life—or lack thereof—he punched in his mother's number. "Hey, Mom," he said when she answered. "Yeah . . . I've missed you too."

———

Jade sat on an overstuffed recliner across from Logan in Sebastian's cabin, cradling a mug of coffee in her hand. They were in the spacious living room of the lovely home, and she felt a little stab of envy that he had such a nice retreat. *The Clementine Times* might be struggling, but Sebastian didn't seem to be, not when he owned two homes, and she was living in an apartment because she was still paying off debt.

Whose fault is that?

She looked at Logan, who was perched on an equally comfy-looking couch. Once again she noticed how fit and healthy he looked. Although she was confused and skeptical, she was glad to see him this way.

"Thanks for coming," he said, looking her directly in the eye. "I wasn't sure you would talk to me."

"I'm not sure I should," she murmured. Then a little louder, "I can't trust you."

"I know." He ran his hand through his short black curls. "I wouldn't trust me if I were you."

She stilled at his unexpected admission. In the past when she said that to him, he always responded by blaming someone else, giving excuses, or saying she was being unfair. It was good to hear some acknowledgment of her feelings, but she still kept up her guard. "Why did you have to leave town? Is it about money again? Because I can't—"

"I don't need money. I've had a job for nine months now."

Her brows lifted. He'd never held one for that long before. "Where?"

"Walmart." He rubbed one palm over his jeans. "I started as a stock boy, then moved to cashier, and now I'm working in the sporting goods department."

"Do they require drug tests?"

"Yes, since I'm still living in a halfway house. I'm fine taking them." He set his untouched coffee on a small wooden table next to the couch and faced her. "I'm doing good, Jade. Real good."

"Then why were you in such a hurry to see me? I thought you were in trouble."

"I figured you would."

"Logan—"

"Because I knew you'd believe that before you'd believe I was clean, sober, and gainfully employed."

He had a point.

"I don't blame you for thinking the worst of me. I spent so much of my life being wasted, trying to figure out how to get wasted, or hustling for money to stop being wasted. But I know better now. Being clearheaded is amazing. I didn't realize how much of a foggy, angry mess I was."

"You drove all this way to tell me this?"

He nodded. "I wanted you to see I'm sincere this time. I've turned my life around for real. And I'm going to fight to keep on the straight and narrow for good."

"I'm so happy for you," she said. It was like a miracle. No, it *was* a miracle.

Logan grinned. "I have you to thank. If you hadn't cut me off, I probably wouldn't have hit rock bottom. Not as fast as I did, anyway. It was either stay locked up, OD, or do something with my life. I got into a good rehab program and finished it this time. Graduated with flying colors, according to my counselor."

Jade wanted to weep. While she'd held out a sliver of hope that her boundaries would help him, she had done it more for herself. "I didn't want to," she said. "I really wanted—" Her voice caught. Talking about the failed adoption at this point was useless. But maybe they could be the tiny family she'd always wanted, now that he was on the right track. She set her drink down and sat beside him, putting her arms around his shoulders. "I'm proud of you, little brother."

He hugged her back. "Thanks, sis."

They let go of each other, and Jade was ready to pepper him with questions about his new life when she noticed the apprehension in his eyes. It triggered her own nerves. "That's not all you wanted to tell me, is it?"

"No." He drew in a deep breath. "Your mother wants to talk to you."

Jade froze. Even her heartbeat went almost completely still. She couldn't have heard him correctly. "Lydia?" she squeaked out.

"Wants to see you."

"No." She jumped up from the couch. "No, no, no—"

"Jade, just listen—"

"No!" She spun around. "How do you even know what she

wants?" She gasped. "You've been talking to her? Why would you do that?"

Logan went to her. "We met in rehab. Ironic, isn't it? Out of all the rehab places in Little Rock, Lydia and I would be at the same one at the same time. We got to talking after group one day and put the pieces together. She misses you, Jade. She knows she has a lot of making up to do, and she wants to start the process."

"Don't listen to her. She's a liar, drug addict, an alcoholic—"

"Me too," he said quietly. "I was and am all those things."

"But you were just a kid." Her voice quaked. "You had a rough life—"

"So did you."

"Because of her!" She backed away. "Would you have contacted me if she hadn't manipulated you into it?"

"She didn't manipulate me. I offered."

Jade noticed he didn't answer the first part of her question.

"Lydia's changed. You have to believe me."

"No, I don't."

He stilled. "You're right. You don't have to. Go see her and find out for yourself. Then you'll see she's different."

"She's making you do her dirty work. If she wanted to reach out to me, she would have."

"Would you have let her?"

They both knew the answer was no.

"I want to pave the way. That's all. Just give her a chance."

"How long were you in rehab together?"

"Two and a half months. But we've kept in touch ever since."

"You've known her less than a year?" She threw up her hands. "What did she do to get to you?"

"She got sober," he said, his expression pleading. "Just like me."

Jade shook her head, not only at Logan's words, but to ward off the tiny part of her heart that wanted to believe him. She could tell he had changed, that he was different. And while she knew he would forever struggle with his addictions, she felt in her soul he was sincere.

Her mother never had been. "She used to say that to me too, Logan. She'd get clean enough to pull me out of foster care and back home. Things would be okay for a little while. But it never lasted long. She'd have men over, get drunk, do drugs. The school or a neighbor would call Child Protective Services . . ." Jade whirled around, fighting for composure. He didn't need to hear all this. His early childhood had been similar.

But that didn't stop the memories from assaulting her—the CPS people picking her up, taking her to a home, starting the cycle all over again. Once she'd called them herself. There were visits with social workers, going to court, seeing Lydia in jail. That had stopped when Jade turned sixteen. She was *done*.

"Jade . . ."

Her brother's gentle voice brought her to her senses. She swallowed her anger, like she always had, and turned to face him. "I understand what you're trying to do," she said, her tone icy steel. "The answer is no."

Defeat crossed his features. "Is that what you want me to tell her?"

"I don't care what you tell her." She snatched her purse off the couch and walked to the door, then turned around. "I hope you can stay sober, Logan. I believe you want to. But if you don't, I won't be there to pick you up." Her heart burned inside. "I can't."

"Understood. I have to earn back your trust, and I will."

More than anything, she wanted to run and hug him again. But she couldn't, thanks to Lydia. Any sign of weakness could be seen as a softened stance, and she couldn't give in. Not now, not ever. "Have a safe trip home," she said, unable to resist being completely cold to him.

His throat bobbed. "You too."

She opened the door and walked into the bright sunshine to her rental car. Only when she got inside and drove off down the mountain did she allow herself to cry.

Chapter 11

After an hour-long phone call with his mother—he really needed to call her more often—Seb looked forward to some peace so he could focus on work. He had a to-do list a mile long, and he'd been interrupted enough for one morning. Talking to her had been a good break, though, even if she hit the phone call running with questions about his dating life.

"I'm busy, Mom."

"I realize that, dear, but you need to learn to delegate more. Then you'd have time to pursue a girlfriend."

Nothing better than being forty years old and talking about his nonexistent love life with his mother. "I don't need a girlfriend." He needed a new printing press. More employees. More advertisers. More circulation. More—

"Don't you want one?"

"Sure," he said absently, shifting another pile of papers around on his desk.

"You don't sound like it."

Their whole conversation wasn't about dating, thank goodness. But considering his talks with her and Evelyn Margot, along with Jade showing back up in his life, he was finding it hard to get the dating/girlfriend thing out of his mind. He hadn't pondered his future much outside *The Times*, and it was uneasy territory. Owning the newspaper had consumed him, and he'd been fine with that. Dating while keeping the paper afloat would have added more complications to his life. Ones he didn't need.

But there was one thought he couldn't kick out of his mind. What if he and Jade had worked out? What if they'd gotten married and had a family? What if . . . ?

He shouldn't care. He didn't care. He was still single and hadn't come close to having a serious relationship in the past ten years. He dated a few people here and there, but he hadn't met someone he was really interested in or worth risking his heart for. And yeah, he had to admit there were times when he was lonely, when it was hard to be single while everyone around was matched up. Except for his sister and Bo. Bo was taken now, and there was a possibility Evelyn and Haskell would get together. *And then there was one . . .*

But he had no regrets. Seb wasn't the love 'em and leave 'em type, and running a newspaper had taken up so much of his focus, he didn't have time for a relationship. Just because Jade had boomeranged herself back into his life temporarily didn't mean his feelings had changed on the subject.

A knock sounded on the door. "Come in," he said, expecting it to be Tyler or Isaiah.

Instead, Flora entered, a big grin on her face.

His mood immediately lifted at the sight of her. He got up from his chair and gave her a big hug. "It's good to see you," he said.

"Same here." She squeezed him tight and let him go, then looked up at him. "Everything all right?"

"Oh yeah. Perfectly fine."

She put one hand on her hip. "And I'm Halle Berry's prettier twin."

Seb chuckled and gestured to his chair. He always gave up his seat for her, starting back when he bought the paper from Buford. "Things are fair to middling, but they could be worse. What do I owe the pleasure of your visit?"

Flora sat down and folded her hands on the desk, her grin slipping into a slight frown. "Retirement isn't what it's cracked up to be."

"You've been retired for what, a week?" He sat across from her. "Give it time."

She paused, staring at his messy desk before looking at him again. "You need me, Seb."

"Of course I do."

"I want to come back."

His gut clenched. He'd always been honest with her, and while it was embarrassing to him as a businessman, he admitted, "I'd love nothing more, but I can't afford you. We both know that."

Flora leaned toward him. "I thought I'd enjoy retirement. Having the time to travel with Carl, work in my garden, play cards with Mama. Things I put off when I was working. Turns out Carl prefers to fish, and I'm fine with that since he's been catching some really good trout lately. He's got a secret fishing hole he won't tell anyone about."

"Sounds like Carl."

"And Mama is busy with her own social life. She meets with the seniors once a week at the community center in Bixby, and then with her friends from church to do other activities. She's busier than I am. Turns out I don't have a green thumb either. Already killed five plants and I have no idea how. But the bigger reason I want to come back is that I miss *The Times*. More than I ever thought I would."

Her words were gratifying and drove the point home that his small-town paper wasn't important only to him.

"With that said, I have a proposition for you. I'd like to come back to work on a volunteer basis for two days a week."

He could hardly believe his ears. "Really?"

"Yes, really." Her smile returned.

A lightness released from his shoulders at knowing Flora was back. She couldn't make money appear out of thin air, but she was an excellent bookkeeper and willing to do a job he really, *really* didn't want to do.

"And don't you dare say no. I know you're tempted."

"Don't worry, I'm not." He bounced to his feet and went to his desk. "I'll give you the ledger right now."

"I can only imagine the state it's in," she said, half joking as she got up from his antique chair.

"I haven't touched it," he said. Which was true, since he'd only read some of it over before getting demoralized. He never thought he'd appreciate his avoidant side, but in this case, it worked out and he was more than happy to transfer the bookkeeping back to her. He searched his desk and scooted the paperwork around on one side. "Huh," he said. Then he checked the other side. The ledger wasn't there either. "I could have sworn I stuffed it in here somewhere."

Flora laughed. "It's just as likely you stuffed it someplace else." She got up from the chair and put her purse over her shoulder. "I'll come in after Memorial Day. That'll give you plenty of time to find it."

He rubbed his neck, frowning. Where was the book? Maybe this was his wakeup call to organize the office and stick with it. "I can't thank you enough for helping me out again."

"My pleasure." She patted his arm and headed for the door. "Don't feel bad, Seb. We all can't be good at everything. See you at the hoedown."

"Give Ms. Florine a kiss for me."

"Sure will."

He did another look-through of his desktop, then sat down again, puzzled. Perhaps he took the ledger to his car when he left for the Clementine Inn yesterday. But that didn't make sense. He did everything he could not to deal with the accounting, and he couldn't imagine why he would have brought it along to Mabel's interview.

When he searched the rest of his office and came up empty, a sick feeling hit him, along with the realization that he shouldn't have been so careless. Could it be at the house? Or in his car?

A knock sounded at the door. "Come in," he said, doing another quick search in case he missed something.

The door opened and Jade walked in.

———

Still numb from her conversation with Logan about Lydia, Jade entered Sebastian's office and stopped a few feet from the door. She didn't want to talk business, but she had a job to do—one that she was bungling badly. Much like her conversation with Logan. She hadn't changed her mind about seeing her mother, but she could have handled it better. As she drove back to Clementine, the distance between her and Logan felt like a chasm, and she hated it. Just when she had another chance for a family, it was taken away from her. *Thanks, Lydia.*

"Jade?"

Sebastian's deep, soothing voice reached through her tumbling thoughts. He was behind his messy desk, a folder in his hand, looking directly at her with concern, and a flash of something else. Something gentle. Kind. So Sebastian.

Something I don't deserve.

Her back straightened and she sat down in front of him, un-invited. "I'm here to talk business." She barely recognized her stony tone. Before he could push back, she said, "My company is prepared to offer you a deal—"

"Are you okay? Scratch that, you're not."

She flinched.

He set down the folder. "You talked to Logan."

How had he picked up on her mood so quickly? She was doing everything she could to be stoic. To pretend her brother wasn't trying to betray her.

Harrington. They had to talk about Harrington. Then she could go back to Atlanta and forget about Arkansas. She did it once, she could do it again. "I . . ." She looked at her hands. They were shaking uncontrollably.

Sebastian got up from his chair and went to her, then held out his hand.

She looked at it. "What are you doing?"

"Trying to help you."

Her gaze lifted to his, and all she saw was the Sebastian she used to know. The wonderful man she dated, the one who had been her rock for a short blissful time. The one she didn't have the strength to resist. She slipped her hand in his and stood. He immediately let her go, but for the split second that she felt his strong hand in hers, she felt a little grounded again.

They left the building and went to his vehicle that was parked in the front space she'd taken yesterday. She suddenly recognized it. "You're driving the same car?"

"Yep. It's been good to me. Just ignore the mess inside."

She looked at the clutter in the back seat. The disaster was so Sebastian too. "Where are we going?"

"You'll see."

Twenty minutes later, he turned into the Cherry Hill Car Wash—a grand opening banner stretched over the front of its three self-serve wash bays. She hadn't seen this one in the phone book this morning, but she had planned at some point to visit the wash she'd found in Westin since Clementine didn't have one.

"You remembered," she said, amazed.

He headed for the auto wash. "Of course I did."

"Because it's weird that I love them."

He shook his head. "I never said it was weird."

That was true. Another point in his favor. "You didn't have to do this for me."

"My car needed a wash." He paid for the service.

"I'll pay you back."

"Don't worry about it."

The green light came on and he slowly moved the car into position.

They didn't say anything, and for a few moments she was in her happy place. Then she remembered the last time they'd been in a car wash together, making out in this very same car as thick bubbly soap cascaded over the outside. Her cheeks heated. She glanced at him, wondering if he was thinking about that time. From the way he was staring straight ahead, his expression blank, she couldn't tell.

They remained quiet through the rest of the rinse and wax cycles, and for a little while, Jade was able to set her troubles aside. But soon the dryers kicked on and she was back to reality. When the drying cycle finished and they were leaving the car wash, she said, "Sebastian, about Harrington—"

"I'll make you a deal."

She perked up. "Really?"

Turning onto the road, he nodded. "We'll talk about it—"

Yes?

"On Tuesday."

"Tuesday?" That was almost four days away. "Why not now?"

"Because that's when I'm free."

She sat back in her seat. What was she supposed to do for four days? Then she remembered the ledger. Hopefully she would find it right away. All right, that would take up some of the time. But the whole weekend, plus Memorial Day? "Sebastian—"

"Nope."

"Seb—"

"Uh-uh."

"Please—"

"Nada."

"Oh, come one." She grimaced. "Are you trying to get me back for—" She clenched her teeth. That had slipped out.

"For dumping me?"

She noticed the muscle in his jaw jerking. "Yes."

"No," he said quickly. "Obviously it was the right decision. For both of us."

Ouch. Although his words shouldn't have hurt. Not after ten years. Not when he was a successful newspaper owner, despite the downturn in the publication business. Dips and highs were common in all businesses. Mabel thought the world of him. Jade wouldn't be surprised if everyone else did too.

"Right," she said. "I'm happy in Atlanta."

"And I'm happy right here."

That ended the conversation until they were back at *The Times* office, parked in his spot. The one thing she wasn't happy about was his insistence that he talk to her about the Harrington deal on Tuesday. Then again, at least he was willing to talk. "I guess

I shouldn't look a gift horse in the mouth," she mumbled as he turned off his car.

"Nice cliché," he said. "Not one of my favorites, though."

She hadn't meant to say that out loud, but when she saw the slight smile on his face, she couldn't help but return it. "Thanks," she said. "For the car wash, and for agreeing to hear me out."

"Sure thing." He glanced at his watch.

Time to go. She opened the door. "See you Tuesday then."

"See ya."

She hesitated. Why couldn't she be as unaffected as he was? Because he was happy. *And I'm . . . not.*

———

Seb watched Jade hurry to her rental, convincing himself that he was just making sure she made it safely to her car, even though it was parked only two spots away. He certainly wasn't staring at her because he thoroughly enjoyed looking at every single inch of her. No, sir, and no way.

He finally shifted his eyes when she pulled out of the parking space, and once he knew she was out of sight, he slumped in his seat. What did he just do? And not just agreeing to discuss Harrington. His mind wouldn't be changed by Tuesday. He told her that to hold her off for a little while, because even though she seemed better after the car wash than when she came to his office earlier, there was still something wrong, and he suspected it had to do with Logan.

He thrust his hand through his hair. Once again he was getting involved, at least mentally. Possibly somewhat more, since his sudden idea to take her to the Cherry Hill Car Wash had been helpful. For her anyway. Not him. All he could think about was their make-out session the last time they were in a car wash together, in his same

167

Altima. Almost every detail, despite it happening ten years ago, filled his mind, affecting him in ways he did not need with her inches away from him. It had been near torture fighting to keep the past back where it belonged. But he did it and had even managed to coolly send her on her way when they got back to *The Times* office.

Which was good. That can of worms, to use one of his favorite clichés, had to stay sealed shut. Their relationship was over, and they both admitted it was for the best. He now had the closure he didn't realize he needed—or he would once they talked on Tuesday. By then, hopefully whatever was going on with her brother would be resolved and she would return to Atlanta to give Miles Harrington Seb's final verdict. Then they would both leave him alone.

He should be glad. Happy. Ecstatic.

Why wasn't he?

Chapter 12

On Saturday afternoon Jade pulled onto a grassy parking space at Wilson farm and turned off the Nissan's engine. The Memorial Day Hoedown was in full swing, and it looked bigger and grander than she thought it would be. Mabel explained that it wasn't just the hoedown that attracted visitors to the area on Memorial Day weekend. There were plenty of other things to do in the Ozarks on the first official weekend of summer—hiking, camping, canoeing and kayaking, antique shopping, fishing . . . The list was endless. From the size of the crowd, it seemed like this year's hoedown was the main attraction.

After leaving Sebastian yesterday, she went back to her room at the Clementine Inn to look for her briefcase, which was still missing, and she was starting to lose hope, although she wasn't going to give up her search. Mabel had promised to keep an eye out for it.

For the rest of that afternoon, she did something she'd never done before. She walked the hiking trail behind the inn. Her preferred form of exercise—when she had time to exercise—was aerobics, along with taking an occasional spinning class at her local gym. Walking had always been a boring activity, especially if there wasn't a specific destination in mind. Meandering through a neighborhood or in the woods seemed pointless.

But she couldn't just fritter time away in her room, and while she had her laptop with her, she wasn't in the mood to go over Harrington Media spreadsheets and financial statements. So she took a walk. A long one, making two circuits of the hiking trail, breathing in the mountain air, working up a decent sweat, and managing to set aside her problems enough that she could experience the sights, scents, and woodland activity surrounding her. It didn't give her the same type of peace she had in a car wash, but it was soothing enough that when she returned to Atlanta, she was going to search for a nearby hiking trail.

When she returned to her room, she took a shower and ordered a small mushroom pizza from the pizzeria up the street Mabel had recommended. Then she tackled what she'd put off all afternoon—calling Miles to give him an update. When she told him Sebastian wouldn't discuss the deal until Tuesday, he exploded.

"Seriously?"

"He's busy—"

"How busy can he be? It's just a simple conversation."

Nothing was simple when it came to Sebastian, despite him being a straightforward, unpretentious man. "It's also a holiday weekend. There's lots of activity in Clementine."

"Oh yeah," he sneered. "It's a regular boom town."

Jade frowned. She didn't like Miles's tone or how he kept putting down Clementine. He was turning into an exceedingly unpleasant man. "What do you want me to do?"

"Stay until Tuesday," he grumbled. "But I expect you to work on him in the meantime. Go where he goes. Hang where he hangs. Be a thorn—or a rose—in his side. Whatever you have to do so he talks to me."

His metaphor was weak, but she understood the mission. That was why she was here. *The Clementine Times* would have someone reporting on the hoedown, and chances were high that Sebastian would be here. Even if he wasn't in an official capacity, Mabel said almost the entire town attended the event every year.

She flipped down the car visor and looked at the small mirror. Nose—empty. Teeth—clean. Hair . . . She draped a lock over her ear, then brushed down some flyways. Maybe she should have put on a little lipstick . . .

She snapped up the visor. She wasn't trying to impress Sebastian or anyone else. Besides, he wouldn't notice if she wore lipstick. She doubted he paid attention to her physical appearance at all. She grabbed her crossbody bag, got out of the car, and headed to the hoedown.

Country music blared through the speakers, and the smell of carnival food hung in the air. The farm was huge, the crowd even bigger. She wasn't sure where to start.

Then she saw a group of teenagers with foot-long hot dogs on sticks. Those looked kind of good actually. She started for the food stalls when Sebastian's sister appeared in front of her, decked out in hoedown-appropriate attire—a knee-length blue jean skirt, black cowboy boots, and a white collared shirt tied at the waist.

"Hello," she said, her high ponytail swinging as she smiled and held out her hand. "We haven't been formally introduced yet. I'm Evelyn Margot, Seb's sister."

"Ah," Jade said, pretending she didn't already know that bit of info. If Evelyn Margot found out that Jade had been in Sebastian's office while she'd been taking his computer, she would be sunk. "We met the other day, right?"

"Sure. He mentioned that you two used to *work* together."

Jade stilled. He'd been talking about her? How much had he

said? And exactly what did he say? This could be good, bad, or both.

Evelyn smiled. "Don't worry, he didn't tell me your deepest secrets."

Thank goodness. Not that he knew her deepest secrets anyway. Well, he knew at least one—Logan. That was enough.

"I've got to run, but I wanted to make sure I formally met you. Are you going to be in town long?"

"A couple more days."

"Maybe we can get coffee sometime." She backed away.

"Uh, sure."

"Great, see you around!" She waved and hurried off, only to spin around again. "Seb's over by the bouncy castle."

A little stunned by Evelyn Margot's surprise invitation and her eagerness to tell Jade Sebastian's whereabouts, she turned to the kid's area. The giant hot dog would have to wait. As she neared the play area, she heard a man's voice through a loudspeaker.

"Square dancin' time! Our dauntless dance instructor, Ms. Eugenia Pickles, is here to guide you along. Even if you don't know your do-si-do from your promenade, come join the fun. She'll whip you into shape!"

The woman took over and soon the band was playing while she was calling out different dance moves. Or so Jade guessed. She'd never square-danced before. She hadn't danced much, period.

Jade made her way through dozens of kids and parents and walked toward the bouncy castle. Teens and adults were manning different stations—face painting, beanbag toss, knock the cans—

Pop, pop, pop, pop!

She jumped and saw a group of young children jumping rear-end-first on balloons, giggling as they popped them with varying success. Cute. She searched around for Sebastian, expecting him to be hanging around the perimeter of the area, talking to people and taking notes.

"Higher, Mr. Hudson!"

She turned to see him by a large swing set, pushing a laughing little girl on a swing.

"My turn!" shouted the boy in the next swing. There were two other boys in the remaining swings, and Sebastian dashed by, giving each one a firm but gentle push.

Jade watched as he continued to swing the kids. She hadn't spent enough time around children to guess their ages, but these had to be early elementary. Clearly they were having a great time, and she didn't blame them. It looked like fun.

After a couple more pushes, he helped each kid slow down. The boys ran off while he lifted the little girl off the swing. She put her arms around his neck and hugged him tight. He planted a quick kiss on her cheek and set her down.

Something in Jade's heart moved. He had his hand on his hips, grinning as he watched the little girl dash away. Unexpected warmth spread through her body. She couldn't help but smile, just as he turned toward her.

Their eyes locked, like they had in his office during their re-union. This time, though, it was different. There were no mixed feelings or apprehension or regret. Not on her part. Her smile grew.

He ambled over to her, his cobalt-blue-and-red plaid shirt hugging his fit torso, the sleeves rolled up to his elbows, exposing strong forearms. Her gaze traveled to the rest of him. *Oh. My. Word.* Just jeans and hiking boots but . . . swoon.

"Didn't expect to see you at the hoedown," he said, moving to stand in front of her.

Me neither. And that was the reminder she needed. She was here on business, not to swoon.

"Did Mabel convince you to come?" he asked. "She's the unofficial hoedown ambassador."

"No. I, um, just wanted to see what the fuss was about."

"Mr. Hudson?" A young boy tugged on Sebastian's pants leg.

"Oh, hey, Jason." He crouched so they were at eye level. "What can I do for you?"

"I want to swing too—"

"Jason!" A harried-looking woman hurried over, holding a baby on her hip. "Mr. Hudson's busy right now." She put her hand on top of the child's mop of blond hair. "Sorry about that," she said to Sebastian.

"I don't mind." He glanced at Jade. "I can swing him for a little bit."

"Thanks, but David should be here soon. He got off work about half an hour ago." She gave him a weary smile, then looked at her son. "Daddy's almost here. He'll push you on the swing."

"Okay!"

After they walked way, Sebastian turned to her. "Between you and me, I'm glad for the break. Swinging kids is hard work."

"Are any of them yours?" Jade blurted, then winced at the slipup. "Sorry. That was . . ."

"Straightforward?"

More like dumb. "Yeah. Let's go with that."

He chuckled. "No kids. No wife either. You?"

"Neither. I mean, no kids or husband." As per usual, this was going swimmingly. "I'm starving," she said quickly, needing a distraction. Or escape, if she continued her absurdity.

"I could eat," he said. "Time for a work break anyway."

"You were working?" she asked as they left the kiddie area.

"Up until the swing kids held me hostage."

She side-eyed him. "You're blaming the children?"

"You have to admit they're pretty cute. That's how they disarm you." They took a few steps and he asked, "So, were you lost?"

"What do you mean?"

"Just wondering why you were in the kids' area."

Good question. How should she answer it? "I ran into your sister. She said you were over here."

"Of course she did." He glanced at her again. "You didn't come to the hoedown on a whim, did you?"

Time for some honesty. "No. I told Miles you wanted to wait until Tuesday."

"And he didn't like that." He put his hand on her arm, stopping them both. Square dancing music blared in the background. "Is he pressuring you?"

"Not exactly."

"Then what's he doing?"

"His job, Sebastian. Just like I'm doing mine. Or trying to anyway." He tilted his head. "I'm not making it easy."

She was about to agree with him, because he definitely wasn't. Instead, she said, "I never expected you to."

Sebastian's only response was to nod, and neither of them said anything as they continued walking to the food stalls.

As they passed by the carnival games, she was glad for the silence. It wasn't as awkward as it could, or should, have been. It was rather . . . nice.

Suddenly she stopped short in front of a Skee-Ball booth. Excitement coursed through her. "I haven't played Skee-Ball in years." She turned to Sebastian. "Do you mind?"

Looking a little surprised, he said, "Go ahead."

Two of the games were empty, and she walked right up to them, digging in her purse for her wallet. "How much?" she asked the attendant.

"A quarter for five balls, fifty cents for ten, a dollar for twenty."

She almost laughed. The short, stout, and slightly bored sixty-ish man was trying to make it sound like a deal. She handed him a dollar.

Sebastian appeared in the spot next to her and handed the attendant a dollar bill. "Twenty for me too."

She glanced at him.

His eyebrow arched.

"Game on?" she said with a grin.

"Oh yeah. It's on."

The attendant dumped the appropriate number of brown balls into each of their wells. The counters zeroed out. "One," Seb said, crouching slightly. "Two . . ."

"Three!" She quickly grabbed a ball and started rolling, sliding into battle mode as she grabbed the balls and zipped them up the incline, immediately in a groove. When she tossed the last one, her counter buzzed and she looked at Sebastian, who still had five balls left. She did some quick math. Even if he hit one hundred points with each ball, he'd never catch up.

"We have a winner," the attendant blandly announced. He pulled down a fuzzy pink polar bear, a little bigger than a loaf of Wonder Bread and handed it to Jade. "Congrats."

"Thank you," she said, accepting her prize. She clutched the bear to her chest, not caring if she looked like a little kid. She couldn't help it. And it wasn't about beating Sebastian. That was a tiny bonus. It was about the thrill of finally getting a win, when lately she seemed to be racking losses.

Three kids came up behind them, so they both moved to the side. "Congratulations," Sebastian said with a grin. "I didn't realize you were so good. You smoked me."

She grinned. He was genuinely happy she'd won. "Thank you."

"You must have played a lot as a kid."

She touched the polar bear's black nose. "It's going to sound silly," she said, not looking at him. "I used to go to ShowBiz Pizza and play when I was in college with a couple of my friends. They liked the electronic games, but I'd play Skee-Ball the whole time." She lifted her gaze. Sebastian had such an amazing smile. "The pizza was pretty good too."

"That was in Little Rock, on Rodney Parham, right?" At her nod, he added, "Did you play there when you were a kid too?"

And just like that, the thrill was gone. Some of it anyway. It wasn't his fault, though. He didn't know about her past or how she'd never gone to a carnival or a fair until she was an adult. Her foster families never went, and of course Lydia wouldn't have taken her. "No," she said quickly. Refusing to let the past destroy her mood, she managed a half smile. "Still hungry?"

"Yep. Let's find something good and we'll celebrate your win."

Her full smile returned, along with a little toe curling again. There really was no ego with this man. "Lead the way."

———

Kalista looked out the back kitchen window at Viv's house at the huge crowd of people roaming outside. Men, women, and children of all ages were swarming Bo's farm, and the noise was so loud she could hear it in the house, including the Flippin Biscuit Boys playing their nonstop country music. She'd begrudgingly helped Viv with the rest of the preparations yesterday but resisted being a part of the event. It was one thing to be stuck in a small town, another thing to be a paper delivery girl, a third thing to be without her phone and money. Attending a hoedown was crossing the line. She was suffering enough.

To make things worse, Viv and Bo didn't have cable or internet, and the only radio stations she could find either played the same country music or were just people talking. She was bored. Like, really bored.

She was also starving, and just like the sounds of the hoedown permeating the house walls, she could smell the different foods being cooked and served outside. There was some food in the house, but other than peanut butter, grape jelly, and white bread, the pantry and fridge were filled with ingredients. Kalista had never cooked a meal before in her life.

The back kitchen door suddenly opened, and she spun around to see Tyler walk inside, a camera hanging around his neck. He was three steps into the kitchen when he froze. "Uh, hi," he said. "I didn't know you were in here."

A rush of deliciousness drifted in, like someone was smoking meat. Or maybe it was a campfire. She didn't know the difference, but whatever it was made her stomach growl. "Duh, I live here." She rolled her eyes. "I already told you that."

His goofy smile slipped a little. "I figured you were out enjoying the hoedown."

"Obviously not." Her stomach growled again. Annoying. "What are you doing 'ere? I'm sure Viv won't appreciate you barging into her house."

"She said I could use the facilities. There's a record number of people here, and they're short a couple of Porta Potties."

TMI. She waved her hand toward the hallway and said, "It's on the left," before looking out the window again.

"Thanks." He dashed down the hall.

Her mood darkened and she crossed her arms. Why was she being so stubborn about going outside? All she had to do was go find something to eat—preferably something healthy. This was a farm after all. Viv had asked her several times this morning if she was going to join in the fun. Kalista refused. She wasn't here to have fun. With the exception of being with Viv, her time here was miserable.

She couldn't keep her mind off Abbie and Ryan cheating on her either, or the fact her stepmother was enjoying her life of leisure on Daddy's dime while Kalista was stuck peeling a five-pound bag of russets last night for Viv's potato salad entry in the Hoedown Potato Showdown.

Tyler entered the room and brushed back his bangs. "Thanks," he said with another full smile. "Much better than the porta john."

She didn't answer.

"Are you coming outside for the Sadie Hawkins dance? It's in an hour."

"The *what* dance?"

"Sadie Hawkins. That's where the girls ask the guys to dance." He was blushing, but it was hot and humid outside, so maybe that was the reason.

"Does the band play more than just banjo music?" she asked.

"They stick with the classics. Ms. Pickles is teaching square dance lessons right now. Would you like to learn?"

She rolled her eyes again.

"I could get you an oxtail sandwich. Those are delicious."

Ooh, he was getting on her nerves. "Look, I realize you're my boss, but we're not on the clock right now. And no, I don't want to learn square dancing. I don't want to Sadie Hawking, or whatever you said. I definitely don't want to eat a bunch of fat, greasy food. Just leave me alone. Got it?"

Tyler pushed up his glasses. "Sorry to bother you," he mumbled and hurried outside.

Kalista turned and faced the window. Tyler's problem was that he was too nice. Excruciatingly nice, and that made her even more cranky. And a tad bit guilty. At least now he wouldn't keep asking her stupid questions.

She let out a sigh and rubbed her temple. Maybe she should apologize to him on Monday. Better yet, she should just pretend it didn't happen. That's what she usually did when she made a mistake—she ignored it, hoping other people would too. Then she didn't have to apologize at all.

She was about to go back to the tiny living room and pointlessly flip through the five channels Bo had on his TV when she saw a tall, good-looking guy walking across the backyard, looking lost. An idea hit her—she could offer to help him. Maybe they could hang out. *And see what happens.*

Grinning for the first time today, she hurried to the bathroom, touched up her makeup, and made sure her hair wasn't a frizz ball. Ugh, it was, but she didn't have time to redo it. At least she looked cute in a Viv-approved light pink sundress. She slipped into her sandals and went outside.

The guy was farther away, scanning the crowd, and she quickly caught up to him. "Hello," she said in her most alluring voice. "Can I help you with something?"

He turned to her, looking a little surprised. "Do you know Jade Smith?"

Jade Smith. That name sounded familiar . . . Oh! The lady she had lunch with the other day. She was still in town? "I haven't seen her," she said moving closer to him. He smelled good too, and his red T-shirt looked great on him, despite the pig image front and center. Viv had called it a Razorback, and she'd seen plenty other people wearing shirts and hats with the emblem on it. He had on long khaki shorts, but his high-tops weren't name brand, so she subtracted a few points from his overall appeal score.

"I can help you find her," she said, despite having no idea if Jade was even here. But hanging out with a good-looking guy was better than being stuck inside staring at chicken wallpaper all day.

He tilted his head as if unsure. Then nodded. "Okay."

They walked through the crowd, the happy screeches of children playing in the bouncy castle, the sights and smells of a cookout and the country music in the air. More than half the people were wearing boots of some kind—mostly old cowboy or rain boots. They were all having a blast.

Things were looking up for Kalista too. Way up. "What's your name?" she asked him.

"Logan. How do you know Jade?"

Humph. She was puzzled that he hadn't given her a flirty look yet. Batting her eyes, she answered, "Work. How do you know her?"

"She's my sister."

"Huh?" The fair-skinned redhead who needed a wardrobe makeover was this guy's sister? It didn't compute, and now she wondered if she had the wrong Jade Smith in mind.

He looked down and smiled a little. "We look just alike, don't you think?"

"Uh . . ."

"I'm kidding." Logan's smile widened. "We're foster siblings."

"Oh." That made more sense.

He returned to scanning the crowd, his smile replaced with singular determination.

Desperate to make conversation, she asked. "Have you had lunch yet?"

"Yeah. Ate something before I came here."

That was disappointing, because now that she had breathed in the full effect of all the different hoedown foods, she was beyond starving. "How about a snack?"

Logan stopped walking and turned to her. "I really need to find Jade. Thanks for your help, but I think I can search faster on my own."

"But . . . wait . . ."

He hurried off.

Kalista scowled. Now what? She guessed she could find Viv and hang with her. Hold up. What was that amazing smell?

Turning around, she saw a food stall with the words Funnel Cakes in bright red paint on the front. From the long line, she knew they must be good. Her stomach was roaring now. Forget avoiding carbs and sugar—she needed food. *I need one of those cakes.*

She quickly got in line behind a man who was smoothing down his bald spot. The sun warmed her skin as country music blared out of the speakers, along with an enthusiastic female voice who added an extra syllable to every word she spoke.

"Time to do-si-do, y'all," she called out.

That must be the Pickle lady Tyler mentioned. Kalista craned her neck toward the dance floor. There were too many people crowding the perimeter for her to view the dancers, but she could see the band playing and the lady speaking into the microphone onstage. She looked to be in her seventies and was wearing a short red-and-white checked dress, the hem flaring out as she skipped back and forth in front of the band.

"That's it," she said, crooking her arm. "Next, you fellas are gonna swing that pardner. Not too fast, though. Junior Simpkins, I'm talking to you! Dora Mae ain't no rag doll!"

The crowd laughed, and Kalista thought she heard a faint, "Sorry, Ms. Pickles!"

"Great hoedown, Mayor Pancake!"

The man in front of her waved at a couple passing by. "Glad you're enjoyin' it!"

The line inched forward at a slug's pace. Kalista crossed her arms. At this rate she'd have her trust fund before she'd reach the booth.

A tall man in blue jean overalls and a ragged straw cowboy hat approached, a scowl on his face. He was the first person she'd seen so far who didn't look blissfully happy, other than Logan.

"Hey, Mayor," he said, his drawl even more pronounced than Ms. Pickles'. He stuck his thick thumb underneath one of his overall straps, a toothpick in the corner of his mouth. "I need to talk to you about that town hall last week. I ain't happy with your decision to annex part of the country road."

"Now, Butch." The mayor continued to smile. "You know I don't talk business at the hoedown. Make an appointment with Betsy and we'll discuss whatever you want." He shook the big man's hand.

"All right, Pancake. I'll do that."

"It's Panchak," the mayor muttered, but he sounded more good-natured than upset. As the man walked away, Pancake glanced over his shoulder, then did a quick double take at Kalista. "Hello, young lady. Don't believe I've seen you around these parts before."

I'm in hee-haw hell. Why did everyone around here sound like they lived under a haystack?

"Is this your first visit to Clementine?"

"It is."

"Welcome. I'm Mayor Panchak." He held out his hand. "Glad you could come to our little ol' hoedown."

"Thanks," she said, surprised at how nice he was being to her. In fact, every person she'd met so far had been nice on one level or another. Especially Tyler. *Too nice, remember?*

"The funnel cakes are always popular," he said as the line moved forward again. "They're the best . . ."

Kalista followed the mayor's gaze as he seemed to forget he was talking to her, then saw him smooth his bald spot again.

"Hey, Haskell," a woman said as she approached and stopped in front of him.

Haskell Pancake, er, Panchak. What a name.

"Evelyn," he said, his voice lower and less formal. He was still smiling, though.

"I, uh," she glanced at Kalista, then looked at him again. "Can I ask you something? In private?"

"Sure." He stepped out of the line.

"I can wait until you get your cake," Evelyn said.

He scoffed. "Already had three today. Won't hurt to miss the fourth."

They walked away, and the line was finally making some progress. When Kalista reached the window, she was practically starving. "One funnel cake," she said to the attendant. "Small."

The lady manning the booth looked at her like she'd grown a third ear. "We make one size and one size only."

Kalista's eyes widened. She'd seen the plate-sized portions as people had gotten their cakes. No way she could eat all that . . . not at once anyway. "Okay, a one-size-fits-all will be fine."

Within a minute, a fresh golden, crispy funnel cake appeared on a paper plate. The woman sprinkled a mountaintop full of powdered sugar over it. "That'll be two dollars."

Oh no. Kalista didn't think to bring any money. Wait, she didn't have any money, and she didn't think to ask Viv for any.

"Ma'am, there's a line behind you."

She smiled, trying to play it off. "I'm Viv's stepdaughter," she name-dropped. "She's good for it."

"Who's Viv?"

"Bo's fiancée."

The woman's thick brows furrowed. "I don't know any Bo or Viv."

"Bo owns this farm," a teenage kid behind Kalista said.

"I don't live 'round here," the woman said. "We just come to different festivals in the area. And this funnel cake is still two dollars, ma'am."

How embarrassing. She couldn't even pay for a lousy funnel cake. "Never mind," she said, moving to step out of line.

"I got it."

She turned to see Tyler standing close by, reaching into his pocket. He pulled out his wallet, handed two dollar bills to the funnel cake lady, then walked away.

Kalista grabbed her plate and hurried after him. "Tyler!"

But he didn't turn around. Just kept on walking.

How confusing. If he was still mad at her, then why did he pay for her cake? And if he wasn't mad, why did he ignore her?

The wafting scent of fried dough and sugar distracted her thoughts, and she sniffed the plate. It smelled heavenly. She took a big bite and almost fainted from the deliciousness. "Where have you been all my life?"

Chapter 13

As he and Jade went to the double-deep-fried corn dog booth, Seb's thoughts spun. He hadn't expected her to be at the hoedown, or to look so enticing. Her outfit was simple—cap-sleeved hunter-green top, perfectly fitting jeans, the same tennis shoes she wore during her dumpster dive, that luscious auburn hair falling in waves over her perfect shoulders. He couldn't recall what he had for breakfast this morning, but he couldn't stop memorizing every physical detail of Jade Smith.

Then there was the Skee-Ball game. He played a few times when he was a kid, and he was never all that good, preferring ring the bottle and baseball toss games. But he was willing to give it a try anyway. Then he saw the competitive spark in Jade's eyes, and a jolt went through him. This was the side of Jade he knew was buried deep beneath her business demeanor. Fun, playful, and for a few minutes, relaxed. He didn't even mind that she won in a spectacular, and possibly embarrassing—for him—manner. He wouldn't care if she beat him ten more times if he could regularly see her smile as brightly as she did when she won the neon pink polar bear.

Then he'd asked her about playing the game as a kid, and the light dimmed. He was unsure why, although she had recovered well.

"Why is it so important to you?" Jade asked, breaking the silence as they neared the Corn Dog Castle.

He jerked his head at her sudden question. "What?"

"Keeping *The Clementine Times*?"

Back to business again. He looked at her, the polar bear tucked in the crook of her arm. Adorable. Oh well, he'd bite, but as soon as she said the words "deal" or "Harrington," he was done. He could talk about *The Times* all she wanted, but he wasn't going to spoil his day with acquisition discussion. "It's—"

"Jade!"

She groaned as Logan closed in on them. "What's he doing here?"

"All right, ladies!" Thurman Story, the hoedown MC, came through loud and clear over the microphone. "It's what you've all been waiting for—time to get yer feller for the Sadie Hawkins dance!"

Already? Nuts. Despite telling Evelyn Margot that he didn't duck the dance, he always totally did.

"You've got five minutes to hit the dance floor."

Seb felt a cold hand slip into his. He looked at it, then at Jade's determined expression.

"Let's go." She tugged him toward the dance floor.

"Wait," Logan called after her. "Jade, I need to talk to you—"

"You want to dance?" Seb asked, baffled.

"Yes." She was practically dragging him now, shooting a look over her shoulder at her brother.

This wasn't the first time Seb had been asked to participate in the Sadie Hawkins dance. In fact, he'd been asked every year, by more than one single woman, although several of them had been close to his mother's age. A few years ago he developed a plan to make himself scarce. He would have already implemented it by now, if it weren't for—

"Jade!" Logan continued pursuit.

She pulled on Seb, and as they passed by the stage, she dropped her polar bear on the edge, then moved to the middle of the dance floor until they were engulfed by couples.

"All right, Biscuit Boys, let it rip!"

The overall-clad band began a moderately paced country song, punctuated by Jubal Fontaine's twangy jaw harp.

Seb and Jade faced each other.

"Now what do we do?" Jade asked, looking bewildered as couples swirled around them.

"We—" Seb pitched forward as someone rammed into him. They couldn't just stand and chitchat anymore. He put his hands on her waist. "Dance."

It was his turn to tug, pull, and lead Jade around the parquet floor, every type of cowboy boot known to mankind thudding in concert with the lively music.

"What kind of dancing is this?" she said over the din.

He shrugged. "No idea. I don't dance."

"Me neither. But I needed to get away from Logan."

He tried to ignore the twinge her words caused. Then again, why would he expect that she wanted to dance with him instead of using him as the equivalent of a getaway car? "He seemed eager to talk to you again."

Jade's face pinched. "I don't want to talk to him right now."

It was on the tip of his tongue to ask why, but he pulled back. *No getting involved.* He didn't need to know what was going on with those two.

Out of the corner of his eye, he caught Junior Simpkins and his girlfriend, Dora Mae, barreling toward them. Junior was the size of an NFL linebacker and Dora Mae was hanging on for dear life.

"Here we go." Seb lifted Jade and turned her, narrowly missing a collision with the ungainly couple. Junior and Dora Mae didn't seem to notice. They only had eyes for each other.

Seb was noticing something, however. Jade was now close to him. Real close. Pressing against him close. Mmm, nice.

"Sorry," she said, pulling back.

"My fault." He muttered the words, so he doubted she heard him. For the next turn around the dance floor, they didn't talk or look at each other. Just held on like two seventh graders who lost a bet at their first dance.

"Let's slow it down, y'all." Thurman did his best impression of a countrified Barry White as the Biscuit Boys switched to a ballad. A few of the couples moved off the floor, but somehow he and Jade were in the middle of the throng, still surrounded. There was nothing left to do but—

"Hey, bro."

Seb turned to see Evelyn Margot and Haskell Pancake dancing right next to them.

"Having fun?" she said, winking at Seb.

He was about to say something smart-alecky when Haskell smoothly moved them both on. He wasn't as big as Junior, but he did have some weight on him. The man was surprisingly light on his feet.

"Sebastian?"

His head swiveled to Jade. Their gazes met. *Whoa.*

"You don't have to dance with me anymore. I'm sure Logan gave up."

From the frantic way Logan had tried to get her attention, Seb wasn't so sure. He also didn't care about her brother right now, or that Jade was going to keep trying to take *The Clementine Times* away, or that he had no business enjoying holding her this much. Common sense took a nosedive too, because he tightened his hands on her waist. "What if I want to?"

———

Jade wasn't sure she heard Sebastian right, and not because of the Biscuit Boys' harmonizing violins filling the air. Her heart was pounding in her chest and had been since she made the snap decision to avoid Logan by dragging Sebastian onto the dance floor. She quickly realized her mistake. If they were on the dance floor, they'd have to dance or get run over.

So they danced. It was awkward, a bit stumbling . . . and wonderful. The pressure of Sebastian's strong fingers lightly pressing on her lower back made her pulse go into overdrive. The movement wasn't sensual, and they were surrounded by other dancers, including Sebastian's sister, she discovered. But being in his arms again was just as amazing as it used to be.

But she had to reel her feelings back in. Somehow she had managed to, only to have them resurface again when he said he wanted to dance with her.

She couldn't give in.

She shouldn't.

He smiled—a gentle, soft, heartstring-tugging grin that made her toes go crazy curly and made her want to give in and let go, something she hadn't done in a long, long time. *Or ever.*

Her hands were on his biceps, and she tentatively moved them up, up, up until her wrists rested on his shoulders. That made him smile more, which compelled her to move closer. Before she knew it, the minuscule space between them was gone.

"You okay?" he said, his eyes not leaving hers.

Managing a nod, she said, "Yes." She was more than okay. She was in heaven.

The Biscuit Boys played their final note, and the crowd applauded, breaking into whatever magnetic connection they just had. Sebastian dropped his arms, and she followed suit.

"Thanks, uh, for the help." Her mouth felt like cotton, and she could barely move it.

He nodded, the sexy smile gone, his expression emotionless. "Gotta interview the band," he said, stepping away.

"Okay. See you—"

He walked off.

"—later." She sighed and followed the rest of the dancers off the floor, trying to get her bearings. When she stepped onto the Wilsons' thick green lawn, she realized she'd blown another chance to discuss the Harrington deal. She'd intended to stick to her promise to talk about only the newspaper. Then Logan showed up, and she lost her wits.

Maybe she should wait around for Sebastian to finish with his interviews. But would he even want to talk to her by then? She was almost sure he would change his mind, having had some time to think about it. He didn't owe her anything.

Jade headed to her car, not bothering to eat anything or talk to anyone. She'd been right about Logan, though. He was nowhere to be seen. That was two wins today, although she felt guilty for evading him.

Then again, if she hadn't, she wouldn't have danced with Sebastian or had those few sweet moments in his arms, even if it was under false pretenses and didn't mean anything.

Her temples started to throb.

She drove back to the Clementine Inn, and as soon as she pulled into the parking lot, she realized she'd forgotten her bear. Disappointment hit her. It was a cheap toy and didn't mean much . . . Except it did. Well, it was gone now. Hopefully it had found a home with a child. That thought made her feel better.

When she saw Mabel in the lobby, she went to her, holding out little hope that her briefcase had been found. Sure enough, Mabel hadn't seen it. "It will show up, sugar," she said. "Don't you fret."

Jade nodded and mustered a weak smile, then went to her room. She flopped on the bed, not bothering to take off her shoes, an absolute no-no in her world. She had too many things to think about . . . to fret about.

Her briefcase and Sebastian's ledger. Finding a way to convince him to talk to Miles, although that was becoming as remote as finding the briefcase. Then there was Logan. And Lydia. *No. No Lydia.* She refused to think about her.

Nothing was going her way, and to make it all worse, she wished she was back on the dance floor with Sebastian. For those fleeting moments there was no business failure, no financial trouble, no family heartache. Just the two of them. Like it used to be.

But it would never be that way again.

Chapter 14

On Sunday morning, Kalista stifled a yawn as the preacher at Clementine Community Church droned on. When Viv insisted she join her and Bo at service, Kalista resisted. But her stepmother was firm, and here she was, sitting on a hard pew, fighting to stay awake. She'd only been to churches for weddings and her great-grandmother's funeral. She'd been so young when Grammy died that she didn't remember it. The weddings had always been about having fun, not paying attention to a sermon.

At least they were sitting in the back pew so she could people-watch. There were two sets of pews with one aisle in the middle, and when she scanned the other side of the church, she was surprised to see Mr. Hudson and Tyler sitting on one of the middle pews. She hadn't seen either of them walk in earlier. Good, now she'd have a chance to thank Tyler for buying the funnel cake instead of waiting until tomorrow morning.

She glanced at Viv and Bo seated next to her, holding hands. Viv had been exhausted after the hoedown, and this afternoon people from the community were coming over to help with the cleanup. Her potato salad had won first place, so she was happy, and Kalista was happy for her.

After the service, Viv and Bo were visiting with other people in the greeting area outside the sanctuary. Kalista slipped away to search for Tyler. When she didn't see him in the building, she went outside and spotted him in the parking lot.

"Tyler!" she called out, waving to him as he reached his car.

He looked up, then got inside his car and drove off before she could make her way to him.

Rude. She put her hands on her hips. All she wanted to do was talk to him, but he was ignoring her now. How could he be so nice to her one minute and so insulting the next? What a weirdo.

"Ready to go?" Viv appeared by her side.

"Totally," Kalista said. She couldn't wait to get out of here.

For the rest of the afternoon, she helped clean up outside. Although she was wearing a tank top and shorts—she was shocked Viv didn't make her go back inside and change her top—she was sweating profusely. Thankfully there was a table with water bottles on it, so she went to grab a cold one. She took a gulp, feeling a stinging on her shoulders. When she glanced at her left one, it was bright red. Terrific. Now she was burned, and then she'd blister, and then she was going to peel. Yuck. How could she have forgotten sunscreen?

When the cleanup was done and everyone went home, Viv prepared a simple supper of ham sandwiches, corn on the cob, and of course, leftover potato salad. Kalista gave up trying to stick to any kind of low-carb, sugar-free eating in Clementine. It was impossible, and she was starving after all the physical work anyway. As usual, Viv's food was delicious.

Bo didn't stay very long, and both he and Viv still looked tired. Once he left and Viv went to her room, Kalista was by herself. Back home she was so busy doing stuff that she rarely had to sit alone in silence. Even if she was by herself, she either had the TV on or was listening to music on her iPod. Daddy had even taken that away. *He truly wants me to suffer.*

She looked for a snack. Dinner had been filling, but she felt the need to eat. At least it gave her something to do.

Then she spied the phone on the wall. Other than the time she called Abbie after her father had shut off her phone, Kalista hadn't tried to reach anyone. Oddly enough, she hadn't been tempted to until now. Surely Daddy wouldn't mind if she made one little phone call on her day off. She'd have to keep quiet since Viv was asleep in her room down the hall.

Should she call her father? No, he would be too busy, probably with Bettany. She didn't want to get into an argument with him anyway. And she wasn't calling Abbie—not after she betrayed her with Ryan, something she still didn't understand. If he liked Abbie, why had he strung Kalista along? They hadn't been exclusive, but that didn't mean he could go out with her best friend behind her back. He owed her an explanation.

She dialed his number, and he picked up after the first ring. "Hello?"

She gripped the receiver at the sound of his voice. Now what? She couldn't just open with *"How dare you cheat on me,"* even though she wanted to. "Hi, Ryan."

"Oh, hey, Kalista." He sounded nervous.

Good.

"How's your vacation going?"

"Just perfect," she snapped. "Especially after I found out you cheated on me with my best friend."

Silence. Just when she thought he was going to hang up on her, he said, "I'm sorry."

Huh. She expected a load of excuses or for him to be like Abbie and put the blame on Kalista for his hurtful behavior. "You are?"

"Of course," he said. "What kind of guy do you think I am?"

A *cheating one.*

"For the record, Abbie and I aren't together anymore."

A tiny feeling of triumph filled Kalista. "That was quick. You guys lasted what, two, three days?"

"Three and a half."

"Why did you break up?"

"I thought she was different."

"In what way?"

"I thought she wasn't like you."

Ouch. "Ryan, that was low."

"I don't mean it that way. Well, maybe I do."

"I'm hanging up now—"

"Don't," he said. "I want to explain."

She wrapped the cord around her index finger. "Go on."

"I needed a change."

Her chin drooped. "From me."

"From everything. I can't live my life as a party guy anymore. I need a new direction—any direction than just filling my life with empty junk. When I mentioned that to Abbie after you left, I thought she felt the same way—that she was tired of being aimless too. Turned out she was just telling me what I wanted to hear so she could go out with me. To hurt you."

"What? Why?"

"I don't know, and I'm not getting in the middle of it."

She was in shock. Ooh, she was calling Abbie next to find out what was going on. She was the worst best friend ever. But now Ryan was free again. "I'll be home in August," she said, starting to smile. "We can pick up where we left off."

"I like you, Kalista, but you're just too immature."

"I don't think so. We're the same age!"

"Our ages don't matter. What are your goals in life? What are you doing other than shopping, parties, more shopping—"

"I do other things." She had to think for a second. "The spa. I go to the spa. And the beach. I love the beach."

"Don't you want to do something more important?"

"The spa is important."

He sighed, and she could imagine him running his hand through his sun-kissed blond locks like he always did when he was annoyed. "I registered for college classes. My parents made me apply back in the fall, but I didn't think I was actually going to go. I don't know what my major will be, but I want to get a degree. I also started working for my dad."

Ryan's father owned a huge computer software business, but Kalista didn't know anything else about it because business talk was boring. "I thought you said you would never work for your dad."

"I changed my mind, and I actually like having a job."

She almost told him about her carrier job, then stopped herself. Their conversation was already embarrassing enough.

"We had some fun times together, but I'm moving on. Sorry if that hurts your feelings."

Kalista didn't answer, and her feelings hurt deeply. No one wanted to be called immature or lacking substance. But at least he was telling her the truth, unlike Abbie. "It's okay," she said.

"Really? I thought you'd be mad and yell at me."

She probably should be. For some reason, she wasn't. "Thanks for keeping it real."

"Good luck, Kalista, with whatever you decide to do with your life."

She hung up, conflicted feelings washing over her. Her father had called her immature too, and that made sense coming from him. But having an eighteen-year-old say the same thing hit differently, because a couple of weeks ago, Ryan had been just fine engaging in the same things he berated Kalista for doing.

Except now that she looked back on their relationship, she remembered there were instances when he would beg off going to a party, and a few times when they were at the beach with their friends, he seemed disconnected, like he was preoccupied. She'd barely paid attention to it back then, but for some reason it was clearer now. This wasn't a last-minute decision. He really had been thinking about it for a while.

Kalista got up and pushed the chair back to the table. She should call Abbie and demand to know what the problem was between them. Then again, why bother? Their friendship was over. The reason didn't matter anymore.

She went to the bathroom to brush her teeth, then paused to look in the mirror. Not only had her shoulders gotten sunburned, but her face had too. Of course that would peel as well, but for once she wasn't panicking about it. Lotion would help, and it wasn't like she was going to see anybody during the week other than Viv and Bo in the evenings. And Tyler at work. Maybe Mr. Hudson if they happened to run into each other. But mostly Tyler.

Tyler. An overly nice, enthusiastic guy who worked not just one job but two and seemed to enjoy both. Up until yesterday in Viv's kitchen, she hadn't seen him upset, downcast, or irritable. Just happy. He was her age, and he was writing newspaper columns, making sure people got their newspaper on time, dealing with subscriptions, and all the other things that went along with his many responsibilities. He did it all with a great attitude. A mature attitude.

She shook her head, so lost in her thoughts she didn't realize she was still looking at her reflection. What did people think when they saw her? She'd always assumed they were jealous because she was so pretty, wore great clothes, and knew how to have a good time. Now she suspected people saw her differently than she viewed herself. At least Ryan did. Abbie too.

Was that what Tyler thought? That she was shallow and immature?

Why should I even care? It wasn't like he was handsome. Well, that wasn't true. He was nice-looking in a dorky kind of way, and when he smiled, he was *really* nice-looking. He also had great hair. She'd noticed that right away.

Flipping off the light, she headed to bed even though it was barely sundown. She didn't care what Abbie, Ryan, or even Tyler thought about her. She didn't need to change. *I'm just fine.* The only person she had to accommodate was her father, and that was only for a few months. There was nothing wrong with liking clothes and spa treatments and parties.

She shoved the covers over her body, wincing when the fabric swished over her painful shoulders. Humph. There were plenty of people back home who liked her. Even if they didn't, she could find new friends. There was always someone in LA who was willing to hang out with a multimillionaire's daughter.

A lump formed in her throat. She didn't need this kind of negativity in her life. Forget them. *Forget all of them.*

"You had some good luck today," Seb said to Logan, who was putting logs in the fire ring on the back patio. Logan had called Seb after church, asking him to come to the cabin. Seb obliged, and the two of them fished for the rest of the afternoon. They barely spoke to each other the whole time they were sitting on the bank of the river that was a few miles away from the cabin. But it was peaceful, and Seb wasn't going to push Logan if he wasn't willing to talk about what had happened between him and Jade yesterday at the hoedown. From the kid's silence, Seb assumed he didn't.

The lack of communication forced Seb to entertain his own thoughts, and of course he was thinking about Jade. More specifically, their dance. Holding her had transported him back to when they were together, when just thinking about her made him happy. After they parted, his arms felt empty as he headed to talk to the Biscuit Boys. Even as he conducted the interview, he had to resist seeking her out again. By the time he went back to his office to write up his notes and meet up with his team to get the Monday issue of *The Times* ready for print, he was second-guessing putting her off until Tuesday. He needed to nip the whole Harrington conversation in the bud, and he had intended to do that after church. Logan had interrupted that.

After they fried up their fish and ate them with a side of Viv's award-winning potato salad that Seb had brought with him, Logan seemed to be in a more talkative mood.

"Thanks for coming over," Logan said, staring at the newborn fire. "And for letting me stay a little while longer."

"You can stay as long as you need to."

"I have to leave soon. I only had a couple days off. I was going to leave yesterday, but I decided to try talking to Jade again. Mabel told me she was at the hoedown." He sighed. "I guess she's really mad at me now."

Seb tried to find some words of encouragement. "Siblings fight. Can't be avoided. It's been a while since Evelyn Margot and I have gotten into it, but when we were younger, some of our arguments were epic."

Logan nodded but didn't look Seb's way.

A few minutes ticked by and he thought Logan was done talking. Which was good, because Seb's curiosity was getting the best of him, despite his vow not to get involved. It was hard seeing the young man so down, and Seb didn't have any advice for him. Jade's MO seemed to be cutting people off. She was doing it to Logan. *She did it to me.*

"Jade really needs to see her mom."

That was the last thing he expected Logan to say. "What?"

"I take it she didn't tell you about Lydia."

He shook his head.

Logan filled him in on how and where he met Lydia, and that they had been in touch since they were discharged from rehab.

As Logan told his story, Seb tried to remain impassive. But hearing about his and Jade's relationship, their time in foster care together, the kid's struggle with drugs and alcohol, and how Jade had bailed him out until she refused to do it anymore was shocking. She'd never said a word about any of that when they were together.

"She tried to adopt me," Logan said. "Right after she moved to Atlanta." He looked at Seb, his dark brown eyes full of somber appreciation. "When it didn't happen, I was really angry at her. She'd given me hope and then let me down. I went off the rails even more after that."

Seb was stunned. "Do you know what happened?"

He shook his head. "She's never said, and I don't want to ask now. I love her. We're family no matter what. But I have to repair our relationship. I want to prove to Jade that I'm a better man now."

Seb could see that he was, despite not knowing him well.

"I didn't mean to dump all that on you." He rubbed the back of his neck. "I'm not sure what to do anymore. I just know that if Jade doesn't talk to Lydia soon, she'll regret it, possibly for the rest of her life." He paused. "I don't suppose . . . Forget it."

"Go on," Seb said. "Say what you want to say."

Logan turned to him, hope in his eyes. "Could you talk to her? Tell her how important it is that she see her mother?"

Seb exhaled. He easily read between the lines—there was something seriously wrong with Lydia. Possibly fatal. Logan didn't seem inclined to elaborate, and Seb would respect that. The kid also seemed desperate. "What makes you think I can convince her?"

"I don't know if you can." He shook his head. "I'm sorry. I shouldn't involve you in this. I just thought you might have some sway."

It dawned on Seb that Logan still knew very little about his relationship with Jade. "Do you know why she's in Clementine?"

"I figured she was here visiting you."

So she hadn't told him about the Harrington deal. And Seb didn't think he needed to know. "She is. But we're not close." They never had been. Today had proven that.

"Oh. I guess I got the wrong impression. I thought you two had been . . ."

"Together?"

He nodded, looking a little sheepish. "My girlfriend tells me I can't pick up signals for squat, so there's that. Forget I said anything. I'll figure something out."

Seb didn't respond and the conversation switched to benign topics—whether the Razorbacks would have a good football team this fall, how they were both looking forward to seeing Matt Damon again in the upcoming *The Bourne Supremacy* movie, and Logan filled him in on a couple of new restaurants that had recently opened in Little Rock. Since moving back to Clementine, Seb rarely went to Arkansas' capital city. Like Buford had always said, the less hustle and bustle, the better.

Shortly before sundown, Seb had to call it a day. "Early morning at the paper," he said.

"But it's Memorial Day."

"And a Monday. Our hoedown special goes out tomorrow."

They both stood, and Logan shook his hand. "Thanks again," he said, appearing less melancholy. "For the cabin, and for listening."

"Glad to do both." He started to head inside, then paused. He'd been fighting the idea ever since Logan had brought up Jade and her mother, hoping it would go away. It only intensified. He turned around. "I can't promise anything," he said, "but if the opportunity presents itself, I'll talk to her about Lydia."

Logan broke into a huge grin. "You will? Whoa, man, thanks so much." He pumped Seb's hand again. "Seriously, thank you!"

Seb was gratified that he could give Logan a little hope, even though it would probably be fleeting. He had no influence on Jade. She hadn't even trusted him enough back then to tell him about her family. Ten years wasn't going to change her decision.

He made his way down the mountain road, his promise to Logan still on his mind by the time he reached Clementine. He wouldn't see Jade until Tuesday, so there was no reason for him to keep thinking about a possible conversation concerning Lydia. What he needed to do was turn his place upside down and find that ledger. He'd already searched his car. It wasn't there, and he'd upended all the clutter in his back seat—something he had to address soon. But the ledger came first. Flora would be back at work on Tuesday, and she would rightly read him the riot act if he didn't find it by then.

But even as he neared his little bungalow on his quiet street, he second-guessed himself. Maybe he should talk to Jade about Lydia sooner than later. If her mother was in crisis, she should know, right? Now that he understood the issues between Jade and Logan, there might be a chance she would listen to a neutral party. It didn't sit right with him to say nothing when he knew what was going on, even if he was one hundred percent sure Jade wouldn't appreciate it.

He groaned and pulled into his driveway, then backed right out, turned around, and headed for the Clementine Inn. *So much for not getting involved.*

Chapter 15

Later that evening, Jade sat in her room, nursing a cup of chamomile tea courtesy of Mabel. Her closed laptop lay on her bed, her phone still in her purse. This morning on a whim—and she almost never, ever did anything whimsical—she grabbed one of the free maps of the Ozarks in the rack near the inn's front desk, got in her little rental, and took off. She'd spent the day driving around Clementine and the adjoining communities, partly to pass the time, partly for the distraction. She rejected the idea of reaching out to Sebastian again and would just be patient and wait for their meeting on Tuesday. At this point, she was sure he was just humoring her, but at least she could tell Miles she'd done all she could.

The drive had some unexpected benefits, other than saving her from staring at the four walls of her motel room. This area of Arkansas was gorgeous. The temperature was milder than the day before, and she kept the windows rolled down as she drove, enjoying every minute. She couldn't remember the last time she'd done something so random and seemingly pointless.

Jade glanced at the half-eaten apple pastry on the bedside table, then at the three small bags she put on top of her closed suitcase.

During her journey, she'd stopped at a few surrounding towns. Most of the shops were closed because it was Sunday, but she found a couple that were open due to Memorial Day weekend. She purchased a glass paperweight in the shape of a cat for Charlotte, who owned a very loved and spoiled feline named Sir Meow. She found two lovely silk scarves for herself and purchased a small trinket for Mabel to thank her for being a good host and dealing with Jade's constant questioning about her lost briefcase.

Her stomach soured. The briefcase was gone, and she had to accept it. She also had to tell Sebastian about the ledger. Great, now she felt nauseous. But it was her own fault for being stupid and deceitful. He'd find out eventually that it was missing, and even though she could go back to Atlanta and not say anything, her conscience wouldn't allow it. She had to face the consequences of her actions, whatever Sebastian decided they would be.

She was also concerned about her job. Miles had given her a break by not calling her today, but even without hearing his voice, she figuratively felt him breathing down her neck. Could he fire her for failing her assignment? She didn't see how, but because he was related to the CEO of the company, anything could happen.

Jade grabbed her laptop and flipped up the lid. Gone was the peaceful, content feeling she allowed herself to experience today, and she was right back where she started since her arrival in Arkansas—tense and keyed up. Oh, and resentful too, because she hadn't wanted to come here in the first place. Her life in Atlanta was far from perfect, but it was better than feeling like an anxious failure nonstop.

She opened an Excel sheet. Other than a car wash, work had always been her prime diversion. Not this time. The numbers on the grid blended together as she tried to concentrate. After several attempts to make sense of what was on the screen, she moved the computer back on her bed and got up, put on her tennis shoes, and grabbed her purse. *Cherry Hill Car Wash, here I come.* Then she opened the door . . . to Sebastian.

"Oh, hey," he said, his fist in the air as if he were about to knock. He dropped his hand to his side. His other hand was behind his back.

She stilled. Never would she have expected him to be standing at her door. "Uh, hi."

He ungainly shifted on his feet, something she'd never seen him do. Actually, she'd never seen Sebastian Hudson anything other than confident.

"Can I come in? Or we can go to the lobby and talk?"

Her optimism returned. Was he here to talk about Harrington? She couldn't fathom what else he'd want to discuss, although she was surprised he wasn't waiting until Tuesday to tell her no, like he'd insisted. Did this mean he'd changed his mind and actually wanted to hear her out? "Here's fine," she said, moving to the side for him to come in.

"Thanks. Oh, here." He brought his hand from behind his back.

"My polar bear!" She took it from him. "You found it."

"You left it on the stage." His expression relaxed a little.

How sweet. She smiled. "Thanks," she said. "I'd forgotten about it."

He entered and scanned the room as she closed the door behind him. "Nice place. Especially that longhorn over there."

Jade smiled at the steer head above her bed and set the bear on the small desk near the window. "You mean Frank?"

Sebastian faced her. "That's his name?"

"That's the one I gave him. Seemed the appropriate thing to do, considering how much time we spend together. It took a little while, but we've gotten used to each other."

He grinned, and she smiled back, some of her apprehension

slipping away. Whether that had to do with Sebastian changing his mind about discussing the buyout or just being in his steady presence, she didn't know. It felt good not to be so uptight.

"This won't take long," he said, turning serious.

Her spirits dipped. That wasn't a good sign. "You haven't changed your mind, have you?"

His brow furrowed. "What?"

"Harrington. It's still no, isn't it?"

He paused. "I promised to hear you out—"

"Wonderful!" She swooped up her laptop. "It will just take me a second to bring up the file with the deal points."

"You don't have a paper copy in your briefcase?"

She froze. Oh no, she forgot she told him she found the briefcase. "This is faster," she blurted, although holding a heavy laptop with one hand while moving her finger on the trackpad was awkward. She was so flustered she couldn't find her cursor, so she pressed harder on the pad, which made the laptop tip.

"Hey." He took the computer from her and closed the lid. "I don't want to talk about Harrington. I'll listen to your pitch on Tuesday, like I said I would."

Jade frowned, confused. "Then why are you here?"

He scooped his hand through his hair but didn't respond right away.

Good thing, because the gesture seized any possible words out of her mouth. Sebastian had the casual, mussy-sexy look down. Emphasis on sexy. Once again she was struck by how much more attractive he was now than ten years ago. Even the faint crow's feet at the corners of his eyes were fetching.

And here she was looking dumpy and frumpy in gray athletic shorts, a plain white oversize T-shirt, and hair piled on her head in a messy pony. A few minutes ago she didn't care about her appearance when she was going to the car wash. Now she was acutely aware that she looked like she'd just woken up. What a fabulous impression.

He shoved his hands in his pockets, which didn't help either. Her gaze followed his movement. He made those jeans look *so* good—

"Lydia."

Her eyes snapped to his. "What?"

"I'm here to talk about Lydia."

Every cell in her body turned cold. "How do you know about her . . . Logan. You talked to Logan."

Sebastian nodded. "He's still at my cabin."

"I don't believe this." She backed away. "What did he tell you?"

"That she's your mother—"

"She was never my mother." Not in the way it counted. Her chest hurt. "How could he do this to me?"

"He loves you, Jade."

She shook her head. This didn't feel like love. It felt like betrayal. Sebastian had no business knowing about her past—Lydia in particular. Logan and Lydia were cooking up something. She was sure of that now. "He put you up to this."

"No, he didn't." Sebastian moved toward her. "I offered to help. I don't know what's going on with your mother, but it's serious enough to have Logan worried, and not just about her. He doesn't want you to have any regrets."

"Too late for that." She was regretting ever allowing Logan back in her life, even if it was just for a conversation. She regretted listening to him, believing he had truly changed. Most of all, she regretted letting Sebastian in her room. Her hands shook so hard she thought they'd fall off.

"Jade."

His deep, comforting voice washed over her, and for a split second she allowed herself to feel its soothing effect. Then just as fast, she threw up her walls. "This is none of your business, Sebastian. You don't have the *right*."

He stilled. Nodded. Backed off. "I just . . ." He shook his head and moved past her. "Sorry."

"Wait." She couldn't afford to be angry with him or let her personal life get in the way of business. It was one thing if she didn't have the skills or tactics to convince him to talk to Miles and quite another if he refused because of Logan or Lydia.

She wasn't sure how her professional brain kicked in through her pain. Then again, she had years, decades of practice shoving down her emotions until she didn't feel them anymore. She turned and went to him. "I apologize," she said, barely aware she'd straightened her posture as if she had on her suit and heels instead of gym wear. "Thank you for being so considerate. I will take your advice under consideration."

His frown deepened. "I—" A ringing sound came from his jeans pocket.

"Go ahead," she said. The interruption would give her time to collect what was left of her sanity.

Sebastian dug into his pocket and pulled out a simple black flip phone and lifted the lid.

"Hudson here. Where? How bad is it? Uh-huh. Oh . . . whoa." His frown deepened. "I'll head there now. Thanks." He hung up and jammed the cell back into his pocket.

"What's wrong?"

"There's a fire. In Chester."

She saw concern in his eyes and tone, but also something else, something she'd seen before when he was chasing down a story. "Go," she said.

He nodded, then paused. "I could use a driver. I've got phone calls to make on the way, and it would be safer if I wasn't behind the wheel."

She didn't even have to think about it. "I'll get my purse."

The next twenty minutes were a blur. She'd never been on a story assignment before, and while it was exciting, her emotions were tempered by the seriousness of the situation. Sebastian made calls to different first responder agencies and police dispatchers, giving her directions in between as they hurried to Chester. When he was done, he snapped his phone shut. "The apartment building is in a rural area," he said. "That's fortunate because it won't spread to other buildings or businesses. But it's bad, Jade. Real bad."

"How did you find out?"

"Isaiah has a scanner, and he was listening in. He would have come himself, but he sprained his ankle square dancing yesterday. Take a left here."

Jade complied.

"Sorry to drag you into this," he said.

"I'm not." Her problems were fading into the background compared to the fire. Suddenly she smelled smoke through the car vents. "We're almost there."

"Yeah." His tone was somber.

Blue flashing lights appeared, and two police cars were blocking access to the road. Sebastian rolled down the window as an officer came over. "Hey, Scott. I'm here to cover the story. Can you let us through?"

Scott nodded. "Just stay out of the way. It's a dangerous scene, and we still have people inside the building."

Jade gripped the steering wheel. Sebastian merely nodded.

Scott moved his cruiser and let them pass. She looked in the rearview mirror as the police car reclosed the gap.

KATHLEEN FULLER

The air was thick with smoke as she pulled into the lit parking lot, getting as close as she could without being in the way of the first responders. Fire and emergency crews were dealing with the blaze. She said a silent prayer for all of them.

"Stay here." Sebastian reached into the chaotic back seat of his car, grabbed a camera case, and looped the strap around his neck.

"But—"

"Stay. Here." He dashed out the door and headed for the ambulance.

Jade sat back and stared at the flames bursting out of the three-level building. Sebastian was speaking with the ambulance crew, and then he moved on to several witnesses standing by. She felt so helpless. But what could she do? She didn't have any first responder experience.

Then she noticed a woman standing separate from everyone else, her head in her hands. Jade's heart went out to her. She might not be able to help with the fire, but maybe she could offer some comfort. She rushed out of Sebastian's car and went to her, ignoring the smoke, ash, and heat coming from the building.

Once she was close, the woman lifted her head. "I've lost . . ." Tears streamed down her cheeks. "I've lost everything."

Oh no. "I'm so sorry." What else could she say? She put her arm around the woman's shoulders and held her for a moment, then heard shrieking.

"My baby! My baby's in there!"

Jade looked up and saw a hysterical woman being guided out of the building. When she tried to run back inside, the firefighter held her back.

Rational thought drained out of Jade. All she could think about was the baby. She ran toward the building.

"Wait!" a male voice yelled. "You can't go in there!"

She ignored it, instinct blocking out everything else. She couldn't let that baby die.

———

Seb had just jotted down a quote when he heard one of the firefighters yelling for someone to stop. "Thanks," he said to the witness, then spun around to see what was going on.

"You can't go in there!" the firefighter hollered.

Someone was running toward the blazing building. A woman . . . a flash of a red ponytail . . . "Jade!" Seb sped toward her.

A firefighter moved to block him. "Mister, you have to stay back."

Seb tried to dodge him.

"Hey!" He grabbed him by the shoulders. "I said stay back."

"Didn't you see her run in there?"

"Yeah. Don't you be stupid too." Sweat dripped off his brow, his respirator hanging to one side. "It's not safe. The building's lost."

No . . . "You have to go after her."

"I'm sorry, mister, I can't. You can't either." The guy looked barely older than Tyler.

When Seb tried moving again, the kid shoved him back. "I'll get a cop over here if you don't stop interfering."

He had no choice but to give in. Everyone, everything was moving in slow motion now as terror engulfed him. *Why, Jade? Why?*

———

Smoke crawled down Jade's throat, her skin searing hot. Thoughts jumbled through her mind as she tried to see through the haze. Yeah, she'd made a dumb decision. A really dumb one. But she didn't care. All she wanted was to find the baby.

A beam crashed to the ground behind her. Fire crackled every-where. And by some miracle, she heard wailing. She ran toward the sound and saw the crib. Scooped up the infant. Held it to her chest and dashed toward the exit.

The red haze and burning heat gave way to cold, breathable air. Jade gasped as people descended upon her. Someone took the baby from her. Another guided her away from the fire. A third appeared in front of her.

Sebastian. Thank God.

"Sir, we need to check her out," a calm female voice said.

"Is the baby okay?" Jade was surprised at how raspy she sounded.

"Yes," he said, still in front of her. He cupped her face in his hands. "Because of you."

Jade touched his cheek and smiled.

"Sir." The woman to her left was more forceful. "I have to take her to the ambulance."

He nodded, his hands slowly falling away. "I'm going with you."

She wouldn't have it any other way.

———

"Thanks for letting Jade spend the night," Seb said.

Evelyn Margot handed him a cup of black coffee. "I'm glad she agreed to stay."

While the paramedics had looked Jade over, he called Evelyn and asked if they could come to her apartment. After what had happened, he didn't want her to be alone. Of course Evelyn agreed. When they arrived, she had fresh clothes and a warm towel at the ready. "You can shower in there," she told Jade, pointing to the bathroom down the hall. Jade had resisted but not too much.

Seb ignored the coffee, still trying to grasp the reality that

Jade had survived. He didn't know how. When he saw the beam crash inside the building, he was sure she was gone. Even now the anguish still lingered. And the fear—the bone-chilling fear he felt when he thought she was dead. Other than mild smoke inhalation, she was unscathed. If she hadn't come out of the building as fast as she did—

"Hey." Evelyn sat down on her bright blue papasan chair. "She's going to be fine."

"I know."

She regarded him for a moment. "However . . . are you okay?"

"Me? Sure." Seb leaned back in the chair, hiding his turmoil.

"Yeah, right." She took a sip from her mug. "You can fool everyone else, Sebastian Percival Hudson—"

He groaned.

"—but you can't fool me. You don't have to be so stoic all the time. It's okay to let yourself feel things."

Ever since he showed up at Jade's motel room, he'd been engulfed in feelings. The first was when she opened the door, looking like she'd tumbled out of bed and more captivating than he'd ever seen her. He wanted to take her in his arms and kiss her senseless.

But he'd gone to her room for a reason, and he had to focus on that, not on what he wanted. Besides, he couldn't have it anyway. And when he saw her reaction after he mentioned Lydia, he knew he'd made a huge mistake. It wasn't just the anger. It was the deep, stark pain in her eyes that made him realize that he should have never said a word.

"You don't have the right."

He absolutely didn't.

As horrible as the fire was, it had given them both an out from the conversation. But then he almost lost her—

"Oh, hey, Jade." Evelyn bounced up from the chair and went to her. "How was the shower?"

"Good." Her voice sounded gravelly. "I feel much better."

Seb rose, unable to keep his eyes off her. That wasn't unusual, considering every time he saw her he struggled with staring, but the outfit Evelyn gave her didn't help. His sister was more petite, and the turquoise sweatpants Jade was wearing were on the tight side, as was the waffle weave pink shirt. He didn't mind that at all.

There was also a bigger, more important reason why he was staring—one that didn't make complete sense. If he looked away, she might disappear again. His chest constricted at the thought.

Evelyn walked to her small kitchen, which was just off the living room of her one-bedroom apartment. "Can you two keep down the fort for a little while?"

He whirled around. "You're leaving?"

"I'll be back in a bit." She slung her purse over her shoulder. "Make sure you cater to her every whim, bro. She deserves it."

"Evelyn Margot—"

His sister dashed out the door.

Sebastian faced Jade and shrugged. "Welcome to my world."

"I like her."

"Me too . . . sometimes." He hesitated, unsure what to do next. "Do you, ah, need anything?"

"Some water would be great." She clasped her hands in front of her.

Seb was glad to see they weren't shaking, like they had in her motel room. "Coming right up." He quickly fixed it and brought it to her. "Do you want to lie down?"

"I probably should."

"Okay. I'll be here until Evelyn gets back." He sat back in the chair.

"You don't have to stay."

He looked up at her. "I want to."

———

Jade couldn't move, the tenderness in Sebastian's eyes holding her in place. In the back of her mind, she was still processing that she had saved a life . . . and had taken a monumentally stupid risk. To his credit, he didn't berate her for that, just brought her to his sister's apartment, insisting that she didn't stay by herself tonight. At first she balked, but now she was glad she'd agreed. She'd rather be here than alone, despite Mabel's hospitality.

He cleared his throat. "Evelyn said you could take her room."

She shook her head, still gripping the water he gave her. "I can't do that."

"Good luck telling her no."

Chuckling, she sat down on the cream-colored love seat. Evelyn's apartment had a bohemian flair and was decorated in warm earth tones. She took a sip of the water, and it cooled her scratchy throat. *You were extremely lucky, Ms. Smith,* the paramedic had said as she filled out forms on a clipboard. *You could have died.*

The reminder gave her chills. She shivered.

"Are you cold?"

"No," she said, looking at him again. It wasn't that long ago that she'd been furious with him. Now, in spite of everything that had just happened, she felt . . . serene. He always had that effect on her.

"I can get you a blanket." He started to stand again. "Evelyn probably has a sweatshirt somewhere—"

"I'm okay, Sebastian. Really."

He nodded, growing silent again, and also looking unsure. He pressed his palms against his thighs. "I'm sorry," he said. "I shouldn't have brought up Lydia—"

"It's okay." She leaned back on the couch, still holding the water. "I'm sorry I got so upset. Lydia and I are complicated."

"Family can be that way."

"She's not family." She stared at the glass. "I don't have one."

"Jade . . ."

She couldn't look at him, couldn't bear to see the pity she heard in his voice. "It's okay. I'm used to it."

He got up and sat beside her. "I wish you would have told me," he said. "You know, when we were together. I could have . . ."

"There was nothing you could have done. You couldn't make Lydia be a real mother or fix Logan's problems. I couldn't even do that."

"You tried."

She lifted her gaze. "He told you that too?"

"Yeah. He said you wanted to adopt him."

Unbidden, tears pricked her eyes. "I took the job in Atlanta because it paid better, but I still ran out of money. Logan's social worker didn't want me to take him out of Arkansas, and the state lawyer didn't think I was able to take care of him. I would have been a single mother to a troubled teenager." She swallowed. "But I would have done it."

"You didn't have to go through that alone."

"I solve my own problems. I always have. I wasn't going to put that on you."

"You could have given me the chance. I would have helped you. Given you whatever you needed."

Her heart soared . . . and she pulled it back. Nothing had changed between them. Her feelings didn't matter. More importantly, even if a second chance were possible, she didn't deserve a wonderful man like Sebastian Hudson. She was too set in her ways, too independent. *Too broken.*

She got up from the couch, needing distance from him. When she was near the kitchen, she turned around, having regained control. To maintain it, she had to do something she abhorred. She had to exploit his kindness, his feelings. She had to manipulate him.

"I do need something from you, Sebastian. I need you to talk to Miles."

Chapter 16

Well played, Jade.

And that's how he felt—played. For the most part anyway. As she stood there, all business, despite her casual outfit and gorgeous, albeit still damp hair, he was stunned how she could flip a switch so fast. A few seconds ago, his heart ached for her. There were so many things he hadn't known about her when they were together. Learning the real reason she took the Atlanta job had been a relief. She hadn't just dumped him on a whim. She had a good reason—her love for Logan.

The knowledge carved out the resentment he'd held against her for so long. Underneath the frost—the protective barrier she developed due to her childhood—was a generous, loving, heroic woman. And he was falling for her, even harder than before . . . until the switch. He'd seen the emotion change in her eyes after he said he would have helped her, and her softness grew an immediate edge when she moved off the couch. Then she went in for the proverbial kill. For a split second he wondered if her vulnerability was just a ruse to catch him off guard.

Except she hadn't been able to completely detach. Even at this distance, he could see a flicker of emotion, of uncertainty. Of desperation. And because he caught it, he was able to speak his next word.

"Okay."

"Huh?"

"I'll talk to him." Seb patted the empty seat next to him. Yeah, he was being a little manipulative himself, but she started it. "I have a condition, though."

She moved to resume her seat, still looking guarded, but much less so. "What's that?"

"I want to tell you why *The Clementine Times* is so important to me." It was also important that she understood why he would inevitably say no to Miles, no matter the price, no matter the circumstance. But he wouldn't tell her that part. He wasn't looking forward to listening to Miles Harrington's greasy sales pitch, but he could go through the motions to help her out. "Are you willing to listen?"

"Absolutely."

He settled back against the couch as she faced him, sitting cross-legged.

He started from the beginning, telling her about working for Buford when he was a kid, much like Tyler did for him now. He skipped over his time at *The Democrat-Gazette*, since there was no point in rehashing, and explained how Buford had offered him the paper.

"You bought it for a dollar?"

"Yep. The deal of the century." He told her about learning the business, about Buford's and Glenda's deaths, about dealing with the ups and downs. "*The Times* is on a shoestring budget, but it wasn't always. We have longtime employees like Paul, Cletus, and

Flora, who just came back on a volunteer basis. We also have some local stringers. Mayor Pancake has a column, Eugenia Pickles donates recipes—"

"The square dance lady, right?"

He nodded. "The point is, even though we're going through a hard time right now, Clementine needs its newspaper. So do the surrounding communities. It's how we stay connected. How else am I going to know that Tilly Henshaw had baby number three last month, Rob Cartwright is giving half-off haircuts every other Saturday, that the Cherry Hill school board is considering renovating the football field, and the Clementine Community Church is planning a potluck on June twentieth."

"What's special about the twentieth?"

"Not sure, although the CCC doesn't exactly need a special occasion to get together to eat." He smiled, but it quickly faded. "I know big companies are picking up the little papers at a discount, and that bothers me. Harrington Media isn't going to care about people who live here. They'll get their news from feeds, their advertising from companies that don't even exist in this area, and of course, their money. I can't blame publishers for selling if they can't keep their paper afloat. *The Times* isn't there. Not yet, and I'm going to fight to keep it that way as long as I can."

Jade didn't respond. He didn't either, wanting everything he said to sink in. There were many other reasons why he wanted to hang on to *The Times*, but he'd given her plenty to ponder.

Finally, she spoke. "I hadn't thought about it that way before. I've always been focused on the numbers."

"Those are important too."

"On behalf of us accountants, thanks for being so magnanimous."

"Hey, I admire you accountants. Since Flora left, I've been trying to make sense of—" He stopped. Jade didn't need to know about his aversion to balance sheets, and she definitely didn't need to know about the lost ledger. Which he still had to find by Tuesday. Egad, he had to get on top of that.

"Not everyone can have the gift of words that you do," she said softly.

He was touched by her compliment. "I didn't know you read them."

"I read all your columns, remember?"

Actually, he didn't. Had she mentioned that when they were dating? Or was he too distracted by her, in a good way, of course? Definitely a good way. It was nice to hear . . . again.

"I understand what you're saying about your community too," she said. "I took a drive today."

He listened as she told him about her trip through the greater Clementine area. When she finished, he said, "I can show you some other places if you're interested."

"Actually, I am."

She seemed surprised by her own statement. He wasn't going to draw attention to it. "How about tomorrow?"

"You're off on Memorial Day?"

No, and he'd planned to work on another column in the morning while doing a third search of his office for the ledger. But that could wait. "Half a day. I can pick you up at the inn around eight. I might even clean up the back seat for you."

She arched a brow. "Is there something special about the back seat?"

He wondered if she was aware she was leaning toward him, her dreamy malachite eyes holding his. He'd meant it as a joke, considering how much of a disaster his messy car was. But "back seat" had suddenly taken on a new meaning, and he was picturing them parked in a secluded, woody spot, climbing into the back seat together and—

"Honeys, I'm home!"

Seb jumped at Evelyn Margot's overly loud and quite obnoxious entrance. Her timing, both good and bad, was another one of her gifts.

His sister poked her head into the living room. "Everyone decent?"

He face-palmed, then glanced at Jade. She was looking at Evelyn, but there was a rosy blush on her cheeks that hadn't been there a second ago. Hmm, maybe he hadn't imagined—or wished—that Jade's enticing expression was real.

Evelyn laughed. "I bought snacks. I thought maybe we could watch a movie."

But Jade was already yawning. When she was aware of it, she stopped. "Sorry."

"It's okay." Evelyn set two plastic Piggly Wiggly bags on the kitchen counter. "I don't mind an early bedtime."

Seb took that as his cue to go. He stood and turned to Jade. "See ya." He almost said "tomorrow," but if Evelyn Margot knew he and Jade were getting together, she wouldn't let him be.

Jade nodded. "See ya."

He passed by the kitchen, where Evelyn was putting away the groceries. "Thanks again. She's gonna be okay."

She gave him a sly look. "Looks like you will be too."

Oh well, so much for Evelyn not figuring things out. He left the apartment, fully intending on going home and crashing. If he got up really early, he could get part of his column done and search the office before picking up Jade.

When he got home, though, he tried. He wasn't in the mood to pen Seb's View Part Deux either. But he was in the mood to write something that he should have been working on a long time ago. He sat down at the dining room table that was never used for actual dining and where his Royal typewriter made its home, a stack of crisp paper nearby waiting to be used. He cranked a sheet into the roller, and his fingers flew.

———

Monday morning, Kalista showed up at *The Times*, still bummed that she had to work on a holiday. Then again, what else would she do? Hang out at Viv's house? That might have been a little fun. Now that the hoedown was over, Viv was focusing on her wedding again, and she had mentioned yesterday that she wanted to start hand-lettering the invitation envelopes this week. She offered to show her how to do the calligraphy, but Kalista didn't want to mess up the envelopes. She could lick a stamp, though.

Kalista was also tired, and that was solely her fault. After her conversation with Ryan, she had trouble falling asleep, so she grabbed a book from the bookcase and started to read. *Pride and Prejudice.* It kind of sounded familiar and she wondered if she was supposed to have read it in school in one of her English classes. She'd paid little attention to her assignments, but she was a decent test taker, even though she rarely remembered the information past the actual test. Two pages into the book and she was fast asleep. Who knew reading was the antidote to insomnia?

Tyler's car was in the parking lot, and a light shined underneath the basement door. When she walked inside, she saw him stuffing flyers into each newspaper on top of the flat stack on the table. "I could have done those," she said.

He didn't look at her. He also didn't tell her to roll up the papers. But if she didn't get moving, she'd be late for her route, so she joined him at the table and started rolling. It was only the two of them, and soon the other carriers would show up. If she was going to do the gratitude thing, she needed to do it now.

"Thanks for buying me a funnel cake." She injected more enthusiasm into her voice than was probably warranted, but she had to get his attention somehow. Coldness was coming off him in waves.

Silence.

His refusal to respond was vexing. Hmm, *vexing*. Good word—she'd read it last night. Totally appropriate.

It was eerily quiet as they worked on their tasks. Kalista was only a quarter of the way through rolling the newspapers when Tyler put in the last flyer. Without a word, he left the basement and went upstairs.

She stopped and watched him go. Instead of being vexed, she was troubled. She'd hurt people's feelings before—some because they deserved it, others accidentally. Either way, it rarely affected her this much. How long was he going to give her the silent treatment? She hated the silent treatment.

An apology was in order. Her least favorite thing. Hopefully that would thaw the ice between them, and they could go back to the way things were when she first got the job and he was so friendly and complimentary to her.

After filling Bo's truck with the papers, she got inside. Driving this thing wasn't so bad, and she was surprised by how quickly she was getting used to it. Totally not as comfy as her BMW, and she'd have to ask Bo to fix the janky air-conditioning before it got really hot, but she didn't need it in the mountains right now.

As she went along the route, she got into a rhythm. She didn't even mind getting out and putting the papers in their special places for their particularly persnickety customers. When she stopped by Mrs. Joyce's house, the woman was outside with her little dog, Pepé.

"Thank you so much, young lady," she said, while Pepé, a fluffy white little thing, sniffed Kalista's sandals. "I'm so glad you delivery people take the time to bring this to my doorstep. I've got a bad hip, and it can be difficult for me to walk all the way to the end of my driveway.

"You're welcome." An unfamiliar yet pleasant feeling came over her. She smiled and went back to her truck.

She didn't bother to turn on the radio since she couldn't get a decent station anyway. Britney Spears was already in her head, and she sang along as she continued her route, feeling completely unbothered and still happy after Mrs. Joyce had thanked her.

The truck lurched. Sputtered. Then completely stopped.

"What the . . ." She turned the key. Nothing. She put the truck in Park, then back in Drive. Still nothing. "Don't tell me this piece of junk is broken down . . . Uh-oh." She looked at the gas tank. The red pointer was aimed straight at the capital E.

She clutched the steering wheel. How could she run out of gas? Back home her father had a chauffeur who took care of filling up all their cars, but she still had to get her own gas if she was out and about. Checking the tank hadn't even been on her radar.

Now she was stuck in the mountains with no phone and happened to be at that one part of her route where there was nobody close by.

Her throat started to close. *I'm gonna die . . . I'm gonna die . . .*

A more rational voice took over. "Don't be stupid," she muttered. Didn't she pass by a cabin a short while back? She got out of the truck, locked it, then walked back the way she came. She wasn't sure how long she'd been walking, but the sun had risen a little higher in the sky, making it easier to see. When she came upon the small honey-colored cabin, she almost fainted with relief. There was a car in the driveway too. Hooray!

She knocked on the door. Knocked again when no one answered it. Then a third time. Were they sleeping? Or not even home? That panicky feeling returned.

The door suddenly opened, and a tall man appeared. "Kalista?"

"Logan! You have no idea how glad I am to see you." Weird that he was here on her route, but there was no time to dwell. "I ran out of gas."

"I didn't know you lived around here."

"I don't. See, I was delivering the paper." She shook her head, still a little embarrassed by her job. "Whatever. Do you have any gas?"

"Sorry, I don't. And I'm kind of in a hurry. Is there anyone you can call?"

She nodded. "Mr. Hudson."

Logan nodded and let her in the cabin. "You work for *The Clementine Times*? Cool. Seb's your boss then."

Kalista frowned. "How do you know him?"

"This is his cabin."

He had a cabin? When she walked inside, she was impressed. He must make a decent amount of money to afford a place like this. She was also struck by how tidy it was, considering the messy state of his office.

"Phone's in the kitchen." Logan went to the couch, where a small pile of clothing was next to a large backpack. He picked up a shirt and rolled it up.

Kalista took the receiver off the hook and dialed *The Times*. Viv had suggested she memorize the number just in case she got into trouble on her route. At the time, Kalista thought that was a stupid idea. What could possibly happen? *Lesson learned.* She let the phone ring and looked at the microwave clock. Six thirty. Too early for Mr. Hudson to be there.

After a few seconds, she almost hung up. She didn't want to bother Viv at this hour because of her own stupidity, but she might have to.

"*Clementine Times.*"

"Tyler! It's Kalista!"

"Oh."

She ignored his bland tone and quickly explained what happened. "I'm at Mr. Hudson's cabin. Logan's here—"

"Who's Logan?"

"Jade's brother."

"Ms. Smith?"

Now that everyone was identified, she said in a small voice, "Can you bring me some gas?"

"You ran out?"

She squeezed her eyes shut. Embarrassing, and irresponsible. "Yes. I'm sorry—"

"Be there when I can."

He hung up before she could thank him. She put the receiver back, then leaned against the counter, her shoulders slumping.

Logan hoisted his backpack over his shoulder. "Can you do me a favor? Would you mind locking up?"

"Sure."

"Thanks." He opened the door. "Nice meeting you."

"Bye." She gave him a limp wave. When he was gone, she sat down on the big brown couch and looked around the living room. No TV here either. She was tempted to do some snooping—something she often did at her friends' houses. Amazing what you could find in someone's medicine cabinet. It would give her something to do until Tyler showed up.

But something stopped her. Mr. Hudson was her boss, and she had to respect his home. He'd hired her for her first job, after all. She owed him that much.

With nothing to do in the house, she grabbed the key and went outside, then locked the door. If she needed to get back in, she could unlock it. Tyler had to be irritated with her, because she was irritated with herself, but a sense of peace filled her as she sat on a large flat boulder near the front of the cabin while waiting for him to show up. She did like being up here in the little mountains. Ozarks, she thought they were called. Birds chirped, a faint breeze rustled the green leaves . . . It was calming. The boulder was big enough for her to lie down on, and when she did, she looked through the tree branches and watched the puffy clouds as they slowly rolled by . . .

"Kalista. Hey. Wake up."

She felt tapping on her shoulder and opened her eyes. Tyler stood over her, his glasses slipping to the front of his nose. She rubbed her left eye. "Did I fall asleep?"

"Yeah." Tyler straightened. "I put gas in your truck." He turned and walked to his car.

"Hang on." She hurried to him.

He hesitated, then turned around.

"I'm sorry, Tyler. I should have checked my gas gauge. I didn't even think about it."

Glancing away, he muttered, "It's okay." Then he jumped in his car and drove off.

Tears pricked her eyes. He didn't give her a chance to apologize for the other day. He didn't even offer to give her a ride back to the truck. It was as if he couldn't physically stand to be around her. That hurt more deeply than what Ryan and Abbie had done.

She walked back to the truck, trying hard not to sniffle. When she reached it and got inside, she turned on the engine and watched the gas gauge go to the halfway point. She blew out a breath and recentered. Never mind Tyler. He could be vexing all day long if he wanted. She didn't care anymore.

She had papers to deliver, a job to do. She put the truck in Drive and drove off to finish her route.

It wasn't long before her bluster weakened. She should still be furious. Sure, she was rude to Tyler on Saturday, but that was only because she was frustrated and hangry. He'd been cruel to her several times over since then, except for buying her funnel cake. Yes, she should be *incensed* that he dare treat her this way.

But she wasn't. She wiped her nose with the back of her hand. She was just sad.

Chapter 17

"How do you like your eggs?"

"Any way you want to fix them." Jade sat on the papasan chair and sipped her coffee. Evelyn Margot didn't have a dining room table, so they would be eating in the living room. After Sebastian left last night, she'd gone straight to bed and slept soundly, something she hadn't done since arriving in Clementine. Miles calling her at the crack of dawn had spoiled her peaceful morning, but she let it go to voicemail. She'd call him later and let him know Sebastian was willing to talk. Miles could cool his heels a little longer.

"Scrambled it is," Evelyn proclaimed.

"Can I help? I don't usually eat breakfast—"

"Oh, you're one of *those*." She chuckled.

Jade knew exactly what she meant. "I do know how to make toast."

Evelyn motioned to the toaster. "Knock yourself out."

As Jade waited for two pieces of wheat toast to pop up from their slots, her mind wandered again. So much had happened in the last twelve hours, and she was still analyzing it. At the top of her thoughts was Sebastian. Despite wanting him to talk to Miles, she'd been shocked he'd so easily agreed. That had made her feel a little less guilty for manipulating him, and it took a ton of weight off her shoulders.

He'd also given her insight to the small newspaper business and how it affected the community, and she'd been impressed. While selling *The Times* to Harrington made financial sense, Jade hadn't considered the human ripple effect until he'd explained it. And if she'd never considered it, having worked at a newspaper before, she was positive Miles and his ilk hadn't given it a thought.

Then there was his offer to show her around and how quickly she'd said yes. Talking with him last night had been like old times. She'd felt completely relaxed in his company, as if all was right with her world, at least for a little while. She still had the ledger fiasco to contend with, and she'd decided to tell him today, after their drive. She probably should confess as soon as he picked her up, but she just wanted a couple hours of peace before he never spoke to her again.

Pop!

She blinked away her reverie and buttered the slices. The thought of telling Sebastian about the ledger strangled her appetite. Maybe he would understand her desperation and that it wasn't totally her fault that her briefcase disappeared. *But it's my fault I stole from him.*

"Um, Jade?" Evelyn said. "Are you sure you know how to make toast?"

"Huh?" She looked down at the hole she'd made in the middle of the bread with the butter knife. "Sorry. I'll eat this slice."

Evelyn dished out the fluffy scrambled eggs, Jade added her pathetic excuse for toast, and they went to the living room. Jade sat down and stared at her plate, her uneasiness growing.

"Eggs okay?"

She looked up at Evelyn and nodded. "They look yummy."

"They are." She grinned and took a bite, then lifted her bunny-slippered feet and wagged them back and forth. "If I do say so myself."

Jade smiled and started to eat. She was right—they were very good. She really liked Evelyn and wished Sebastian had said something about her before. Then again, back then she always shifted any family conversation before it got started, for her own sake.

"So," Evelyn said, putting her empty plate on the oval glass coffee table. "What are your intentions toward my brother?"

Jade froze, the last bite of her eggs halfway to her mouth. "Intentions?"

"Yes. You do have intentions, don't you?"

She wasn't sure how to answer that, because she didn't know how much Sebastian had revealed. Evelyn worked at the paper too, and Jade wouldn't be surprised if she had the same resistant attitude he did. "No?" she ended up saying, knowing she had to tell Evelyn something.

"As long as you're sure." She grinned, but it didn't quite reach her eyes now.

Great, now she was suspicious. Jade didn't blame her. "It's good to see him again." One hundred percent the truth, especially since they weren't at odds right now. That would change soon, but she would do everything she could to apologize and own up to her bad judgment.

"I think you're good for him," she said. "When I got back from the store, I noticed how relaxed he was. He hasn't been that way in a long, long time."

Wow. She was glad she'd put him at ease too.

"Why did you two break up? And yes, I'm nosy. But I love my brother. He's an amazing man, and I don't want him to get hurt. He's had enough of that in his lifetime."

Jade inwardly winced. She set her plate next to Evelyn's. "I took a job in Atlanta. Long distance wouldn't have worked out. We didn't date long anyway." Her answers were clipped, and she refused to elaborate. While she was glad Sebastian had such a loving sister, Jade didn't owe her any more information.

"He said that too. About you not dating very long. Then you're just friends?"

"Yeah . . . friends."

"That's probably for the best. Seb's married to his work. There's not much room for anything else."

Jade could relate. Charlotte had accused her of the very same thing not that long ago. *"One day you're going to realize that all work and no play makes for a dull life."*

"I probably shouldn't tell you this." Evelyn sighed. "I promised him I wouldn't say anything to anyone, but since you're not a Clementonian, it will be okay. Seb doesn't just write newspaper columns. He's also a novelist."

"He finished his book?"

Evelyn looked surprised. "You knew about that?"

"He was working on it when we were together. I didn't know it was done, though. He never mentioned it to me." Although he didn't really have a reason to.

"Here's what drives me bonkers about Seb. He holds everything in, and that includes his accomplishments. The only reason I know that he published a novel was because I asked him straight out how he was keeping *The Times* in business. I'm the advertising manager—I know where most of our income comes from—and for several years, we weren't making a dime of profit. I asked our bookkeeper, Flora, about it, but she didn't know either—just that money kept showing up in the business account.

"I can be persuasive when I want to be, although Seb calls it nagging. Whatever. He finally admitted that he sold his book and had made money on it. Of course I wanted to take out a full page ad and publicize it, but he refused. To this day he won't tell me a thing about it. I'm sure he published under a pen name too, because I can't find any novels written by Sebastian Hudson or any iteration of his name. Believe me, I tried."

Jade believed her. But she was confused. "Why would he keep that a secret?"

"I can only guess." She pushed off her slippers and folded her feet under her. "He's humble to a fault. You probably already know that."

She did. Even before they started dating, she'd heard people at *The Democrat-Gazette* talking about his writing. And she'd read every one of his articles, then his columns when he switched to writing Seb's View. She wasn't surprised to hear his book had done well. He never promoted himself, though, and brushed off any praise that came his way.

"He also doesn't like notoriety. He's just a small-town guy who loves his town. I can't even imagine him doing book signings or being interviewed. He'd probably break out in hives. As for financially supporting the paper, I guess he didn't know what else to do to keep *The Times* solvent. That newspaper is his life."

Jade mulled over Evelyn's words. His resistance to Miles and any other corporate takeover made even more sense. Not only did he have financial skin in the game, but he had an emotional attachment to the paper and the community. And then she showed up and kept pushing—nagging, really—for him to consider selling it. If she'd known all this, she would have refused Miles's assignment.

"Whew, it felt good to finally talk about that." Evelyn smiled. "Mum's the word, though. He'd be super mad if he knew I said anything."

Jade made a zipping motion over her mouth. "It's safe with me."

They finished their coffee and Jade got ready to return to the Clementine Inn, where Sebastian would pick her up in an hour. Evelyn had kindly washed her smoke-filled clothes, and when she changed into that outfit, she felt much better. Evelyn's clothes had been a bit too tight, although Jade appreciated her giving her something to wear.

When she was packed up and ready to go, she thanked Evelyn. "You've been so kind. I really appreciate it."

"Thanks, but it's no big deal."

It was a big deal, and she could see humility ran in the Hudson family.

"How long are you staying in Clementine?" Evelyn asked.

"I'm going back to Atlanta tomorrow." An odd feeling of disappointment came over her. Strange, because since her arrival in Clementine, she couldn't wait to go home. Now she wished she had more time.

"Oh. I was hoping you weren't leaving so soon. I just thought..."

"Thought what?"

"That you might be the one that got away." She waved off her words. "Not sure where I got that idea. Seb rarely talks about his personal life. I didn't know about you until you showed up. I don't mean that in a bad way."

"I know." Jade wasn't offended, but it did give her confirmation that their relationship hadn't been serious. For him anyway, despite his spontaneous admission of love during their last conversation.

"I'd better let you go before I put my foot in my mouth again." Evelyn quickly hugged her. "Take care, and don't be a stranger."

Jade returned her hug without responding. It was nice to hear, but there was no reason for her to come back. Sebastian had agreed to talk to Miles, and her assignment was over. By tomorrow evening, she would be headed back to Atlanta, where she belonged.

But until then, she was going to enjoy her time with Sebastian for as long as she could.

———

SEB'S VIEW PART DEUX
JULY FOURTH REMINISCING

It's almost that time again, fellow Clementonians, for the July Fourth parade. The entire town is festooned with flags and banners, and Mayor Pancake's decoration crew has outdone themselves this year.

July Fourth was a little more than a month away, and Seb wasn't sure why when he woke up this morning he was inspired to write about his most prominent memory of summers past, but he'd learned long ago that when inspiration struck, he needed to follow. He'd edit the details later.

Main Street is dripping with red, white, and blue, and the Clementine High School marching band has been practicing their patriotic songs with musical zeal. If you see a band member, give them a pat on the back. They relinquish part of their summer to bring us the best in high school marching band entertainment, and it's a crying shame they haven't been chosen for the Macy's Thanksgiving Day Parade yet. Hope springs eternal.

I was never a musician, but I have my own vivid Independence Day memories from when our quaint town was even quainter. One in particular sticks out in my mind the most.

Clementine, 1978. My ten-year-old self moseyed into Wright's Soda Shop and Sundries to get a chocolate malt. I was skinnier than a pencil lead, and for some reason Mr. Wright thought that was the only qualification needed to shimmy up the medium-sized flagpole right outside his store. He wanted to replace his tattered, well-worn Old Glory and had offered me the princely sum of one dollar and fifty cents to do the job. When I hesitated, he sweetened the pot with free chocolate malts for the rest of the month. Against my better judgment and because of my weakness for milkshakes, I foolishly agreed.

He handed me a flag that strangely smelled like motor oil and supervised while I tucked it under my arm and climbed up the pole. The task was easier than I thought, and with increasing confidence I climbed until I was almost to the top. Then I made a tragic error.

I looked down.

And at that moment I realized something I'd never known about myself. I was terribly, horribly, incredibly, and all the other appropriate adjectives afraid of heights. It didn't matter that the flagpole wasn't that high—probably twelve feet, if that. My body refused to move.

Mr. Wright promptly responded to my lack of progress.

"Why'd ya stop?" he yelled, shielding his eyes from the afternoon sun, perspiration puddling on his balding head.

I sympathized, drenched with a combination of flop sweat and exudation from Arkansas in midsummer. I also remained mute.

"Sebastian?" His tone changed from quizzical to concerned. "You okay?"

I was *not* okay. I couldn't climb up. I couldn't go down. I was in the grip of paralyzing fear.

At that point Mr. Wright started yelling in earnest. I don't remember what he said, only that his loud bellowing brought out a sizable crowd that included three of my buddies who'd been walking around town wasting time.

"Are you stuck?" Roger Brown stated the obvious.

"Whatcha doing up there?" Billy Johnson queried.

"You're gonna be in trouuuuuble," Evelyn Margot hollered.

From my perceived atmospheric position, I thought my sister was my buddy Christopher. This wasn't the first time I mistook her for a boy. When she was five, she gave herself a Marine-esque haircut, on purpose. That day she had on a Razorbacks baseball cap that hid her then shoulder-length hair. True to form, she was being annoyingly unhelpful.

There was a sudden cacophony of voices, and when one unidentified adult claimed that he would call the fire department, that was all it took. The idea of being rescued in front of my friends, a few curious townspeople, and—gasp, Evelyn Margot—spurred me into action.

I wiped one damp palm on the flag, then the other. I quickly climbed the rest of the pole, affixed the flag, and wobbled toward earth, sliding down the last third of the way. When my sneakers hit terra firma, I expected accolades. Or at least a thank-you. Instead, the crowd moaned.

I felt a tap on my shoulder. I turned to see Evelyn Margot standing there in her pink Stay Groovy T-shirt, grinning. "It's upside down, dummy."

The egg timer rang, and Seb shut it off. He'd set the timer before starting his column because he didn't want to be late picking up Jade. He removed the sheet of paper from his typewriter and finished getting dressed. Nothing was far in Clementine, and he had fifteen minutes before he was supposed to be at the inn. It would take ten minutes to get there. He didn't want to be too early. Or too late. He wanted to be casually on time, whatever that meant. It was the best he could come up with since he didn't want her to notice how eager he was to see her.

He was quite alert, considering he'd only gotten three hours of sleep. That wasn't Jade's fault. Or maybe it was. The second he got home last night, he planted himself in front of his Royal and hammered out almost three chapters of his follow-up novel, which was now exactly almost three chapters long. For the past eight years, he assumed he'd avoided working on it because he was so busy with *The Times*. There was also a little fear too. His first book had exploded out of the gate—something he hadn't anticipated. Now he wondered if part of his reticence had been writer's block. He sure busted through it last night.

He'd hold off contacting his agent, though. After a couple years of encouragement, they agreed to temporarily part ways, although she was still willing to rep his writing if he ever finished something. He wasn't foolish enough to think that one breakthrough night had set him on the right track. And if Jade was the reason he was able to move forward . . .

Seb shook his head and searched for his car keys. Where had he left them? Oh, right. In the bathroom, duh. He grabbed them off the sink and left his small bungalow, trying to temper his anticipation. But it was hard. Last night with Jade had been another breakthrough—a personal one—and he was looking forward to being with her and not thinking about work or buyouts or even the past. He wasn't naive enough to believe they were going on a date, and he refused to call it one.

Could it lead to something else?

Once again he gave his head a shake. He had to stop doing that, imagining things that weren't likely to happen, even if thinking about those things made him feel good. And hopeful. Wow, when was the last time he felt truly hopeful about anything?

Eleven minutes later he pulled into the inn's parking lot and saw Jade waiting outside. His heart thumped. He'd never get over how beautiful she was, and he was glad to see she had dressed casually. They were entering the no-business zone.

He got out at the same time she spotted him, and she headed toward him as he zipped over to the passenger side of the car to open the door for her. "Morning," he said, glad he was sounding nonchalant.

"Hi." She smiled.

Another thump. Yes, this was going to be a good day.

For the next two hours, he drove through the Ozark Mountains, mostly on back roads since she mentioned she enjoyed them during her Sunday drive. Conversation was casual and easy, and she asked plenty of questions about the area, particularly Clementine. He was glad to oblige.

Around ten thirty he asked, "Are you hungry?"

"A little. Evelyn made breakfast this morning."

"Eggs?"

Jade nodded. "They were delicious."

"She's known for those. I don't know what kind of cooking magic she does when she makes them, but they're amazing." He glanced at her. She had sunglasses on and the same outfit she wore to the hoedown. Her hair was pulled back with a dark green headband and her fair complexion was radiant. Kind of like he was feeling right now. *Whoa. Dial it back, Hudson.*

Food. They were talking about food. "There's a café in Jasper that's pretty popular. Excellent pie."

"Coconut cream?"

"To die for."

She grinned. "I'm in."

He drove them to the Crescent Ridge Café and enjoyed a lunch of hamburgers, french fries, and of course, pie. He wasn't into sweets, so he didn't get a piece. That didn't stop Jade from offering him a bite.

"Trust me, you'll love this." She held out a glob of white-and-light-yellow cream on her fork.

Their surroundings might be different, but everything felt familiar, reminding him of the lunches they shared at the Sports Page in downtown Little Rock. He took the bite, barely aware they were sharing a fork, something they used to do. "Not bad."

"What?" She shoved the tines back into the slice. "This is the best pie I've ever had, and I thought the Clementine Diner's was exceptional."

Seb enjoyed watching her finish the dessert. The only hiccup was when the check arrived and she insisted on splitting it, canceling his expectation that he'd take care of the bill. They each paid for their own meals.

It was near noon when they got back in the car, and by the time they'd return to Clementine, it would be almost one o'clock. He still had a pile of work waiting on him, along with finding the ledger. He turned to her. "We need to head back."

She nodded, glancing his way.

Was that disappointment he saw? Or, rather, wished for.

Jade slid on her sunglasses, and he started the Altima. They were both quiet on the drive back to the inn. Seb didn't want to push conversation, and they had talked plenty today. All surface things—nothing too personal. Probably for the best.

But when he pulled into the parking lot, reality hit. She was going back to Atlanta tomorrow and this was probably the last time he'd see her. Even if she did decide to talk to Lydia and Logan again, they lived in Little Rock. There wasn't a reason for her to come back to Clementine.

Seb pulled into a space to the left of the inn. The parking lot was almost empty, and he assumed people were out enjoying the last of the holiday weekend. This was it. Goodbye. That's all he had to say, and then he'd be on his way to *The Times* office. To work. Again.

He opened his mouth. Closed it. Then shut off the engine.

"Sebastian?"

He turned to her, and the question he'd been dying to know the answer to bubbled to the surface. "Why didn't you get married?"

Chapter 18

Y ou're stunning, Viv." Kalista watched her stepmother turn around in front of the tri-paneled mirror. When Kalista got back home from work, Viv asked if she'd like to go with her to the fitting. Of course she said yes, and now they were at a bridal shop in Fayetteville, and Viv was getting the final fitting for her wedding dress. "Bo won't be able to take his eyes off of you."

She blushed. "That's very sweet of you to say."

"Because it's true." The stout seamstress was checking the hem that hovered just above Viv's bare feet. "You look incredible."

Kalista had been shopping long enough in her life to know that salespeople would say anything to get you to buy their product and keep you in the store longer to purchase more. In this case the seamstress was absolutely correct. Seeing Viv out of her country clothes and in the tasteful dress reminded her of how Viv used to look when she was married to Kalista's father. *Glamorous.*

"I love it." Viv's voice was soft as she spoke to the seamstress. "Thank you, Eileen."

"It was a pleasure to work with you, Ms. Clark."

Paying close attention to the exchange, Kalista could even see that Viv's interactions with a store employee had changed. She'd been young when she and Viv were on their shopping trips, but she could still remember Viv's attitude. A little haughty, not necessarily snobby, but she definitely had a superior air about her. Kalista probably wouldn't have picked up on it now if she hadn't been around her for the past several days. It wasn't just seeing her in different clothes that made the difference.

"I'll be out in a minute." Viv and Eileen went into the large dressing room for her to change out of the gown, while Kalista browsed through wedding dresses that surrounded the fitting area. She looked at some of the prices, stunned by how inexpensive the gowns were, even the top-dollar ones. She was used to a handbag costing more than some of them. Still, they were all pretty.

Viv appeared. "Ready to grab some lunch?"

"Yes." Kalista was hungry, and soon they were on their way to a restaurant Viv had picked out.

"You're going to like this," Viv said as they entered the eatery. "It will remind you of home."

She was right. There were plenty of low-carb, organic choices, and she landed on a turkey sandwich with goat cheese and sprouts. After Viv ordered a ham and Swiss cheese pita, they got their sweet teas, took their trays, and sat down.

Kalista glanced around the restaurant and saw a skinny guy with olive skin, cargo shorts, and an oversize T-shirt. His black hair was worn in the same style as Tyler's. Her heart skipped a beat, but then he turned around. No glasses. No Tyler.

"Kalista?" Viv's voice grabbed her attention. "Everything okay? You've been pretty quiet today."

Tears welled in her eyes again. She blinked them away. The last thing she wanted to do was cry in her alfalfa. She planned to tell Viv she was fine. What came out was, "Is there something wrong with me?"

"Of course not. Did someone say that to you?"

Suddenly everything spilled out. Her conversations with Abbie and Ryan, along with telling Viv how she treated Tyler in the kitchen on Saturday and that he could barely be around her now. "Am I really that bad? Am I"—she sniffed—"immature? That's what Dad thinks. Ryan too."

Viv folded her hands on the table, her food barely touched. "I think you're a product of your upbringing," she said as if she were weighing each word.

"I don't understand."

"Remember how I told you that I needed to get out of the modeling world? That I couldn't take the life anymore?"

Kalista nodded.

"That's what I mean. That entire lifestyle where everything is fleeting, competitive, and . . ."

"Shallow?"

"That's a good word for it. I'm not criticizing people who like that kind of life. Your father always has. When he asked me if you could stay here for the summer, I was happy. To get you away from LA, even for a little while, was worth it." She smiled.

"That's why you agreed?"

"You're the closest thing I've ever had to my own child. That was due to the decisions I made about my career. Being a model and having a baby—those things don't sync up very well. By the time I got out of the business, I had already divorced your father. He wasn't interested in having more kids anyway. I was kind of lost for a while. The one stable thing I had during those years was my relationship with you."

"Really?"

"Yes, and I'm glad your father never interfered with that. In fact, when he called me, he thanked me for being in your life."

Kalista fell back in her chair. "I didn't know any of this. I always wondered why you and dad divorced." Because she couldn't help it, she added, "Was it because he cheated on you? I'm sure he's cheated on all his wives."

"No, Kalista," she said softly. "I cheated on him." She paused, letting the words sink in. "I never loved your father. Looking back on it now, I think there might have been some affection there for him, but I didn't love him like he needed or deserved. Maybe if I hadn't been so immature back then, we could have made it. I could have learned to love him. He does have a lot of great qualities, but the truth is, I married him because he was rich."

Kalista was so shocked, she couldn't say anything.

"I don't want you to blame your father for the divorce. I want to make that clear. I think part of my infidelity was that I felt lonely. He was very busy making the money I thought I wanted so badly. But ultimately I wasn't the wife I should have been." She hung her head. "I'm ashamed to say all that, but it's true. I'm sure you think I'm a terrible person."

"Viv, I could never think of you that way. You're the only one of my dad's wives that ever stuck around or ever did anything with me. Paid attention to me. I don't remember my own mother, and I love you for being the mom I never had." Tears slipped from her eyes. She'd never been this emotional before. Maybe when her real mom died, but she'd been so little back then.

Viv took her hand. "I'm glad I could be, Kalista." She gave her hand a squeeze before letting it go. "Raymond did ask for one other thing."

"What's that?"

"To be nicer to Bettany."

Kalista rolled her eyes. Leave it to her wicked stepmonster to ruin the moment. "No. Way. Do you know she's barely older than I am? Ick."

A tiny smirk appeared on Viv's lips. "He does have a type. I'm not asking you to be . . . best friends, but you could give her a chance. It's not easy becoming a stepmom."

"I'll think about it." She didn't have an intention to take the request seriously. Wasn't she suffering enough? Well, not suffering exactly. Lunch was good, and staying with Viv was really nice. She was even getting used to the house and was feeling more confident about her job.

The only snafu was Tyler. She thought about asking for Viv's advice, then changed her mind. She needed to forget about him and stick to it this time. She was spending way too much energy on a dorky guy with glasses. He wasn't even her type.

As of right now, she wasn't going to think about Tyler Hernandez anymore. Not ever. Ever. And never.

"Want to get pedicures?" Viv asked.

Kalista grinned. Finally, she was going to do something fun.

———

Jade's eyes grew wide. Leave it to Sebastian to keep throwing her loops.

During the ride back from Crescent Ridge Café, her stomach churned with dread, the scrumptious pie she'd just eaten making it worse. All morning she'd been able to forget about the ledger. Sebastian had made that easy. It felt like they'd picked up right where they left off ten years ago, even sharing a bite of food the way they used to.

For the first time ever, she allowed herself to think about what would have happened if things were different. If she had told Sebastian about Logan and hadn't run off to Atlanta to make more money, only to ultimately fail to adopt him. If she had trusted him enough, would they still be together? Would she, Seb, and Logan have been a family?

When he pulled into the inn's parking lot, she ceased her thoughts. There was no point in what-ifs. She was just grateful to have spent this time with him. A complete one-eighty to how she felt almost a week ago. Then he parked his car, and the time had come. She had to confess to taking and losing the ledger. She shoved her shaking hands under her thighs.

Then he knocked her off guard with his question. Her automatic answer was something he could relate to—she was too focused on work and her own security to have a social life. She turned to tell him that.

His tender gaze caressed her, making the words disappear and uncovering the real truth. Sebastian Hudson had her heart. He always had. *He still does.*

Suddenly he turned away. "Doesn't matter," he mumbled, opening the car door. "I'll walk you to the inn."

The encompassing warmth she'd felt a second ago vanished, making her think she'd imagined the moment. She probably had. Anything to keep the sick feeling at bay. She got out of his car, and he met her on the passenger side.

"I guess this is goodbye," he said.

Jade nodded. "Thanks for talking to Miles."

Seb shrugged. "I'll see what he has to say."

They both knew he wasn't going to agree, and Jade was fine with that. Actually, she was glad. Sebastian *was The Clementine Times*. He deserved to keep it.

She swallowed, ready to tell him about the ledger. She lifted her eyes to meet his. She'd been enough of a coward. "Sebastian . . ."

Her words, her thoughts, everything around her disappeared as their gazes met. Her pulse danced—no, it *do-si-do'd* as he took a step forward. Bedroom eyes. *He has bedroom eyes.*

She willed his mouth to meet hers, pressing against him, kissing him with so much emotion she wanted to weep. His arm went around her waist, drawing her closer, slightly arching her back while his fingers dug into her hair as he returned her kiss. The hollow emptiness inside her began to fill.

At some point he pulled away, but not very far. "I missed you," he said, his already deep voice husky and deliciously low.

She smiled, fully relaxing in his arms. "I can tell."

"Yeah, I'm not exactly hiding it."

He wasn't. And he was perfect.

He traced his fingertips down her cheek. "Stay, Jade. An extra day or two. Three, even. Let me get to know you again."

Her instinct was to say no. Her default setting whenever it came to doing something for herself. She was a logical woman who worked with numbers and understood objectivity and order. Objectively, she had to go home. She had work to do. She had . . . nothing else.

Yet, in Clementine she had this sexy, dependable man, right in her arms. *Right where I want him.* Taking a day or three off wouldn't hurt. She had plenty of vacation time accrued. "Yes," she said. "I'll stay."

His eyes lit up and he kissed her again. "Then it's a date."

"When?"

"Tonight." He grinned and backed away. "Pick you up at six."

She giggled. When was the last time she'd done that? "What are we doing?"

"We'll figure it out."

Sebastian got in his car, and she stepped away. There would be time to tell him about the ledger. Time to get to know each other, and he would be more apt to understand what she'd done. She waved as he drove off, and she headed toward the inn. Floated, actually.

When she walked inside, the inn was empty, and no one was manning the counter. She tapped the little metal bell and waited for someone to show up. Now that the hoedown and Memorial Day weekend were over, she might be able to extend her reservation. She reached for her purse. *Oh no.* She thought she'd put it over her shoulders, but she must have left it in Seb's car. A moment of panic, then she remembered she'd be seeing him tonight. That made her smile.

"Jade!" Mabel appeared behind the counter, grinning from ear to ear. "You're not going to believe this."

It had been an unbelievable morning so far, that was for sure. "Try me."

She put a briefcase on the counter and grinned.

Jade's briefcase. She shot a shocked look at Mabel. "How did you find it?"

"That's the unbelievable part." Mabel still beamed. "One of our guests that stayed for the weekend saw it on the floor after they had checked in. She thought it was her husband's. She was so mad at him for bringing work with him on vacation that she took the briefcase and hid it from him in the hotel room. When they were packing to leave this morning, she gave it back to him, and she was mortified to find out it wasn't his. You weren't here when she returned it, or I would have given it right back to you."

Jade couldn't believe it. She stared at the briefcase, making sure it was truly hers. This solved everything! Now that she was staying in Clementine for a few days, she could sneak the ledger back in Seb's office. He would never know what happened. She almost fainted with relief. "Thank you," she said to Mabel. "Thank you so much."

"I'm just glad someone didn't steal it. Not on purpose anyway."

The inn's front door opened as Jade grabbed the handle.

"Jade, you forgot—"

She turned at the sound of Sebastian's voice and saw he was carrying her purse. She grinned and picked up the briefcase. "Thank you—"

Suddenly the latch gave way, spilling everything onto the floor.

Including Sebastian's ledger.

Chapter 19

Seb's gaze landed on the ledger that fell out of Jade's briefcase. His jaw dropped. He'd turned his office, house, and car upside down looking for it. All this time she had it, and he definitely, absolutely, without a doubt knew he wasn't the one who gave it to her.

Jade fell to her knees, scrambling to pick up the papers. And his ledger. "I can explain," she said, jumping to her feet.

His eyes narrowed. "You'd better."

She paused, clutching the open case, loose papers and the ledger book pressed against her chest. "Can we talk somewhere else?" she squeaked.

He glanced at Mabel, who looked unsurprisingly confused. He and Jade were blocking the front entrance too. He gave Jade a sharp nod.

"We can go to my room—"

That was the last place he wanted to be right now, despite his yearning to have her alone and all to himself again the minute he drove away from the inn. When he heard a phone ring in his car shortly after he left the parking lot, he saw her purse on the floorboard and quickly turned around. Work could wait—it wasn't going anywhere. They could start their date right now.

"No," he said, then stalked off to the empty eating area. He heard papers rustling behind him as she followed. When he reached the other side of the room, he turned around. "How did you get my ledger?"

Her porcelain skin turned ashen, and she laid the briefcase and papers on the table but still held the ledger. She glanced at it and gave it to him. "I took it."

His jaw tightened.

"I know it was wrong, but it was kind of an accident."

"How do you *accidentally* steal something, Jade?"

Her hands were practically shaking off her wrists, but she didn't bother to hide them. She told him about sneaking into his office, presumably to find out where he was so they could talk about Harrington again. She didn't find a calendar—because he didn't own one—and then noticed the ledger.

"I just took a peek," she insisted. Her voice was trembling too. "Then Evelyn and Tyler showed up, and I panicked. I ducked under the desk—"

He held up his hand. She was sounding ridiculous, and he didn't care about the rest. She went behind his back, stole his financial records, and kept them for days. *Days.* She had plenty of opportunity to tell him if it was just an "accident."

His heartbeat ground to a halt. It had all been a ruse, and he'd fallen for it. He wasn't crazy enough to think she ran into the burning building to save that baby so she could convince him to listen to Harrington. But she'd taken advantage. He'd even been aware of it at the time.

His mistake was to believe everything after that. That she cared about his determination to keep *The Times* alive. That she was interested in seeing and experiencing the community he loved. That she had kissed him . . . and meant it. A brick to his face would have been less excruciating.

"Sebastian." Tears swam in her eyes—those stunning eyes he'd gotten lost in moments ago when she was in his arms. "I'm sorry. I was going to tell you—"

"When?" he exploded. "Tonight? Tomorrow? Were you even going to stay?" He shoved his hand through his hair, pulling at the ends. "I bet you were planning to get on a plane tonight."

"I promise I was going to stay. I still am—"

"Don't bother." He blew past her, gripping the ledger. He had no idea if Mabel was still behind the counter, and he didn't care. He had to get out of the inn. He had to get away from Jade. He had to figure out how to *breathe* again.

He jumped in his car, slammed the door, and drove off. When the furious haze cleared from his eyes, he slowed down, pulled over to the side of the road, and stopped. The ledger was still in his lap. He looked through it, making sure nothing had been removed. Nothing had, but there were things Jade could have copied down. Account numbers, notes Flora had written to help guide him. She could have taken a picture of all of it. She probably had.

Seb threw the book on the seat, then slammed his fist on the steering wheel. He'd read Jade Smith all wrong, again. Forget his girl picker. His entire perception process was busted. He'd let down his shields and she plowed on through until she got what she wanted.

He'd been stupid enough to believe she wanted him. Not once, but twice.

A car whizzed by. He couldn't stay on the road. He didn't want to go to work. Or home.

Seb yanked down the gearshift and headed for the mountains.

———

"We're ready to preboard flight 6845 to Atlanta. All preboarding customers proceed to the front."

Jade crossed her arms as a woman in a wheelchair pushed by an attendant passed her, followed by two mothers with their young children. She barely noticed them as she stared straight ahead, waiting for her turn to board, her suitcase next to her. The briefcase had gone into the dumpster as soon as Sebastian left.

Her chest tightened. Her throat too. The second Sebastian refused to listen to the rest of her explanation and apology, she knew it was over. And she only had herself to blame. She had to fight not to go after him. It would have been a waste of time.

There was only one thing left for her to do. Go back to Atlanta. Where she belonged.

She wasn't sure if Mabel had witnessed her and Sebastian's altercation, but the woman had been subdued when Jade settled her bill, and there was no, "Come on back, ya hear," from her before she walked out of the inn. She'd been able to get a last-minute seat on tonight's final flight to Atlanta. It had cost her a pretty penny, and she wasn't going to expense it. She'd take the hit, and any other ones that came her way. She'd *earned* them.

Her seat was in the last row on the plane, and she began to fidget. She didn't want to wait. She was in a hurry to leave Arkansas behind again, like she had ten years ago. She wouldn't look back. She hated looking back. She would put Logan, Lydia, Clementine, and everything else behind her and not give them a single second thought . . . including Sebastian.

The pain in her heart deepened. It didn't matter how much she tried, she couldn't ignore the sense of betrayal in his eyes before he stormed off. As she always did, she tried to rationalize. Even if she hadn't stolen the ledger, after three days she would still be here, waiting to board a flight back to Atlanta. Spending more time with Sebastian would have delayed the inevitable.

Her cell rang, and she yanked it out of her purse and shut it off, not bothering to look at the caller ID. She still hadn't called Miles back, but she'd see him tomorrow. She doubted it was Logan. He hadn't tried to contact her since the hoedown on Saturday.

She knew for sure it wasn't Sebastian.

A harried woman who looked to be in her early seventies sat down next to her. "Mind if I plop here?" she said, carrying a large tote bag and sounding a little breathless.

Jade nodded and returned her phone to her purse.

"Thank you. I ran all the way from the TSA checkpoint." She took in a deep breath, then pushed her fluffy silver bangs from her forehead. "I hope we don't have to deal with those X-ray machines for much longer. I miss when you could just come into an airport, check your bags, and get on the plane without standing in line and . . ." She sighed. "Sorry. I'm in a mood."

Jade nodded.

"But it's going to get better." She grinned, revealing a gold tooth on her bottom left incisor. "I'm off to visit my grandbabies. I haven't seen them in years." She leaned closer to Jade. "Family feud. I shouldn't have let it go on so long. I missed their early years, and now they're all teenagers. All because of a peach cobbler recipe."

"Must be some cobbler."

"Darn tootin' it is. You have to use a certain kind of peach, you see. From Guy, Arkansas. The sugar-to-cinnamon ratio is the key—"

Jade's stomach curdled and she tuned out the woman as she described her recipe. She didn't want to think about food. Or pie. Or sharing a bite with Sebastian. Or his searing, toe-curling, earthquaking kiss—

"Anyway, I ended up calling my daughter and apologizing for getting mad that she put my recipe in her church cookbook without my permission."

She glanced at the woman, who was smiling at her.

"Life is too short to fuss over peach cobbler, or anything else. Now I have no regrets."

"Rows twenty through thirty, please board."

"That's me, twenty-nine." She got up from her seat. "Safe travels, young lady."

"You too."

Jade watched her go, managing to be happy for her. But not seeing family because of a recipe sounded ridiculous. There were far more serious reasons to be estranged.

She stilled. Regrets. She had plenty. An entire past full of them. Some more recent now, and one that overrode them all. Weariness washed over her at the thought of adding them to the weight of the rest. What else could she do, though? She couldn't fix the past. The doors were all closed . . .

Except for one.

"Rows thirty through forty, ready to board."

Jade looked at her boarding pass. Row forty, seat C. She glanced at the line of passengers waiting to get on the plane. She needed to join them. She needed to go home.

She got up and grabbed her suitcase. But instead of getting in line, she left the gate, digging into her crossbody bag for her Razr. With one hand she pulled it out and flipped open the cover, then punched in a number and put it to her ear, never breaking her stride.

"Jade?"

Relief washed through her. She wasn't sure he was going to pick up. "Hi, Logan."

On Tuesday morning Kalista made a decision—she couldn't ignore Tyler for the summer, not until after she apologized and paid him for the funnel cake. That meant she had to ask Viv for the money, but she told her it was for coffee at the Clementine Diner and not to pay Tyler back. During her tell-all at lunch yesterday, she hadn't mentioned the funnel cake and didn't see the need to. Paying him back was the right thing to do, even though she never had to pay anyone back in her life before.

Another first was feeding the animals with Viv that morning. Viv hadn't asked her until now, and Kalista guessed it was because of her new job. She yanked on the black rubber boots Viv had given her and trudged to the pig pen. Slopping the hogs, as Viv called it, was the most unglamorous thing she'd ever done. They smelled. They snorted. They rolled in the mud and smacked their snouts as they gobbled down their food.

They were kind of adorable too, in a messy, stinky way.

When Viv went to spread chicken feed by the coop, Bo came over to Kalista, who had dumped the last bucket of feed over the fence and into the trough. "You look like you've been doing this your whole life."

She glanced at him and smirked. "It's not exactly rocket science."

"No, but it's important." He rested his forearms on the red metal gate and looked ahead. "I want to thank you, Kalista."

Stunned, she said, "Thank me? Why?"

He turned to her. Bo wasn't a looker, that was for sure. He was bald, his stomach protruded too far over his belt buckle, and he always wore overalls that were a little long in the legs. But he was a very, very nice man and treated Viv like a princess. "I'm glad you came here. Clementine ain't no LA, and we ain't fancy here either. It's got to be hard. I'm sure you're missing your family and friends."

Kalista barely nodded. She'd lost her best friend and boyfriend in the span of three days, although she could say good riddance to Abbie and good luck to Ryan, now that she wasn't so hurt. Bettany hadn't called and checked on her, not that Kalista expected or wanted her too. Neither had Daddy. Him ignoring her was expected. Out of sight, out of mind, apparently. "I guess," she mumbled.

"I hope you're able to make some friends here. You've sure made my Vivian happy too."

Now she could genuinely smile. She looked past Bo and watched as Viv sprinkled crushed corn nibblets on the ground, the chickens pecking around her. She looked like one of those Disney princesses who could enchant animals. Her stepmother was definitely in her element.

"How's work?" Bo asked. "Seb treating you well?"

Seb? Oh. Mr. Hudson. "I haven't seen him much. I mostly work with Tyler."

"Yeah, he's a great kid. Nicest guy you'll ever meet."

Humph. Bo was already that, in Kalista's mind. The jury was still out on Tyler. He'd been nice to her for a couple of days. Now he was rude, rude, rude.

"Well, gotta get back to the tractor." He grinned at Kalista. "See you at supper tonight."

"See you."

Kalista stayed and watched the pigs for a little while longer after Viv went inside. She was getting a little used to the smell. Or immune to it. Then she realized she was stalling. Time to go to *The Times* office and take care of business.

She drove to Clementine and parked Bo's jalopy in a spot in

front of the building, and the truck was almost straight between the lines. She grabbed her pink Chanel purse and climbed out of the vehicle. Before she'd left Viv's, she'd gone through her suitcases and looked at the clothes she brought. The shorts were too short, the skirts too high, and the shirts too tight—for work anyway. Even though she wasn't throwing papers today, she wanted to look appropriate in case she ran into her boss. Viv loaned her a super cute, light pink dress with capped sleeves and a mid-knee hem.

She walked inside and faced two stairwells—one up and one down. She was unsure where to go first. Tyler could be downstairs in the circulation area or upstairs where the offices were. He might even be on assignment—something she hadn't thought about until just this moment. She put her finger on her chin and tried to decide.

"Kalista?"

Spinning on the heel of her white ballet flat, she turned and saw Tyler. "Hi," she said, giving him a smile and a quick, unnecessary wave. At least she didn't have to hunt him down.

"What are you doing here?"

Flat tone, flat expression, flat . . . everything. It was like he'd turned into a robot.

Let's get this over with. She dug inside her purse for her almost-empty wallet and pulled out the money. "I owe you for the funnel cake." She presented him with the two dollar bills.

He eyed them like he'd never seen cash before.

"Take it!" She thrust it out at him. Why was he such a weirdo?

Tyler shook his head. Even the movement was emotionless. "You don't have to pay me back."

"Yes I do." She hadn't anticipated he wouldn't cooperate. She envisioned him accepting the money and her apology. Then she'd feel better about herself. "I'll pay you back for the gas too."

He didn't say anything, just turned and headed for the bottom stairs.

Ugh, he was infuriating. She marched over to him. "Why are you so mean to me? I know I was rude to you on Saturday. And it was dumb not to check my gas gauge. But that doesn't mean you can treat me like dirt on your shoe."

Tyler pressed his lips together and glanced away. "It's . . . hard to be around you."

So she was right. He thought the same thing Daddy and Ryan did—that she was immature and shallow. Oh great, more tears. Apparently she was also a crybaby. "Got it," she said, her throat hurting. "I won't bother you again."

His eyes grew wide before he turned and headed down the stairs.

She clutched the dollar bills and looked at the empty stairwell. She'd never felt so alone.

Chapter 20

Jade exited the elevator at Baptist Health Medical Center. When she called Logan yesterday, he'd been shocked that she was willing to talk to him. *"What made you change your mind?"* he'd asked as she fast walked to the car rental counter to arrange for another vehicle.

She didn't know how to answer because she wasn't sure. She still wasn't. Maybe it was the lady in the airport who had mentioned her peach cobbler regrets. Or maybe it was because she was filled to the brim with shame and remorse over what she'd done to Sebastian and her own credibility. Maybe it was because she was so tired of the past constantly hovering over her, no matter how much she tried to ignore it or lock it away.

She knew one thing for sure. *I'm tired of being alone.*

Logan apologized for not having a place for her to stay since he was still in the halfway house. That was fine—she didn't mind getting a hotel room. She needed time and space to clear her head. She still had to call Miles and then ask her supervisor for a few days off. She'd planned to do that anyway when Sebastian had asked her to stay.

"Can we meet for coffee in the morning?"

"No." He went quiet, then said. "I'm going to the hospital."

"Are you okay? What happened? I'll come see you right now—"

"It's not me." Another silence. "It's Lydia."

She balked at first, then surprised herself when she agreed to listen as Logan explained her mother's situation. She had liver failure and needed a transplant. She'd been on the list for years and was almost to the top, but it looked like she wouldn't make it.

"That's why I wanted her to see you," he said. "She doesn't have much time left."

Jade went numb. "Okay."

"*Okay?*" he said, irritated. "She's your mother—"

"I know!" Her voice cracked. How was she supposed to feel? Sad? Angry? Worried? She didn't know. She had zero connection to this woman anymore.

"I can meet you around noon," he said. "I wanted to make sure I talked to her doctor, and he usually rounds in the morning."

"Why are you helping her?"

"She's got no one else."

His words hit her square in the chest. She was still thinking about them as she rounded the corner to the hall where Lydia's room was located. Two people were standing halfway down the hallway, speaking to each other in hushed tones. She recognized Logan immediately, but not the tall, winsome black woman he was with.

She paused, her pulse hammering in her head. She told herself she was just here for Logan, that she had no intention of visiting Lydia. Jade wasn't prepared to see her. She didn't want to see her.

Logan looked up. He said something to the woman and hurried toward Jade. "You're here," he said, smiling a little but seemingly confused. "I thought we were meeting later."

"I wanted to talk to you," she said, coming up with an excuse that was only partly the whole truth.

He glanced over his shoulder. "The doctor isn't here yet, but I can tell Tameka to text me when he shows up. There's a waiting area on the other side of the hall—"

"How is she?" Jade's eyes widened, stunned she'd asked the question and even more surprised that she needed to know.

He looked at her, somber now. "Not good. She's got cirrhosis, and it's causing a lot of swelling. They're trying to get fluid off her."

Jade nodded, still composed. "How long does she have?"

"Doctor's not sure. If she doesn't get a transplant, maybe a couple weeks?" Tears filled his eyes. "I hate this for her."

She swallowed. "She did this to herself, Logan."

"You know, if you're going to dog her, just go." He stormed off.

Her temples were pounding. Logan didn't understand. He met Lydia when she was sober. He didn't know her drunk and wasted, only caring about herself. She was probably faking all this for attention, playing on Logan's sympathies—

Stop. Stop, stop, stop!

Jade whirled around and dashed away from the hall. She saw a small private waiting area and ducked inside, grateful it was empty, and dropped onto one of the chairs, her head falling into her hands. Lydia had faked a lot of things, particularly parenthood and sobriety, but she couldn't fake liver failure. The woman was dying, and instead of being empathetic, Jade attacked her. How could she be so coldhearted? Oh, and a thief. She couldn't forget she was that too.

A soft knock sounded on the door. Jade lifted her head and saw Logan. "Can I come in?"

She nodded.

He sat down next to her, leaning his elbows on his knees. They didn't say anything for a long time. Jade didn't mind. Her brother had a solid way about him. That was new, and much different from the volatile kid he'd been in the past. He seemed grounded. *Like Sebastian.*

"I'm sorry," Logan said. "I shouldn't have snapped at you."

"Yes, you should have." She leaned back in the chair, fiddling with the strap of her crossbody purse. "I was out of line."

He sat up and faced her. "Yeah. But it's understandable."

Jade sighed. "Not to me."

"When I first met Lydia in rehab, she took me under her wing. At the time we didn't know our connection to you, but she watched out for me, encouraged me, made sure I was sticking with the program."

Jade fought the stabbing envy. Lydia had been more of a mother to him than she was to her own daughter.

"After we found out who we were, she filled me in on some things."

"I don't want to hear her excuses—"

"Good, because she didn't give any. She took responsibility for everything she'd done to you."

Sure she did. "That's called manipulation, Logan."

"I know manipulation. I'm an expert at it. But I get it—you can't trust her. Just like you can't trust me. And I understand if you don't want to see her. I'm just glad you're talking to me now. We're family, Jade. I don't want to lose that again."

Her eyes stung. *Family.* As a kid, she longed for a permanent one. As an adult, she tried to make a legal one with Logan. And the one biological family member she had—that she knew of anyway— was just down the hall, hanging on to life.

Logan stood. "I told Tameka I'd get her some coffee. She's been amazing through all this."

Jade managed to smile. "I take it she's your girlfriend."

He nodded. "We met at work about a month ago. She's a cashier and is going to UALR to get her degree in education. She has to go to work at three, but she's been here for me as much as she can."

"Then you'd better make her the best cup of coffee she's ever had."

Logan grinned. "When do you go back to Clementine?"

She frowned, then remembered she hadn't told him where she was when she called him from the airport. "I'm not. I'm heading to Atlanta, probably tonight."

"Oh." His smile dimmed. "What about Seb?"

Her heart pinched. "He's . . . working."

"Hopefully you two can get together soon. He's a cool guy." His smile was back. "After the doctor shows up, Tameka and I will take you out before you go. There's a great restaurant out in the Promenade that does Mediterranean fusion. How's that sound?"

"Sounds great. What's a promenade?"

"Outdoor shopping center. A lot has changed since the last time you were here." He left the room.

Jade stared at the picture of watercolor lilies on the opposite wall. She could be in Clementine right now, talking to Evelyn Margot, eating chicken tenders at the Clementine Diner, taking another drive in the country. *Being with Sebastian.*

She shook her head. She could do none of those things ever again. *I did it to myself.*

After a few more minutes, she got up. She had a few hours still before she, Logan, and Tameka went to lunch, and she tried to figure out what to do. She could go back to the hotel and do some work. There was always work to be done. Or she could go shopping. Hit a café for a cappuccino. Take a drive. Find a car wash, for sure. She definitely needed to decompress. There were plenty of things she could do to fill the time.

She left and turned to go back to the elevator. She had taken three steps when she halted. Looked over her shoulder. Why couldn't she leave?

Regrets. She had enough to last a lifetime.

Jade drew in a deep breath . . . and went to Lydia's room.

Plink. Plink. Plink.

Seb stared at the slowly moving river and tossed another stone. He had no idea how long he'd been here this morning. He didn't care either. After he left the Clementine Inn yesterday, he drove to his cabin, intending just to spend a few hours there and go back to work. He had another column to write, since the July Fourth one he'd impulsively penned was too early to go to print. Then there was the article about the fire, and he also needed to get things set up for Flora when she came in the next morning. At least he didn't have to search for the ledger anymore.

Plink. Plink. Plink.

But he didn't go back to Clementine. He turned off his phone for the night, then turned it on again to text Evelyn Margot that he was taking a few days off and she would be in charge of *The Times* until he returned. He hit Send and turned the phone off again.

Normally, being at the cabin brought him peace, particularly when he was outside. But all he felt was turmoil. He did take a stab at writing another chapter in his novel but managed to get out four words before hanging it up. Yeah, he was moping. Big-time. And the best way to get out of a mopey mood was to dive back into work. He probably could do just that if everything didn't remind him of Jade and her duplicity.

Seb went over and over what had happened, from the moment she showed up at his office in Clementine until the ledger fell out of her briefcase. Every single time it came back to one thing—his gullibility. The past rolled through his mind, including their relationship ten years ago. Jade was extremely independent and could be aloof. But once he got to know her, he saw her vulnerability, and that was his Achilles' heel.

Not just with her. Giving Logan a place to stay without knowing anything about him. Hiring Kalista because Bo asked a favor, not because she was the best qualified. He'd only fired two people in his life, but there were a few others he should have given a pink slip to, and he kept them on, costing him time and money. Even now, despite his dangerously low bank account and every single cent he'd made on his book going to the paper, he was trying to figure out ways to keep *The Times* in business. If he didn't stop, he'd go completely broke.

"There you are."

Seb groaned but didn't turn around. *Evelyn Margot.* Of course.

She plopped herself right next to him on the semi-grassy patch of embankment.

"You're supposed to be at work," he muttered.

"So are you."

"What, I can't have a vacation?"

Evelyn scoffed. "Sure you can. But Sebastian Percival Hudson—"

"For the love of—"

"—never, ever takes a vacation. What gives, bro?"

"Mind your own business."

She did a double take. "Wow. It must be bad if you're almost growling at me."

He should apologize, but he didn't have it in him. He tossed a couple more stones into the water.

"You're scaring me a little," she said. "I called you five times. You didn't answer."

"Phone's off."

"Yeah, I know. Talk to me, Sebastian. I know you hate doing that, but I need to know that you're okay. Because right now you're definitely acting like you aren't."

Seb turned from her, pressing his palm to the back of his sun-warmed neck. "I don't know if I can do it."

"Do what?"

"Keep *The Times* going."

"Sure you can. I know things are bad, but you've always found a way."

"Not this time." He turned to her. While he never wanted to see Jade Smith again, she had done one thing for him—snapped him back to reality. For years he'd been riding on hope that things were going to get better with *The Times*. That he could save it. "The press is down again," he said. Paul had called him on the way to the cabin yesterday and given him a dismal report on Ol' Bessie.

"I know. He and Cletus are working on it. They'll have it fixed for Thursday's edition."

"What if they don't? Or what if it breaks down permanently? I don't have the money to buy a new one."

"We can farm out the printing."

"Right. And then we go to digital. Better yet, let's just put the whole thing on the internet."

"Why not?" She held up her hands. "Lots of newspapers are going in that direction."

"Then it wouldn't be *The Times*!" He stared at the river. "Not Buford's anyway."

"Or yours." Evelyn looked at her lap and tugged on the fringed hem of her sixties throwback top. "Why didn't you tell me about this before?"

"Because I thought I could handle it." He grimaced. He remembered the first thing he told Buford when the man offered him the paper. *"I'm not a businessman."* He sure proved that. He also proved that he couldn't trust his own judgment—professional and personal.

"What are you going to do?"

"Sell." He scrambled up off the bank. When he finally got around to turning on his phone, he was sure he'd find a voicemail from Miles. Jade had accomplished her mission. But he wasn't selling it to Harrington. No. Way. There were other media companies that had wanted *The Times* over the past couple of years. He'd contact one of them.

"And that's it?"

He went to the cabin, ignoring her.

"You can't do this!"

Halting his steps, he turned around. "It's my paper. I can do what I want."

Her eyes narrowed. "That's not fair. What about your employees?"

"I'll make sure y'all stay on. That will be part of the deal."

"Sebastian—"

"It's done, Evelyn. I've already decided." The fact that he'd decided just this moment didn't matter. She might be right about moving to digital, and that might keep the paper in business. But he couldn't bear to see Buford's lifelong work, and his own too, go through such a drastic change. Not when he was at the helm.

She jumped in front of him, her hands on her hips, glaring at him. "This isn't like you. Something else happened. Something . . . Where's Jade?"

"She's got nothing to do with this." He stalked toward the cabin again.

"Now I know she does."

He opened the sliding patio door, resisting the urge to slide it shut in Evelyn's face. His sister didn't do anything wrong. Not this time anyway. Actually, not in a long time. Their relationship had always been solid. But part of being her brother was to let her have her say, no matter how long it took, or how much he didn't want to hear it.

"Where is she, Seb?"

"Atlanta." He went to the kitchen counter, grabbed his phone, and turned it on. Might as well start making calls now.

"She really left? I thought—"

"What?"

"Well, Mabel saw you two kissing in the parking lot. She told Clyde, and you know he can't zip his lips for nothing—"

"Stop," he said. Fantastic. Now most of Clementine had gotten the news that he and Jade were making out. "Just . . . stop."

"When are you going to see each other again?"

"We're not."

"But I saw how you two were—"

"What?" he shouted. "*Looking* at each other? We're not googly-eyed teenagers. We're not . . ." His chest felt like a concrete block had fallen on it. "Anything."

Evelyn grew quiet. Tilted her head. "Oh, Sebastian," she said, her expression filling with sympathy. "She was something to you."

He gripped the phone, not looking at her. This was painful—not just Jade's betrayal, but that Evelyn Margot had figured out his feelings so easily, with an assist from Mabel and Clyde. Painful and humiliating.

She went to him and put her arms around him.

Against his will, he hugged her. After a few minutes, he pulled away. "Thanks," he said gruffly.

She nodded. "Anytime."

He didn't feel better, but it was good to know Evelyn had his back. "Don't say anything to the staff," he said. "I don't want them to worry while I find a buyer."

"I won't." Her voice sounded thick. "I wish there was another way."

Seb did too. But there wasn't, and it was past time he accepted it.

Chapter 21

Jade looked at Lydia but didn't move closer to her bed. She barely recognized the frail, sallow-complected woman, her face and abdomen swollen. Her former blazing red hair that had always been chemically enhanced from a drugstore box was a dull, yellowy orange. Her eyes were closed, and Jade didn't know if she was sleeping or . . .

The lump in her throat grew. During her childhood, she'd witnessed Lydia in various states of health, mostly bad ones. But even when she was using and drinking herself to oblivion, she hadn't looked as bad as she did now. Reality slammed into her. *Mom is dying.*

Lydia's eyes opened, and as if she sensed someone in the room, she turned her head. "Who's there?"

Jade clasped her shaking hands. She could still leave. Lydia didn't know she was here, and she'd tell Logan not to say anything to her. He and Tameka had taken their coffees and gone to the waiting area. Jade appreciated their respect of her privacy, but it might be for nothing.

"I know someone's there," she said weakly. "Come on in."

She stepped from the shadows and neared the bed.

Lydia's eyes widened. "Jade? Is that you?"

All she could do was nod.

Her mother smiled. Jade noticed she was missing some teeth—one on the top and two on the bottom. From drugs? Liver failure? It just added to her pitiful appearance. She took a couple steps forward, still keeping her distance.

"I can't believe you're here." She kept her gaze on Jade's as if she had never seen her before. "Did Logan talk to you?"

"Yes."

"He's a great kid. It's so fortunate we met." Her eyes shifted to the seat by her bed. "Do you want to sit down?"

No. She wanted to leave, but not because she was angry. Not anymore. It was hard to be mad at someone who was suffering. All she felt was compassion, and she didn't want that feeling. Not where Lydia was concerned.

"Or you can stand." Lydia managed a faint smile. "I'm just glad to see you. I wish it was under better circumstances." Her voice was breathy too, as if she were struggling to fill her lungs with air.

Jade looked at the wires coming from different places on her body, hooked up to several machines. She had no idea what they were for—just that they were probably keeping her alive somehow.

"I guess Logan told you about my liver. I pickled it, Jade. All this"—she lifted her hand slightly, revealing the white cords attached—"is my doing."

That was the first time she'd heard her mother take responsibility for anything without blaming someone else.

"There's still some hope," Lydia continued. "I'm first on the list now, according to the nurse who was in here a few minutes ago."

She stopped speaking and licked her lips. "Never thought I'd have to wait for someone to die so I could live."

Jade's hand went to her aching heart. She sat down on the chair, fighting tears.

"Hey, I didn't mean to make you cry." Lydia sighed. "I've done enough of that. And I don't want our visit to be sad."

Was she serious? "You're dying, Mom. How is that not sad?"

"I'm still here. And I want to get to know you again. Tell me what you've been doing in Atlanta. How's your job? Are you married?"

"No," she said, shifting in her chair. "I'm not married."

"Well, I'm sure a pretty woman like you will find a nice man soon enough."

She already had. And because of her decisions, she lost him . . . twice.

Jade answered her questions, and Lydia told her about how she'd landed in rehab after falling off the wagon. "I'd been sober for six years," she said.

Jade's mouth dropped open. "What?"

"I got clean in '98—"

"And you didn't tell me?" All this time she'd been sure Lydia was still using. Still bouncing from man to man, jail cell to jail cell, living life on her own terrible, selfish terms.

"I wanted to. But the last time we spoke, you said you never wanted to see me again."

That was true. Lydia had called her, begging for money. Jade didn't have it to give, since she was still bailing Logan out and paying legal bills. The last straw was Lydia not bothering with even the most surface pleasantries. No "Hello. How are you doing? I miss you." Just a demand for cash, as if she were entitled to it.

"Logan told me that you said the same thing to him."

She looked at her lap. "I had to."

"I know. And you did the right thing, for both of us. When I got clean, I was able to see what I'd done to you. I was ashamed, and still am. I thought more about what I wanted than what my own child needed. By some miracle you were able to live a normal life and be successful on your own. You didn't need or want me."

"Mom—"

"You had every right not to. The reason I stayed away was I knew you were better off without me. Simple as that. I ended up drinking again, but I got myself in rehab real quick. I didn't want to lose my spot on the transplant list." Her eyes started to close. "Sorry, honey. I get tired easily."

"It's okay. You can sleep if you need to."

Lydia nodded off for a couple of minutes, then woke up again. She turned to Jade. "I hope someday you can forgive me. I do love you. I was terrible at showing it, and if the Lord gives me a little more time, I want to . . ."

Jade wiped her eyes as Lydia dozed again. Her emotions tumbled all over each other as she tried to process everything. For the first time, she actually believed her mother. *She loves me.* She reached for her hand, something she hadn't done in years. Decades.

And she wasn't letting go.

———

Two weeks after Kalista had tried to pay Tyler back—he was still refusing to acknowledge her existence—her life had settled into somewhat of a rhythm. She helped Viv and Bo with the morning chores and had been very excited to find out one of Bo's sows was pregnant and would give birth in a month. She was excited that she would get to see the piglets.

She was also pleased to help Viv with the wedding plans—particularly addressing envelopes in calligraphy once she felt brave enough to learn. She was surprised how much she enjoyed penning the fancy script, and when Viv decided she wanted calligraphy on the thank-you notes too, Kalista eagerly offered to do them all. She was also learning to cook . . . a little. That wasn't as much fun as calligraphy, but she could make a good baked potato and some passable spaghetti and meatballs.

Daddy still hadn't called her, and Kalista still didn't have access to her phone. She didn't care as much anymore, now that she was diligent in checking her gas tank and had read almost all of the Jane Austen novels on Viv's bookcase. She didn't bother with the TV anymore, or the radio. It was more fun to sit on the front porch and read.

She did wish she would hear from Daddy. Didn't he miss her, even a little? She kept that to herself, though, and she refused to call him. She shouldn't have to chase down her own father.

Her paper delivery job was going well too. She could hurl a newspaper with almost flawless accuracy, and she had started taking treats to little Pepé, at Viv's suggestion. He literally ate them out of her hand. How sweet.

But nothing between her and Tyler had changed. Not on his end anyway. Unfortunately she had suddenly and without warning been obsessing over him—covertly watching him when he was working with the other carriers or talking to Cletus and Paul. She'd even taken to lingering after coming back from her deliveries so she could catch a glimpse of him. Since he was oblivious to her, she didn't have to worry about getting caught, and she could admire him from afar. The more she was around him, the cuter he was. Not just cute. *Le* cute. Cute infinity. And when he took off his glasses to wipe them on the edge of his T-shirt . . . *le sigh.*

"Kalista?"

She glanced up from the envelope she'd been addressing and looked at Viv. "Yes?"

"Everything okay?"

"Sure." It wasn't. However, everything wasn't bad either. "Why?"

"You were sighing."

She was?

"Have you heard from Raymond at all?"

"No." She applied the fountain pen tip and made a black swirling O.

"Hmm. Maybe I'll give him a call."

Kalista's head popped up. "Why? Did I do something wrong?"

Viv gave her a sweet smile, one that made Kalista warm inside. Like she was loved. "Not at all. I think you've acclimated faster to Clementine than I did. I was just wondering if you were feeling homesick."

She thought about it. "Not really." She went back to writing.

"You don't miss home? Your friends?"

"A little. I miss the beach." But even as she said that, it wasn't the beach parties or being seen at them. She missed the sound of the waves, the sand in her toes, the salt in the air.

"I like the beach too." Viv picked up her pen. "But I'm glad everything is going well for you."

Kalista was about to nod, then stopped. "There is, um, one thing."

"What's that?"

"Do you know Tyler Hernandez?"

"April and José's boy? Yes, he's a very nice young man."

If she had to hear one more time how nice Tyler was . . . "I think . . . I think I kinda like him."

"Ooh." Viv put down her pen and rested her hand on her chin, curiosity sparking in her eyes. "Do tell."

Now *this* was the Viv she remembered—the one who liked a little bit of drama. She told Viv about how she was rude to him at the hoedown, and ever since then he wouldn't talk to her. "I even tried to pay him back for the funnel cake. Twice. He wouldn't accept my money."

"That sounds like Tyler."

"But he acts like I don't exist." Her mood was deflating. It was hard to admit she wasn't appealing to him. "He even said it's hard to be around me."

"He said that?"

"Uh-huh."

She sat back up. "That *doesn't* sound like him. Are you sure he said those exact words?"

"Yes." Why was she pushing this point? "He doesn't want to be around me. Ryan didn't either. Daddy definitely doesn't—"

"Your father loves you."

"He sent me away."

"To learn how to be an adult. And you've made a lot of progress."

"Thanks," she mumbled. But that still didn't change the truth. She was unlikable.

Viv got up to get a glass of tea.

Kalista resumed her calligraphy. What else was there to say? She couldn't make Tyler like her. Which was a shame, because she really, really liked him. Everybody else at work did too, and he seemed to like them. The only person he had a problem with was . . . *her*.

When she sat back down, Viv said, "Have you tried talking to Tyler?"

"Yes, a couple of times. I gave up, though."

"Maybe you're giving up too soon."

"Viv—"

"I've got an idea. It's a little sneaky, though. And you'll have to tell him everything that's on your mind . . . and heart."

That sounded scary. But if it would get him to talk to her again, she was willing to do almost anything. She didn't expect him to like her. That was an impossibility. But it would be nice if he stopped ignoring her. "Okay."

She grinned. "Here's what we're going to do."

———

"That's wonderful news, Logan." Jade tucked her Razr in the crook of her neck as she pushed the elevator button on the bottom floor of the Harrington Media building. When she returned to Atlanta a little over a week ago, she'd gotten a new briefcase with a flawless latch—she'd tested it several times at the store to make sure. She put her cell back to her ear. "Any news on the transplant?"

"No," he said. "But the doctors are more optimistic about her prognosis now that she's not retaining as much fluid anymore. They're surprised too. They'd been so sure she wasn't going to make it."

A chill went through her. "What changed?"

"I think it was you, Jade. Those three days you spent with her perked her up. Like she had something to live for again."

Jade doubted that, but Logan sounded convinced. The elevator door opened. "I'll check back later today," she said. "Gotta run, I've got an appointment first thing this morning."

"Good luck. Love you, sis."

"Love you too." She hopped on the empty elevator and hit the button, then leaned against the wall, relieved. During her stay in

Little Rock, she'd spent hours with Lydia, and they'd gotten to know each other again. Jade found out things about her mother's childhood that mirrored her own. Lydia had repeated the patterns, and she was thankful Jade had broken them.

On her last day, the doctors said she was well enough to be released. She did look a lot better—definitely less swollen. Jade wasn't sure about her staying in her apartment alone, but Logan had asked for early release from the halfway house, and because of his stellar recovery, it was granted. He moved in with Lydia, and Jade couldn't thank him enough. Since her return to Atlanta, she called them both every day, sometimes more than once.

She smiled. They were family. *Her* family.

The doors opened and she hustled to her cubicle. She wasn't used to taking time off, and because it had been unexpected, work had backed up. She was plowing through it, though, and she would finish if she worked the weekend. But she wasn't going to. Not this time. She planned to go to Peachtree City, rent a golf cart, and drive the paths that connected the shopping villages in the city. It was a little more than half an hour away, but she'd never visited before. There was always work to do instead.

"Mornin' sunshine." Charlotte Rae was standing by Jade's cubicle, holding a mug of peppermint tea.

"Good morning." Jade smiled at her friend and set her new briefcase on the floor.

"Did I mention how nice it is to see you cheery and smiling?"

"A couple times." She sat down and powered up her computer. "But I don't mind hearing it again."

"I don't mind saying it either. How's your mother?"

On her first day back, Jade had filled Charlotte in on her mother and brother, but she didn't go into too much detail and Charlotte didn't ask. She did want to know how her trip to Clementine was, and Jade wasn't sure how to answer. She had landed on "Unexpected" and left it at that.

"I have a proposition." Charlotte grinned.

Jade glanced at her polar bear sitting near her computer. She'd ended up naming her Polly, and while Charlotte had raised a thin eyebrow when she'd brought it into work and set it on her desk, Jade didn't care, and she didn't explain. She needed something tangible from Clementine. From Sebastian. Eventually she'd take it back home and, at some point, donate it. But right now Polly reminded her of better times. "Do I want to hear this?"

"I've found the perfect man for you."

Jade's stomach sank. She should have known Charlotte wasn't going to give up.

Over the past two weeks she'd tried to put Sebastian out of her mind. It was difficult, and even Lydia had sensed she was holding something back when she talked about why she was in Clementine. Jade finally told her everything.

"*That's it?*" Lydia had said, her brow lifting. She could sit up now and was eating a small cup of vanilla pudding. "*You're not going to make things right?*"

"*He's not going to listen to me, Mom. I wouldn't either if I were him.*"

"*But what if—*"

She'd shut the conversation down at that point. Her mother meant well, but she didn't understand, mostly because Jade didn't want to discuss her past mistakes with Sebastian. She wanted to forget the latest one, like she'd managed to do ten years ago. Two weeks wasn't long enough. Two decades might not be either. Not this time, and that was her own fault.

"Charlotte, I'm not—"

"Just hear me out. His mom is friends with my aunt, and he just moved back to Atlanta. He's a lawyer, so you two have your big brains in common. He's thirty-one. A bit younger than you but he's not opposed to dating a cougar."

Good grief. "You told him about me?"

"Of course I did. And he was very, very interested. Oh, and here's the best part. He's hot. *Really* hot. Like I said, he's perfect."

Jade doubted that. Sebastian was perfection. Her heart squeezed as the computer screen flickered to life. "Thanks, Charlotte. I'm not interested."

Charlotte's expression fell and she handed Jade a business card. "Take it. Just in case."

She hesitated, then accepted it, not bothering to look at the information. She set it aside just as her office phone rang. Charlotte nodded and slipped away while Jade answered it. "Jade Smith."

"Hello, Ms. Smith."

Uh-oh. "Hi, Tifanni."

"Mr. Harrington would like to see you in his office as soon as possible."

This couldn't be good. Her interaction with Miles had been brief since she left Clementine. Her quick phone call to him after she left the Little Rock airport had taken only two minutes, if that. "Mr. Hudson isn't going to sell."

"I'm the one who will determine that," Miles countered, not hiding his annoyance. "When can I talk to him?"

She hesitated. Sebastian had agreed to listen to Miles, but that was before he found out she'd taken his ledger. He had no reason to follow through on that promise. Miles was wasting his time anyway. "I couldn't convince him to do that either." Not the truth, but not quite a full lie. That would be her last one.

The silence on the other end of the line was harrowing, and she expected him to rant at her at any second. Instead, he said, "Thank you for trying."

When she got back to work, she expected he would want to meet with her for a more thorough explanation. He'd spent the money on her plane tickets, and under normal circumstances she would have expensed everything else she'd spent on the trip other than the extra flight. Since she failed in every single way, other than reconciling with her family, she would pay for the rest. She'd lost her raise and bonus, but having Logan and Lydia back in her life in a healthy way was priceless. Fortunately Miles had been ignoring her, and she thought she was in the clear. Until now.

"I'll be right up." She hung up the phone and stared at her screen. This was it. She was going to get fired. Or at least yelled at. Although she didn't agree with Miles acquiring *The Times*, she let him—and herself—down.

Bracing for the worst, she made her way to his office. When she entered the reception area, Tifanni was tapping away at her computer. She gave her a quick glance. "He's waiting on you."

Her coldness wasn't a good sign. Jade walked into the office.

Miles stood in front of one of the large windows overlooking the downtown Atlanta landscape. Her hands started to shake as she waited for him to turn around. She thrust them behind her. For a man in a hurry to talk to her, he was taking his time. If he was trying to scare her, it was working—she felt like throwing up.

Finally he turned around, expressionless. Then he took a step toward her, and another one. "I'm not a man who second-guesses himself, Ms. Smith. I also like coming up with creative solutions to problems. I thought I had when I sent you to Clementine. I thought it was a simple assignment, and that you understood how important it was. It became clear soon after you arrived that I may have made a mistake, but I was willing to give you time. I foolishly trusted you."

Jade was stunned. Where was this coming from? "You can trust me, Mr. Harrington. Sebast—Mr. Hudson is adamant about keeping *The Times*."

"Then explain why he's not only willing to sell, but he's also shopping the paper around. To everyone but me."

"What?"

"You lied to me, Ms. Smith." He continued moving until he was standing in front of her. He wasn't as tall as Sebastian, but he could still look down on her.

"But I didn't. I promise, he told me he wasn't going to sell. He said that several times."

"Then he lied to you." His eyes narrowed. "I don't like being stabbed in the back."

Her mind was reeling. Surely Miles was wrong. Sebastian would never sell the paper, much less seek out buyers. "I would never..." She'd been underhanded in taking Sebastian's ledger, but she wasn't that cutthroat. "You have to believe me."

"Then prove it. Go back to Clementine. Make sure he sells the paper to me."

"I...can't."

"Can't or won't?"

She paused. This didn't make sense. Sebastian loved *The Times*. Something must have happened to make him change his mind, but she couldn't imagine what would drive him to go against his principles and give up the newspaper that meant so much to him.

"Got my answer," he sneered. "You're fired. I want you gone within the hour."

"But—"

"You can forget working in this industry too. No one's going to hire a traitor." He turned around and walked back to the window.

Jade froze. There was nothing she could say. Or do. She couldn't fix this or prove her loyalty. Numb, she turned around and left.

Tifanni didn't look at her, and Jade suspected she'd known ahead of time what the meeting was about.

Jade hurried out of the office to her cubicle. She sank down on her chair. Ten years. Two years at PU, then eight when it was sold to Harrington. And it wasn't just this job she'd lost. She'd lost her credibility and her ability to work in media. Probably in the whole city.

Consequences. This was the consequence of stealing the ledger. Losing her job. Her reputation. Sebastian. All because of one horrible decision. It didn't matter that it was an accident—she shouldn't have snuck into his office to start with. The worst part? She knew better and did it anyway.

Charlotte Rae poked her head over the cubicle wall. "I'm getting another cup of tea. Do you want— Oh no." She rushed over to Jade. "You look like death. What happened?"

"I'm fired." She got up and grabbed her briefcase. Opened it and put in the few personal items she had. She didn't even need the standard cardboard box.

"What? I don't understand."

Jade closed the briefcase. "I'll call you later."

"Jade—"

She rushed out of the building. She'd get a call from HR, probably within the hour, to finalize the severance. Heat hit her as she rushed to the parking deck. June had arrived with a vengeance. Reaching her car, she got inside, turned on the engine, and let the air conditioner do its thing.

Fired. She'd never been fired in her life. She expected her financial mind to kick in and go over her bank accounts, her savings, her 401(k), her stock portfolio. None of them were robust, due to paying off debt. Who knew how long it would take for her to find another job, or even decide where to look?

But none of that was at the forefront. All she could think about was *The Times* and Sebastian. She had to find out why he was selling. Calling him was out of the question. Visiting was too. Mabel had seen her last interaction with him, and she was sure Sebastian had told Evelyn Margot about the betrayal.

Wait. Maybe there was someone she could call. And maybe, hopefully, there would be something she could do.

Chapter 22

Kalista waited by Bo's truck for Tyler to arrive. Her hands were damp, and even the mountain air and scent of pine didn't soothe her nerves. It didn't help that it was muggy and hot—something Viv had warned her about the weather once summer was in full swing. She was parked on the side of the road in the middle of her route, not that far from Mr. Hudson's cabin, per Viv's instructions last night. *"You'll have to fake a breakdown,"* she'd said while they were still on the porch. *"That way you can get him alone. There won't be any distractions or an escape."*

"How do I do that?"

"Bo will know. He's inside."

Kalista listened as Bo told her what to do to the engine after she parked it. It was simple—just loosening a wire. She didn't know the name of it or what it was hooked to, she just did what he said. *"Tyler will figure it out quick, though,"* Bo pointed out. *"He's a smart cookie."*

"Then you'll have to work fast, Kalista." Viv smiled. *"Think you're up to this?"*

She wasn't sure, but it was worth a try. He hadn't been happy when she called him about thirty minutes ago, telling him the truck had broken down. She was also sure he'd be even more irritated when he found out it was just a loose wire. It was a risk she was willing to take.

When she saw his car heading her way, she smoothed the dress Viv let her borrow—a cute, conservative sheath she paired with her sandals. Definitely modest, and not her normal delivery girl attire. She'd curled her hair instead of just putting it up in a ponytail, and she'd taken off her overgrown acrylics over a week ago and had given herself a plain manicure. She missed her long nails, though. Regardless of how things turned out in the future, she wasn't going to give up her mani-pedis.

Tyler pulled behind the truck. Sure enough, there was a scowl on his face when he approached her, carrying a toolbox. Scowling didn't suit him. Smiling did, and if Viv's plan worked and she could talk to him for longer than a minute, she might turn his frown upside down.

"Did you look under the hood?" he said, blowing right past her and straight to the front of the truck.

"Um, no." An itsy-bitsy lie because she'd been fiddling with the wire under it when she called him.

"Pop it for me."

"I will . . . in a minute."

He turned around. "What?"

"I'll pop the hood in a minute." She walked toward him, keeping her gaze on his. "After we talk."

Tyler took a step back. "Just pop the hood, Kalista."

"After we talk."

He stepped back again, his foot slipping on the gravel road. The toolbox hit the ground as he flailed, trying to get his balance. Then he fell down the incline.

"Tyler!" She ran after him. How could she be so dumb to park next to the edge of the road like that? When she reached him, he was on his back in a thick patch of grass. "Are you okay?"

He sat up and blinked. "I think so."

"Oh, thank goodness." She automatically grabbed his hand. "I was afraid you were hurt."

"I'm fine." Tyler yanked his hand out of her grasp.

"I'm sorry." Her bottom lip quivered. "I just wanted—"

"What," he snapped. "You want what?"

"To know why it's hard to be around me."

When he didn't answer, she got to her feet. How embarrassing. She shouldn't have listened to Viv, although it wasn't her fault. "Doesn't matter anyway," she said, turning to leave. She'd fix the truck herself. "I already know."

He bounced to his feet. "Huh?"

"You don't want to be around me because I'm immature and shallow. The end."

His brow hit his hairline. "What? No. You're neither of those things."

"I'm not?"

"Of course not." His expression relaxed. "You've never been late to work, I've gotten calls about how nice you are when you deliver the paper, and Mrs. Joyce says Pepé adores you."

"He does like his treats."

"You also cleaned the circulation room without me asking. I'd been meaning to get to it, but I haven't had the time."

"It was kind of fun." In addition to always having a chef, her father had employed many maids over the years. Kalista rarely had to clean anything, but when she decided to tackle the circulation room, she discovered she enjoyed organizing. She'd also gotten a chance to interact with Cletus and Paul, who showed her how the press worked.

But Tyler was confusing her. "Then why do you keep ignoring me?"

He looked down at his feet. Kicked a stone with his sneaker. She half expected him to say, *"Aw, shucks."* Instead, he said, "Because I like you."

Kalista crossed her arms. "You have a funny way of showing it."

"Mr. Hudson didn't want me to get my feelings mixed up with business, so I knew I had to keep my distance. And I tried, but when I saw you at Viv's house during the hoedown . . . Gosh, Kalista, you're so pretty."

"Aw," she said, leaving off the shucks. "Thank you. I'm sorry I made you mad that day."

"I wasn't mad. I was disappointed. I know you're out of my league. So I had to stay away from you. The more I'm around you, the more I like you."

She did a double take. "Wait . . . You like me . . . like that?"

He nodded, finally looking at her, his cheeks red and his glasses slipping to the end of his nose. He pushed them up. "Yes," he said softly. "I do."

Kalista smiled. *Why is he so adorable?* "I'm not out of your league, Tyler."

He scoffed. "Yeah. Right. You're just being nice to me."

Oh, the irony of him thinking she was nice. Then again, maybe she was. She'd changed since coming to Clementine. She didn't mind not having her phone, music, or TV because she'd fallen in love with classic literature. She enjoyed her job when she thought she would hate it, and she loved getting closer to Viv. She even looked forward to slopping the hogs in the morning. *Who am I?*

She smiled. She was Kalista Louise Clark, and the most irresistible guy she'd ever met had just told her that he liked her. But he didn't believe that she could like him. Time to redress his assumption. Ooh, even her vocabulary was changing. *Thanks, Jane Austen.*

"Is there any way I can convince you that I'm telling you the truth?"

His chocolate-brown eyes widened. "Huh?" he said again.

She leaned forward and kissed his cheek. "Does this help?" His little gasp made her smile and boosted her confidence. She kissed his other cheek, letting her lips linger. "Or this?"

He pulled back, not saying anything, still looking shocked.

Oh no. This was a mistake. He was her boss, and he just said he couldn't get involved with her. Just when she was going to apologize again, he said, "I think you missed a spot."

"Where?

"Right. Here." He touched his mouth.

She inwardly squealed and gave him a light kiss. "Now do you believe me?"

He took her hand. "I might need more convincing later."

Absolutely adorable. Although she didn't want to, she dropped his hand. At his surprised look, she said, "We're at work. We have to be professional."

"Oh. That's right."

She turned and headed for the truck.

"Where you going?" Tyler asked.

Grinning, she said, "To fix the engine."

His mouth dropped open. "You know how?"

"Of course I do. I'm the one who broke it."

Seb stared at the computer screen as he read the latest email from Bennett Communications. After coming back from his cabin and beginning his search for buyers for *The Times*, he discovered that everyone was doing business through email now—at least the communication part. That was when he noticed his computer was missing. Evelyn Margot had fessed up, pointing out that it had taken him forever to even notice it was gone. Touché, but he was angry anyway. All she had to do was ask for it and he would have given it to her.

She'd quickly returned it, and he'd given himself a crash course on all things Mac.

He had to admit it did make some things easier. He would never write on one, though.

Writing. Not only hadn't he worked on his novel since Jade's betrayal, but he hadn't written another column. No one seemed to miss it much either. Then again, he'd kept to himself except for the occasional discussion with Flora, who still didn't know about the impending sale and hadn't been able to make money appear out of thin air, which only proved that selling was the right thing to do. He did give out assignments and edited articles, but he was more hands-off than he'd ever been. Subconscious or not, he was pulling away. Hopefully that would make the inevitable easier to swallow.

He leaned forward and read the screen.

Dear Mr. Hudson,

Per your last email, I have put together a final proposal for purchase of *The Clementine Times*, incorporating your requests and suggestions. Once you've read this document and agree to the terms, we will execute the contract.

We look forward to *The Times* joining our family of community newspapers.

Sincerely,
Elizabeth Vuong

Seb sat back, the wheels of his antique chair squeaking. He'd been going back and forth with Bennett, and the negotiations had gone smoothly. His biggest demand was that every single employee and delivery person would keep their job or get a severance if they decided not to stay. He had to take care of his people.

As for him, he would get a nice chunk from the sale. Not as much as if he'd gone with another company, and Harrington had offered the most. But integrity meant more than dollars, and he believed Bennett would do right by *The Times* and the Clementine community. He hoped so anyway. He didn't trust his judgment anymore, but he'd done as much due diligence as he could.

His hand hovered above the keyboard. It was still weird to use something other than a typewriter, but he was getting used to it. He'd learned some shortcuts to avoid the mouse, a gadget he found even more unnatural to utilize. Once he read the document and gave Bennett the go-ahead, he'd finish cleaning up his office. He was being forced to do it now, and he was trying to decide how much of Buford's and *The Times*'s history he needed to preserve. The task had kept him busy, along with the complete overhaul of his house. His days of disorganization and inattention to his surroundings were gone. Something positive that had come out of Jade's duplicity. If he'd been more careful with the ledger, she wouldn't have had the opportunity to take it.

That didn't mean she wouldn't have taken something else.

He shook her from his thoughts. Once he sold *The Times*, he was going on a long break. He'd spend some time at the cabin, but he was looking to get farther away for a while. He'd always thought about traveling out west. Or to a foreign country. He needed a complete change of scenery and plenty of activity to get Jade Smith completely out of his head and heart. Her betrayal should have been enough.

He hated that it wasn't.

A knock sounded at the door and Evelyn Margot came in. She'd stopped putting his portrait outside the door and had treated him with kid gloves. She'd also tried convincing him not to sell, but he was resolute. Thankfully she hadn't brought up Jade. Evelyn didn't know what had happened, and he wasn't going to tell her or anyone else. He didn't need to look any more imbecilic than he already felt.

"Hey, bro." She walked toward him. "Time for our staff meeting."

He frowned. "What staff meeting?"

"The one we're having in"—she glanced at her watch—"two minutes."

"I didn't call a meeting."

"I know. I did." She grinned. "Now chop-chop, you don't want to be late. Bad form for the boss to be tardy."

"I'm busy," he said, looking at the screen again. "You called the meeting, you hold it."

"I am. That's why I'm telling you that you have to be there."

Seb rolled his eyes. "Fine. If it will get you out of my office." He pushed back from his desk as she beamed.

"Trust me, you're not going to want to miss this."

He doubted that. He hadn't held a full staff meeting since Flora's retirement party. But he was intrigued. What was his sister up to?

When he walked into the conference room, Flora, Cletus, Paul, and Tyler were at the table. Their confused expressions told him this meeting was a complete surprise to them too. Plain red folders were on the table in front of them, and another one was by an empty chair.

"Have a seat," Evelyn said to him.

He sat down and reached for the folder.

"Not yet." She stood at the head of the table, more business-like than he'd ever seen her. "You're all probably wondering why I called you here today."

"Yes," they all said in unison.

She blinked. "It's no secret *The Times* is struggling."

Seb scowled. "Evelyn Margot—"

"Before you get in a snit, Sebastian Perc—"

"Don't you dare."

She nodded. "Is there anyone here who's surprised by that news?"

"I'm sure not," Flora said.

"Me neither," Cletus added while Paul nodded.

"It's been pretty obvious," Tyler mumbled.

Great. Flora obviously knew, but to see his staff so aware of his failure was humiliating. He glared at Evelyn. Why was she doing this?

"And would everyone agree that we should do anything possible to save it?"

"Yes," they all said at the same time.

Had Evelyn told them about the sale? He couldn't tell.

"I've found a way." She grinned. "Well, not me. Someone else, and she's here to explain her proposal."

Seb turned to see Jade walking into the room. His breath caught and his jaw tightened at the same time. Whatever she had to say, he wasn't going to listen to it. He started to get up. "Evelyn, out in the hallway. Now."

She shook her head. "Not until you hear Jade out."

He was trapped and he didn't like it. He was also going to fire Evelyn when he was done. If he didn't strangle her first.

Jade went to the head of the table and Evelyn stepped away. The woman was all business in her crimson power suit, white blouse, hair slicked back in a sleek ponytail that accentuated her gorgeous face. How could he still think she was beautiful after what she'd done?

"Hello," she said, placing her fingertips on the table. "I'm Jade Smith. It's nice to meet you all. Thanks for giving me a few minutes of your time." She looked at everyone but Seb. "This won't take long. If you're unaware, there's been a concerted effort by megacorporations to acquire community and local newspapers. This is happening all over the country. The reasons are varied—some companies truly want to see newspapers thrive and are a godsend to the ones that are struggling or completely going under. Others are trying to enhance their own growth and are eager to fold them into their portfolios. I'm not here to make a moral judgment about either, only to confess my part in trying to take over *The Clementine Times*."

Seb was shocked. So was everyone else, and they listened attentively to her explanation of Harrington Media and how she'd come here to get Seb to talk to them. "I wasn't completely above board," she said, moving her hands behind her back.

That was the only indication of emotion from her as she admitted to taking the ledger. "I was wrong. So wrong." For the first time she looked at Seb. "And I'm sorry."

He didn't look away, and he knew he was the only one in the room who could detect her discomfiture. Didn't matter, though. He didn't care if she was sincere or not. The damage was done.

"I understand if you refuse to consider my idea," she said to him, then turned to everyone else.

Seb couldn't take it anymore. He got up and stalked out of the room, straight to his office. She could tell them whatever she wanted. He owned the paper, he was going to do what he thought was right, and he wasn't going to be a part of her conscience cleanse. He banged his fist on his desk. The nerve . . . She was worse than he ever knew.

"Sebastian."

He whirled around and glared at Evelyn, who was holding one of the red folders. "You'd better leave now," he growled. "I'm this close to doing something I'll regret."

She shut the door behind her, unfazed. "You shouldn't have left."

He paced. "How could you do this without telling me?"

"Because it was the only way. You wouldn't have listened. She called me a few days ago and told me everything. Trust me, I was mad. But then she explained her idea and that she could present it to us. It's solid, Seb. It will save *The Times*." She held it out in front of him. "Just take a look at it."

His mind went back to the day Jade had walked into his office and had held out the Harrington folder the same way his sister was holding out this one. "Fine," he said, snatching it from her. "Now get out."

Evelyn complied and shut the door behind her.

Seb stalked to the trash can, ready to drop the folder where it belonged. He held it up, then held back. He was furious with Evelyn, but he knew she loved *The Times* as much as he did, and she wasn't a pushover. So whatever Jade had said to convince her to set up the meeting behind his back had to have merit.

What if Jade was right? What if her proposal would keep *The Times* going? Was he going to let his personal feelings and judgment get in the way of a sound business decision?

He plopped down in his chair, ignored the groaning squeaks, and opened the folder. True to Jade form, the proposal was thorough, organized . . . and good. Really good. He sat back and looked through the prospectus. She was proposing that some form of ownership, either partial or total, was made available to Clementine residents. There were a whole bunch of numbers and equations and business terms he wasn't familiar with, but Flora would be. She could examine the financial merits and plan implementation and give him some insight.

When he got to the back of the folder, there was a handwritten note. He pulled it out, recognizing the script. He almost didn't read it, then forced himself to.

Dear Sebastian,

If you've made it to this note, I thank you for reading the proposal. I wouldn't have blamed you if you didn't. I want to explain to you why I did this.

I found out from Miles that you were selling The Times, and I was shocked and saddened. I know how much you love this paper and Clementine. I couldn't stand the idea of you giving it up. I talked with an acquisitions and merger expert, and she helped me develop this plan. It's only a summary, and there are lots of moving pieces to make it happen. If you and your staff decide you want to go this route, she'll help you with the details.

I'm not good with words like you are, but I'll try anyway. I'm so, so sorry for taking your ledger and for sneaking into your office. I take every bit of responsibility for it. But that's not my biggest regret.

I always seem to get in my own way, and that comes from only trusting myself. I should have trusted you enough to tell you about trying to adopt Logan. I should have told you about the ledger as soon as I took it. I should have let myself do the easiest thing in the world—

allowing you fully into my life. I was a fool, Sebastian. I still am.

I hope this plan will save The Times, and I hope it will in some small part make up for my mistakes. Most of all, I hope someday you can forgive me.

Jade

Seb dropped the letter, dashed out the door, and went down the hall to the conference room. It was empty except for Evelyn. "Where is she?" he demanded.

"She left. Everyone liked the plan, by the way—"

"Later," he said, racing out of the room. There was something more important he had to do.

Chapter 23

Jade sat in her rental car, which ended up being another little Nissan that she enjoyed driving. She blew out a breath and stared at *The Times* building in front of her, once again letting the air-conditioning cool her face. But she wasn't just hot from the warm summer air. Seeing Sebastian again had only confirmed how big of an idiot she was. From the moment she'd had her idea for Clementonians to own the paper, she couldn't stop thinking about him and her regrets. She hadn't expected him to welcome her with open arms, but seeing his hard expression when she walked in, then his quick exit from their meeting pierced her heart.

She had to push her personal feelings aside and explain the proposal, and was thrilled with how it was received. Evelyn had told her they would be in touch with Rachel Lewis, the specialist that had helped Jade put together the proposal, and Jade quickly hurried by Sebastian's office, not looking to see if he was reading the documents. Her job was done, and while it made her feel a little better that the staff was so receptive, she also felt awful knowing that was truly the last time she'd ever see him.

There was nothing else for her to do than head to Little Rock. She was going to spend a week with Logan and Lydia . . . Mom. Then she'd reevaluate her options, as few as they were. Her family was surprised she'd come back so soon. They were happy too, and so was she. Being with them would be a balm to her broken heart. Not a complete one, but she'd take it.

She looked over her shoulder to back out of the parking space when she heard a knock on her window. Turning, she saw a familiar pair of khaki trousers, right at the beltline. Her heartbeat pulsed, but she tempered it. Sebastian was probably here to throw her proposal in her face, although she couldn't see him doing something so melodramatic. She could see him telling her never to come back. No worries there.

He motioned for her to open the door.

Jade drew in a deep breath and did as he asked, although they kept their distance as she stepped out and closed the car door behind her. "I'm sorry," she said, tears forming in her eyes. "I'm so stupid—"

"You're not. The plan is brilliant. I think you saved *The Times*."

Her heart soared.

"What about Harrington?" he asked. "I never heard from him."

"I told him you wouldn't sell. Later he told me you were shopping it around. Why?"

"I'm not a businessman, Jade. I never was. I tried my best to keep things going, but I couldn't keep doing it."

"It's not your fault the newspaper business is in turmoil."

"Maybe not, but I should have done things differently. Talked with a financial adviser. Developed a strategy with Flora. I . . . I don't know what else, but I'm sure there're other things I could have done. I felt beholden to Buford's legacy. He trusted me to keep *The Times* the way it was. I still believe in his vision. I'm just not the one to see it through."

At the defeat in his eyes, she couldn't keep from moving closer. "The mark of a good businessman is to know when to make a change. To put the business above himself. You, Sebastian Hudson, are an excellent businessman."

He smiled, closing the space between them. "And you, Jade Smith, are—"

The sound of a growling engine broke them apart, and a familiar pickup truck pulled into the space next to her, straight as an arrow.

"Great timing, Kalista," Sebastian muttered.

The young woman got out of the truck, pretty as ever with her hair in a pink scrunchy and dressed in a T-shirt and shorts and carrying a small white paper sack. "Oh, hey, Mr. H. . . . Jade?"

Jade gave her a little wave. "Hi."

Kalista halted. Tilted her head.

"Is there a reason you're here on your day off?" Sebastian asked, sounding more than a little perturbed at the interruption.

"I'm bringing Tyler some of Viv's blueberry muffins." She held up the bag. Then she wiggled her fingers at them. "Carry on," she said, and sprinted to the building.

Sebastian turned to Jade. "Where were we?"

She smiled, her toes curling. His bedroom eyes were back. "I know where I want to be."

His brow arched. "And where is that?"

She moved into his embrace and melted against him. "Right. Here."

_____

August

"You're gorgeous," Viv gushed as she and Kalista looked at their reflections in the mirror. They were getting ready for the wedding in the nursery room at Clementine Community Church.

"I don't hold a candle to you, Viv." She'd read the phrase in one of the many novels she'd read over the summer, and it was true. Kalista felt pretty enough in her peach-colored maid of honor dress, despite all the ruffles on the hem and the sleeves. Totally Viv. But Viv was beyond stunning, her simple off-the-shoulder wedding dress fitting her perfectly.

"I'm finally going to be Mrs. Bo Wilson in an hour!" Viv giggled.

Kalista hugged her. "I'm so glad I'm here to see it happen."

"Me too. I'm sure your dapper young man won't be able to take his eyes off you."

She grinned. Tyler *was* quite dapper in his black suit and peach tie. He wasn't in the wedding party—Mr. H. was Bo's best man, and he and Kalista were the only attendants—but he'd been happy to match her dress. After spending almost every spare minute with him over the summer, she was head over heels, and she refused to think about what she inevitably had to do in a few days—go back to California. Her summer with Viv was almost over.

She had a plan, though. At least a semblance of one. She was going to college to major in graphic design. Evelyn Margot had been kind enough to show her how to draw graphics and set advertising and had encouraged her to pursue a degree. *"You'll be great at it,"* she'd said.

Kalista wasn't sure about that, and she had doubts that she'd sail through college. She'd missed a lot during high school, and she'd probably have to get a tutor. But she was determined to get her degree. Her father was on board, and they were now talking weekly—something she'd instigated shortly after she and Tyler got together. She was even cordial to Bettany, but not by much. Maybe they'd grow closer when she returned to LA. *Baby steps.*

Sadness overcame her. She didn't want to leave Clementine, but she couldn't impose on Viv either. California was her home. And then there was Tyler. How could she leave him behind?

"We can talk on the phone," he'd said, cuddling with her on Viv's front porch swing the other night. *"I can come visit, and you can do the same. We'll make it work."* He'd sealed the promise with a tender kiss, and then they stopped talking altogether.

"Someone's waiting to see you," Viv said, going to the door. She blew Kalista a kiss. It was fun to see her so giddy. "See you in a bit." She left, and a man walked in after her.

"Daddy!" Kalista ran to her father and hugged him. "What are you doing here?"

"Viv invited me." He grinned and held Kalista out in front of him. "My baby's all grown up." He kissed her cheek. "You look beautiful."

"Thank you." She paused. "Is Bettany here?"

"No. I cleared my calendar for a week, and I want to spend all that time with you."

"Really?" She tried to be disappointed that Bettany was back in LA. That was the grown-up thing to do. But she couldn't. She never had Daddy all to herself for so long. "Where are you staying?"

"The Clementine Inn." He gestured to two rocking chairs on the other side of the room.

Where else would he stay?

"Can we talk for a few minutes?"

"Sure."

They sat down, her father still smiling. "I'm so proud of you, honey," he said. "Viv's been keeping me apprised of what you've been doing, of course, but I can tell from our conversations that you've matured." He pulled a cell phone from his suit jacket pocket. "I turned your phone back on and got you the latest model." He held it out to her.

She looked at it. It was fancier and bigger than her other phone and had a larger screen. Nice. She shook her head. "I'll get it later," she said. "When I go back to LA."

His brow arched in surprise, but he pocketed the phone. "About that." His expression grew somber.

"What? I still can't come home?"

"You can come home. I just want to know if you want to."

"Of course I—" But she couldn't say the rest. She'd just assumed she had to go back to California. That's where she belonged, right?

"I have an idea," Daddy said. "During one of my conversations with Viv, she mentioned that *The Clementine Times* was open to investment."

"Uh, I guess." She really didn't know all the business stuff, just that Jade had moved to Clementine and was working with Flora. What Kalista had really noticed was how happy Mr. H. was around Jade. His portrait outside his door was always him smiling. The whole mood at the office was brighter.

"I made some calls, and I decided to buy some shares. Well, more than half actually."

"You own half the newspaper now?"

"Yes. I like to diversify, you know."

She frowned. "What does that mean?"

"I'll explain it later. You might want to consider investing in *The*

Times yourself, once you get your trust fund. I can help you figure that out."

Wow, she hadn't even thought about her trust fund lately. The news didn't deter her from her college plans, though. She was determined to go.

"I need someone here to keep an eye on my investment," he continued. "Someone on the inside."

"You want me to stay here?"

He held up his hands. "Only if you want to. Honey, I do want you home, and I want us to grow closer. I promise I'll make the effort to make that happen, whether you're in LA or in Clementine. Most of all, I want you to be happy. You seem much happier here than back home. Is that true?"

Kalista didn't think about it. "Yes, I am." Not just because of Tyler either, although he was a big reason. But there was so much more. She didn't see Viv simply as a stepmother anymore. She was Mom now, through and through, and she loved being with her and Bo on the farm. The piglets that had been born in June were growing like crazy, she had learned how to cook more meals, there were still more books to be read on the bookshelf, and who would give Pepé his treats on Monday and Thursday mornings?

"I'll give you time to think about it," he said, starting to get up.

She put her hand on his arm. "What about college?"

"You still want to go? You're not going to need the money."

His words made her think about Ryan, whom she hadn't thought of hardly at all after they broke up. "I need a goal. A direction. I think college is where I'll find it."

Daddy took her hand. "Seems like you've already found it, kitten. How about we research some local colleges while I'm here? I'll help you find the right one."

"Thank you!"

They hugged and he left. She took another look in the mirror and squealed. "I'm staying in Clementine!" She picked up her bouquet and headed for the sanctuary. *Mom is getting married!*

———

Jade glanced at Sebastian and tried not to stare. She'd done enough of that at Viv's wedding a few hours ago when he and Bo had taken their places at the altar. Kalista was lovely, and when Jade had glanced at Tyler, she saw him tug on the collar of his dress shirt. She doubted it was because he rarely wore one. Viv was stunning, Bo was nervous, and Sebastian was . . . hot. *Real* hot.

The reception had been fun—a small one in the church activity hall. There had been some square dancing at Bo's request, and Eugenia Pickles was both caller and DJ. Jade didn't know Bo could cut such a rug. Thankfully, Ms. Eugenia had played a couple of ballads, and she had danced both of them with Sebastian. Absolute bliss.

Now they were at his cabin enjoying the last few minutes of a gorgeous sunset. He sat casually in the patio chair, his jacket off and no tie but still wearing his dress shirt. Sleeves rolled up, top two buttons unfastened—

"What?" he said, glancing at her.

"Huh?" She quickly looked away.

"You're staring at me."

Busted. She was about to make an excuse or apologize but changed her mind and faced him. "Can you blame me?"

His brow arched and he gave her a sly grin. "It's the shirt, right?"

"It's the whole package, Sebastian Hudson."

He sat up and motioned to her. "Get over here."

She scrambled out of her chair and into his lap. After a long, lingering kiss, she sighed and put her head on his shoulder as he rubbed her back.

"I like this dress," he said, pressing a kiss to her temple. "Green suits you."

"I am Jade, after all." She liked the dress too. It was more feminine than she was used to wearing, with a flared skirt and tight, sleeveless bodice. It put her out of her comfort zone, but when she saw Sebastian's reaction when he first saw it, she knew it was the right choice.

Evening mountain music was all around them, provided by nature, and by some miracle today was cooler than the entire summer had been, keeping the mosquitoes away. Heat would be on the menu tomorrow, but she would take the small reprieve and enjoy being out here with Sebastian.

"When are you leaving tomorrow?" he asked.

"Early. I want to spend as much time as I can with Mom before her surgery."

"I can go with you," he said. "Put Evelyn in charge of *The Times*."

She lifted her head and looked at him. "Thank you, but I'll be fine. The doctors are confident the transplant will be a success. Logan and Tameka will be there too."

He met her gaze. "I'll miss you."

"I'll only be gone a week." Or longer, if there were complications, but she was trusting that there wouldn't be. "You can survive without me."

Sebastian shook his head. "I don't know how I ever did."

Oh, this man. She kissed him again, then reluctantly moved off his lap. She had to head back to her apartment in Clementine and pack for her trip. Once Mom was released from the hospital, she would come back. *To my home.* It was amazing how quickly Clementine had become home. She'd moved here at the end of June, and since then she and Rachel, along with Flora's help, had worked on the shareholder plan while Sebastian continued to run the paper. They'd gotten a surprise last week when Raymond Clark, Kalista's father, had agreed to invest in the paper, with the caveat that it stayed the same. Sebastian assured him that it would.

There was one other surprise she'd learned only recently. Sebastian started working on his second novel again, and when she was at his surprisingly tidy bungalow, she'd seen the pages in his typewriter. When he revealed that he was bestselling-thriller author Jaden Caxon, she couldn't believe it.

"*Everyone in my office read your book,*" she said. "*Charlotte had a conniption for years when the follow-up didn't come out.*"

"*I'm hoping to rectify that,*" he said. "*I'm inspired now.*" He paused. "*Did you read it?*"

"*I didn't have time.*" She walked over to his alphabetized bookshelf, saw the novel, and slipped it off the shelf. "*I will now.*" And she had, and it was amazing. She would do everything she could to encourage him to finish this one.

"Don't leave," Sebastian said. "Not yet." He took her hand and led her inside. After sliding the patio door shut, he faced her but didn't say anything. He just shifted on his feet, looking nervous.

"Sebastian?"

He blew out a breath. "The last time I told you this, it didn't end well."

Now she was concerned. "Told me what?"

His hand cupped her cheek, his thumb tracing her chin. The look in his eyes was different but just as toe-curling. Not bedroom eyes . . . but ones filled with love.

"I love you, Jade."

She could barely breathe as he kissed her with exquisite tenderness. She looped her arms over his neck, her heart bursting with joy. "I love you too."

His smile reached into her soul, and she melted against him. She'd lost Sebastian Hudson twice. Now he was hers forever. *I'm never letting him go.*

Epilogue

One year later

SEB'S VIEW PART DEUX

~~It's with great sadness~~
~~I lost track how many times I started this~~
~~There comes a time in every man's life when he must~~

Nuts." Seb yanked the paper out of his typewriter—gently, as he didn't want to mess up his Royal—and balled it in his hand. He tossed it on the desk and grabbed another sheet. The former page had plenty of space left, but maybe a fresh blank one would spark some inspiration.

"What's wrong?" Jade looked up from her laptop. They were in Seb's office, and she was working at a small table in the corner of the room. It was amazing how much room there was in here now that he'd organized, archived, and yes, just plain pitched a bunch of stuff. Although Jade was now *The Clementine Times* official accountant, fully allowing Flora to retire, she was the one who suggested they share an office. He was more than happy to oblige.

He rubbed his temples. "Writer's block."

"For Seb's View Part Deux?" She frowned. "You never have trouble writing that."

"I do today." He fiddled with his gold wedding band. "It's hard to say goodbye."

"Ah." She got up and went to him, resting her chin on his shoulder. "Then it's to be expected." She nibbled on his ear, sending a shiver straight down his spine. "Is this helping?"

Seb grinned and spun around in his chair without a squeak, thanks to regular maintenance with WD-40. He grabbed her around the waist. "Doesn't hurt."

Jade leaned forward and kissed him, and he was ready to pack up not only the column but also the rest of the day and take her back to the house. The column could wait—

"Ahem."

They both groaned and Seb looked over his shoulder, half expecting Evelyn Margot to be there, then remembered she was still on her honeymoon with Haskell in Branson. Instead, it was Kalista.

"This is a no PDA zone, Mr. H."

"I'm the boss." He set Jade aside, reluctantly. "I can do what I want."

"Oh good, does that mean Tyler and I—"

"*Can't* do what you want."

Jade chuckled and went back to her table while Kalista flounced in, a little disappointed scowl on her face. "I wanted you to look at the advertising mockup before I took it to Cletus downstairs."

Seb eyed the thumb drive she was handing him. "Okay," he said, putting it next to his computer. "I'll go over it."

"Thanks! You both still coming over for supper on Sunday? I'm making biscuits from scratch. Mr. Clyde gave me the recipe."

"I thought that was a family secret," he said.

"I can be very persuasive. See you later. Bye, Jade."

He shook his head and picked up the thumb drive. Looking over this was a formality. Evelyn Margot had trained Kalista well, and she did have a gift for design—a lot more than Seb did. He was inserting the drive into the computer when Jade's phone rang.

She answered it. "Yes," she said. "Oh. What? Really?"

Seb looked up, seeing Jade's stunned expression. Was it Lydia? She was over a year out from her transplant and was doing well. Maybe it was Logan and Tameka—they'd been getting serious over the past several months.

"Okay. Thanks. Bye." Jade closed the phone and set it down on the table. Behind her on the shelf was Polly. Jade had insisted on adding her to the decor, and Seb was happy to oblige.

Uh-oh. It wasn't engagement news. He went over to her. "What's wrong?"

She blinked and looked up at him, then slowly got up from her chair. "That was Mrs. Roberts."

He took Jade's hand. Libby Roberts was the social worker that had been working with them. "And?"

Jade's eyes teared. "We're officially foster parents."

He couldn't believe it. Shortly before he proposed last September, they'd discussed having a family. Jade was adamant about fostering a child, and Seb was open to it. If they were blessed to have a biological child, that would be great, but fostering and adopting took precedence.

He scooped her into his arms. "I'm so happy," he said, kissing her. Then he stilled. "I'm so terrified."

"Me too. I don't know anything about being a mom."

"Logan would beg to differ." He smiled and held her close again. "We'll figure it out, together."

"Yes," she murmured against his chest. "We will."

The rest of the day went by in a blur, and Jade left the office to go home to their cabin and fix supper. Seb had sold the bungalow after their wedding in January. With a child coming, they'd have to find a larger house—something in Clementine proper. Thoughts of his future made him smile.

He stared at his faithful Royal, picked up a sheet of paper, and cranked it in. He now knew exactly what to say.

SEB'S VIEW PART DEUX

Endings are also beginnings. For almost twelve years I've written about Clementine and its people in this column, and it's been my honor to have penned every word. But life, she is a-changing, and I must change with it. I hereby announce that our very own Evelyn Margot Panchak has agreed to take over as publisher and editor in chief. If you have a problem with that, take it up with her husband. I'm sure the mayor will be happy to hear your input. In all seriousness, most of you already knew this, especially those of you who own a part of *The Times*. I just needed to make it official.

I'm also making something else official—this is the last edition of Seb's View Part Deux. Don't worry, *The Times* will still have a column dedicated to Clementine and the greater community's shenanigans. I guarantee you'll enjoy Tyler Hernandez's take on Clementonian life. I've read his debut column. It's a winner.

As for me, I'll be doing some reporting here, some fishing there, and most definitely spending all the time I can with Jade, although she might end up running for the hills after a week of my constant presence. I guess what I'm saying is this—I'm retiring from the newspaper business. It's not an easy decision, but it's the right one. As for my new beginning, well . . . check your local bookstore in two months for *Lies in the Mist*, the follow-up to *Truth in Shadows*, by Jaden Caxon. You'll find my picture on the back cover.

Thank you, my dear friends. I'll see you around.

Seb

He sat back and reread the column with a mix of heaviness and freedom. When he first approached Jade and Evelyn with the idea of retiring, it had been difficult. But *The Times* was in good hands, both financially and creatively. Advertising and circulation were up, and thanks to Jade and Rachel's hard work, the paper was solvent. Evelyn was already helping him out with managing things, giving him time to finish *Lies in the Mist*, which had flowed from his fingertips faster than anything he'd ever written before. The story had been dormant for nearly a decade, and it was more than ready to be told.

Seb unrolled the column out of his Royal and set it on his desk. He took one last look at Buford's picture, saluted him, and stood. He was going home—to make love to his wife, to celebrate the impending arrival of their new foster child, and to start a new adventure.

From his view . . . life was good.

Acknowledgments

Writing *Behind Enemy Bylines* was an education and an adventure! A big thank-you to my editors Becky Monds and Karli Jackson for their help and encouragement in bringing the story to fruition. Whew, we made it! As always, thank you to Natasha Kern for her friendship and support.

Special thanks to Jay and Sloane Grelen for sharing their personal story with me, for being the inspiration for *Behind Enemy Bylines*, and for giving me the inside scoop on the newspaper business. Most of all, thank you for your friendship and famous sweet tea. Thank you to my dear friend Sandy Schemp for sharing her extensive knowledge of newspaper distribution and helping me brainstorm ideas. Did I mention writing this book was an education?

And my deepest appreciation to you, Dear Reader, for joining me on another reading journey. I hope you enjoyed Seb and Jade's story and the blast from the recent past as much as I did writing it. You are all honorary Clementonians!

Discussion Questions

1. Jade finds car washes relaxing. What activity do you do or place do you go when you're feeling stressed?

2. Out of desperation to keep her job, Jade made several bad decisions—sneaking into Sebastian's office, accidentally taking his ledger, then not returning it when she found out she had it. Discuss a time in your life when you made a wrong decision and what would you have done differently?

3. Logan acknowledged that Jade's boundaries had helped him become clean and sober. How would you advise someone who has difficulty setting boundaries?

4. Does knowing Jade's past make some of her decisions understandable? Why or why not?

5. During her summer in Clementine, Kalista had to face some unpleasant truths about herself, and that led to her making changes in her life. What do you think she would have done if she returned to California, instead of staying in Arkansas?

6. Although they don't realize it, Jade and Sebastian have both learned to protect their hearts by ignoring/hiding their feelings. What are some other ways we protect ourselves from hurt and pain?

7. Jade told Sebastian that she always solved her own problems, on her own. Discuss how this line of thinking negatively impacted her and her relationships.

8. Sebastian, Jade, and Kalista all changed due to events in the story. Discuss a time in your life when an event or period of time changed you for the better.

9. Family is an important theme in the story. What does family mean to you?

About the Author

With over two million copies sold, Kathleen Fuller is the *USA TODAY* bestselling author of several bestselling novels, including the Hearts of Middlefield novels, the Middlefield Family novels, the Amish of Birch Creek series, and the Amish Letters series as well as a middle-grade Amish series, the Mysteries of Middlefield.

———

Visit her online at KathleenFuller.com
Facebook: @WriterKathleenFuller
Instagram: @kf_booksandhooks

LOOKING FOR MORE GREAT READS? LOOK NO FURTHER!